"You'd better come in," Ross said, his tone gruff and strangely awkward.

Maddie held her breath. Was he going to set off on one of his rants? She looked him straight in the eye, refusing to be daunted... To her dismay, her heart began beating loudly in her chest.

"About today..."

"Yes?"

He lowered his eyes, concentrating on his bare feet. His toes were long and finely formed, with broad flat nails and a dusting of dark hair above the knuckle joints; they made him suddenly seem vulnerable, those bare feet.

Looking up with a surge of embarrassment, she met his dark gaze again; there was a hint of amusement in his face. "I'm sorry, that's all," he said. "Sorry for being angry with you, especially in front of Bob Nelson."

"Well, he didn't have a bad word to say about you," she remarked.

"He is one of the few who didn't judge me after..."

"I know what you went through," she told him. "And for what it's worth, I wouldn't judge you, either."

"Wouldn't you?" he said, holding her gaze.

He took a step toward her, and suddenly, somehow, she was in his arms.

Dear Reader,

I do hope you enjoy this book. It is the third in my Creatures Great and Small series, set in and around Little Dale and the beautiful Lake District fells in Northern England. I was brought up on a farm in the area and have always loved its timelessness and ancient traditions. To be able to immerse myself not only in the romances I love to write but also in a place that is so dear to me feels like a real privilege. It is heartwarming to know that as time slowly passes us all by, there are places and traditions that never seem to change, places where our ancestors lived and loved, laughed and cried, just as we do now and as our children and their children will do in the future.

Enjoy, and I'd love to hear your thoughts. Feel free to contact me at info@holmescalesriding.co.uk.

Eleanor

HEARTWARMING

The Little Dale Remedy

—

Eleanor Jones

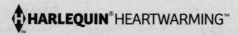

Recycling programs
for this product may
not exist in your area.

ISBN-13: 978-0-373-36776-4

The Little Dale Remedy

This edition published by arrangement with Harlequin Books S.A.

For questions and comments about the quality of this book,
please contact us at CustomerService@Harlequin.com.

Printed in U.S.A.

Eleanor Jones was brought up on a farm in the north of England and learned to love animals and the countryside from an early age. She has ridden all her life, and after marrying her husband at just eighteen years old and having two wonderful children, they set up a riding center together. This is still thriving over thirty years later. Her daughter competes at the national level, and she is now a partner in the business and brings her adorable three-year-old son to work with her every day. Eleanor's son is also married with two children, and they live nearby. Eleanor has been writing for what feels like her whole life. Her early handwritten novels still grace a dusty shelf in the back of a cupboard somewhere, but she was first published over fifteen years ago, when she wrote teenage pony mysteries.

Books by Eleanor Jones

Harlequin Heartwarming

A Place Called Home
The Country Vet
Footprints in the Sand

Harlequin Everlasting Love

A Heartbeat Away

I would like to dedicate this book to
my dear Aunt Gwen

CHAPTER ONE

MADDIE SANK WEARILY into the well-worn, ancient chair by the open fireplace. The grate was black and cold, heaped high with ash and half-burned logs that had once brought warmth and cheer. Now the room was empty and kind of sad, an alien environment. A wave of homesickness washed over her, flooding her mind with images of her mum and dad and the comforts of home, making her question, yet again, why she'd moved here, so very far away from all she knew.

Guilt niggled as she remembered how hard her parents had fought her spontaneous decision to leave behind the love and care they'd lavished upon her, especially since the tragedy turned her whole world on its head. She'd been so determined to try to regain some independence and self-esteem after the accident, though, that getting away was all she'd been able to think of. Perhaps she'd been stupid; perhaps she should have stayed in their care longer. Perhaps it was too soon for this.

Impulsively, she reached for the car keys in her pocket. Of course she could just climb into her car and drive home. But then where would she be? Back in the protected cradle of love that stifled her dreams—that's where. Well, she wasn't prepared to give up on her future…not yet. Fate may have moved in unexpectedly to shatter her dreams on a lonely road in the pale light of dawn, but she wasn't about to give up on everything that mattered to her because of one bizarre accident. If she was focused enough, then anything was possible. She just had to hang on to that thought and keep believing it. She'd worked way too hard to regain even half of what she used to be to give up on the next stage just yet.

Dropping her keys on the small oak coffee table, Maddie took a deep breath and stood up. She pressed a palm to her back to fight the pain that flared up, waiting a moment to let it settle before going into the tiny kitchen to fill the kettle. The sound of water starting to bubble and the fresh aroma of the coffee she unpacked from the box of groceries her mum had provided brought familiarity and contentment, reestablishing the single-mindedness that had brought her this far. This was the right decision; she was sure of it. She had overcome so much already, and she was determined to find a place again in the life she loved…or she'd die trying. Maddie's every instinct told her that Sky View Stables held the key to her future. All she needed was the strength to see her plan through.

Returning to her chair, she sipped her coffee, reflecting on the new job that was just a stepping stone to what she really wanted. She may only have been hired as a general home help, but she intended to gradually try to work with, and eventually ride, the horses there. It might not be the promising horse-racing career she had been forced to abandon, but it was a start, at least. The doctors and consultants had told her riding again would be impossible, and her parents would have a heart attack if they knew what her real goals were but in Little Dale no one knew her history. Here, she had a chance to prove them all wrong; no one would watch her every move, no one would judge her and no one would look at her with sad sympathy in their eyes.

A loud knock took her by surprise. Who could be at the door? She didn't know anyone from around here. Draining her cup, Maddie headed slowly down the hallway with a sense of unease and a sudden awareness of her isolation. The noise came again, louder and more intense as she approached the front door and opened it just a crack. A tall, dark, angry-looking man in his early thirties was on her doorstep, his hand raised high to begin the tirade of knocking yet again. A large dog stood behind him. Hurriedly, she slipped on the chain, gasping in relief as it slid easily into place.

"Yes?" she said, her voice deceptively cool. "Can I help you?"

"What do you think you're doing in my house?" the man roared. "I want you out. Now!"

Maddie felt her anxiety drain away as her anger rose. No one was going to speak to her like that. She'd paid good money up front to rent this place, so what was he talking about? She had every right to be here. That knowledge lent her confidence. "What the hell are *you* doing here is more to the point," she retaliated, meeting his gaze through the crack.

The ferocity in the man's dark eyes swayed her slightly, making her aware yet again of how alone she was out here.

"This is my house," he insisted. "And my

guess is that you're squatting, so if you don't get out right now, I'm calling the police."

Maddie held her ground, knuckles turning white on the door handle. "And you will look like a fool," she told him. "I've rented this place for three months, and I'm fifteen hundred pounds down, so I'm going nowhere. Call the rental company if you like, but I'm not leaving until my lease is up. So stop harassing me...unless you want *me* to call the police."

"What do you mean?" His whole frame deflated just the tiniest bit. "What rental company?"

Sensing the shift in his demeanor, Maddie held his gaze with fresh confidence. "Shouldn't *you* know that?"

He paled beneath his tan as he turned abruptly away. "We'll see," he said, striding off toward the lane without a backward glance.

Maddie shut the door and quickly bolted it, her whole body shaking. There had been something so fiercely intense about the man...and the huge, silent dog behind him had seemed to echo his master's expression. Yet again, she felt so alone. What if he had tried to break into the house? And what did he mean, anyway...

it was his house? If he was really the owner, then surely he'd have known the cottage was rented out.

Hurrying to check the back door and all the windows, Maddie wondered about calling the police herself. He hadn't really done anything wrong though, had he, so what could they do? She peered through the narrow window beside the front door and saw the tail end of his travel trailer pulling away. Well, at least he'd gotten the message for now. She'd just have to see what tomorrow brought.

Walking wearily into the kitchen, she poured herself a strong coffee and sat down at the small table, determined to put her annoying visitor firmly out of her mind.

Maddie's thoughts wandered back to how she'd come to be here, all alone in this cottage in the middle of nowhere. She'd felt jittery on the long journey from Devon to the Lake District, she remembered, driving on automatic, her head crowded with doubts and apprehension. It was only when the sign finally loomed out at her, penetrating the fog that clouded her brain, that her spirits lifted. Little Dale—at last, the place that she hoped held a brand-new start.

The moment she'd seen the sign, she'd felt

everything beginning to click into place. Now though, after her encounter, she was not quite so sure. A pain shot down her back, almost on cue, as if it had been sent to strengthen her doubts, making her wince and worry. She realigned her position, wondering how long it was going to be before her body felt whole again. And what if it never did? She pushed that thought straight out of her head; there was no place in her life for what-ifs.

Was she crazy to even contemplate having a career with horses again? Her parents had certainly thought she was making a huge mistake by going back to work too soon, especially when the job she'd found was so far away from home. She'd felt so guilty when she hugged her mum goodbye. The image of her strained, worried face in the rearview mirror had left a heavy weight in Maddie's heart. But this was *her* life, and she knew what she wanted…had always known. Horses had been her entire life for so long, and the buzz of competition was ingrained into her soul; she couldn't just let go of that.

Rose Cottage had sounded really nice in the ad, and when Maddie arrived in Little Dale, she decided it was probably one of the prettiest places she'd ever seen. The buildings were all gray stone, apart from the village store, which was painted white. They surrounded a small village green with a lovely old church on one side, and there was even a river running through the center of the town, with ducks waddling and quacking on the bank. The town seemed like a friendly place to make a fresh start.

She'd driven another mile before Rose Cottage appeared around a bend. It had felt instantly welcoming, small and quaint with a tiny front garden, standing all alone in beautiful surroundings. The view of the Lakeland hills and wide open sky beyond was amazing.

After arriving at Rose Cottage, Maddie had headed over to Sky View Stables to see Cass Munro. Maddie was starting her new job there tomorrow, helping Cass with chores and with her eight-year-old stepson, Robbie. Cass had turned out to be slightly built, very friendly and approachable and obviously pregnant. She had swung back her shiny dark hair and smiled at Maddie. "Now you know why I need help," she'd said, patting her stomach. "And I didn't want some experienced old nanny type looking down her nose at me, so I hired you."

Maddie had smiled back at her. "Well, I've

certainly had no experience, so you're okay there."

"Perfect. I'll show you round. Do you know much about horses?"

Maddie had considered telling her the truth. *Oh, yes. I was once a promising young jockey, engaged to my boss's son, working with Thoroughbreds and looking forward to a long and successful love affair with the racing industry...until some prat knocked me off my bike early one morning, leaving me for dead on the side of the lane...*

Biting her tongue, though, she had just smiled and given a little shake of her head. No sad, pitying faces and no one to judge her. That's why she'd come here, and it meant keeping quiet about her past, no matter how nice Cass Munro seemed to be. "A bit," she'd said, not wanting to be totally dishonest.

Now, three hours later as nighttime hovered, sitting alone in the secluded cottage after her disturbing visitor left, Maddie tried to focus on how much she was looking forward to tomorrow. Seeing the stable yard at Sky View had reinforced her passion to ride again, maybe even compete in some way, and she wasn't going to let some rude, obnoxious, deranged man upset her. And he *had* upset her, if she was honest with herself, and had frightened her a little. Glancing around the cold and empty cottage, she picked up on a vibe she hadn't noticed earlier. A sad and lonely vibe, as if someone had suffered here.

Taking a deep breath, she lifted her chin and stood up. This was ridiculous; she'd come here to put her future straight again and drive away the emptiness and fear that had filled her life for the past year and a half. It was her own vibe she could feel, simple as that. All that the cottage needed was a glowing fire in the grate, a good cleaning to sweep away the cobwebs and the aroma of the stew her mother had insisted she take.

OVER AN HOUR LATER, tired and aching but feeling so much happier, Maddie surveyed her handiwork. She'd found wood neatly stacked right outside the back door, and now flames flickered red and gold in both the kitchen log burner and the open fire in the small sitting room. The enticing aromas of wood smoke and stew simmering on the stove drifted through the cottage.

She pushed the vacuum cleaner back into the cupboard beneath the steep, narrow staircase then sank into a chair in the kitchen to try to ease the nagging pain that spread through her back and down into her left leg. She'd overdone it; she knew that by the way her leg was suddenly refusing to do what she told it to. Damn her stupid injuries and damn the man who'd caused them. She'd eat the stew and have an early night, she decided— build up a bit of strength for her big day to-morrow.

And as for the fierce and angry man who'd unsettled her with his unexpected visit…well, she'd just have to hope the rental company would sort it out when he called them in the morning. With a bit of luck, she wouldn't even see him again. If he did come back to harass her, she'd just ring the police. And to-night she'd check that all her windows and doors were locked yet again…just to be sure.

CHAPTER TWO

A GRIPING, FAMILIAR pain in the region of his heart made Ross Noble lighten his foot on the accelerator of his big, old pickup truck. How could he have believed he would be able to just drive back into Little Dale as if nothing had happened? As the vehicle slowed down, he glanced in the rearview mirror at Meg, his six-year-old daughter. "Come on, Dad, we're nearly there," she cried, her eyes alight with excitement.

"Perhaps we should just turn around and go back home to Scotland," he suggested.

Her face fell. "But you said that *this* was my real home."

"And it is." He sighed. "It's just…"

For Ross, the area held nothing but sad memories. He had vowed never to set foot in Little Dale again, but his daughter had been born here, and she had a right to know her heritage. She might not remember her mother, Jenny, or her grandma, Anne Maddox, but Little Dale was the place where they all used to live when she was a baby and Ross was only too well aware that Meg longed for a proper family life and other kids to play with. Suddenly, though, he was questioning his decision to bring her back here and questioning his own ability to get past all the bad memories.

Stalling for time, he pulled his truck onto the shoulder and jumped out. "Seems like Red needs to stretch his legs," he told Meg, who was peering out of the window impatiently.

Next to his daughter, his huge copper-colored dog whined softly. Ross opened the back door and let Red out, kneeling down and cradling the dog's big face between his palms. His heart ached with regret. "Am I really doing the right thing, lad?" he murmured. "Or should we just turn around and get out of here?"

Well used to his master's ramblings, Red pushed against him, eager to get out of the confined space. "I know." Ross sighed, giving the dog one last rub behind the ears before slamming the back door. "It's the right thing to do…for Meg's sake. She deserves to know where she came from."

Memories assailed him, of Jenny, his sweet young wife, when she was whole. They had been so in love back then; how had he let it all go so terribly wrong? Perhaps her mother was right; perhaps it really had all been his fault. If he hadn't been so selfish then maybe she'd still be alive today to watch their daughter growing up. He'd been too engrossed in his work, though, to realize how ill Jenny was becoming, how much she struggled with depression after Meg was born...until it was too late.

Ross climbed back into the driver's seat, closing the door with a heavy clunk. How he felt was irrelevant. He'd lost the right to be selfish. Now it was all about Meg. When Jenny died, he'd sworn to dedicate the rest of his life to his daughter's happiness, and he intended to keep that promise. He couldn't expect her to live in a trailer forever, especially not now, when a real house awaited them.

"Well, Meg," he said, reaching across to ruffle his daughter's hair. "You'll soon be home."

"Home," Meg echoed, her bright little face shining. "Isn't it your home, too, Daddy?"

The powerful engine rumbled into life and he nosed the big vehicle back out into the lane, glancing in his wing mirror to make sure that the travel trailer, their home for the past six years, was clear of the verge. "I hope so, Meg."

The little girl grinned, pressing her face against the window, eager to take in all her surroundings.

It would be strange, Ross thought, as the landmarks became ever more familiar, to stay in one place and live in a house again, especially one where so much had happened. But Meg was school-age now, and she needed that stability. When they found out Anne Maddox had left Rose Cottage to her granddaughter, it was as if it was meant to be.

The sign for Little Dale appeared ahead of them. "Well, Jenny," he said under his breath, "are you waiting here for us, watching our every move?"

"Who is waiting?" Meg asked, overhearing.

Ross smiled at her. "Your mum, I hope. She'll be watching over you from heaven, I guess."

Meg nodded slowly. "She's still with Jesus, though, right?"

He cleared his throat to cover up a sudden rush of the emotion he rarely showed. "Yes…

she's still with Jesus. She's helping look after him."

Ross drove slowly through the village, overcome by memories. He'd first arrived at Little Dale from his native Scotland to take a job on a farm. Sutcliffe's, a sheep farm farther up the fell. That's where he first met Jenny. Anne Maddox's sister, Dora, was married to Ian Sutcliffe, and Jenny often came to the farm to visit with her mum. She'd been just nineteen and he twenty-four when they'd met.

Swallowing hard to ease the dryness in his throat, he glanced across at Meg. She smiled at him, and he ruffled her chestnut curls. "Nearly there, Nutmeg."

She wriggled on her seat, squirming in excitement. "How long will it be?"

"Five minutes, I guess," he told her.

She started to count. "How many seconds is that?"

"Three hundred or so. Start again and count slowly."

Clasping the sides of her seat, she closed her eyes tightly. "When I open them we'll be there," she cried. "One…two…three… Tell me when to open them."

The cottage looked just the same, Ross thought with a lurch of surprise. A bit more run-down and uncared for, perhaps, but there were the same low front door, the same small, paned windows, same backdrop of rugged hills and glorious sky. He pulled over, cutting the engine, staring at the place that held so many memories both good and bad. Shame it was the bad ones that stuck in his mind.

"Are we there?" asked Meg, sneaking a peek.

Seeing a movement from inside the window, he hesitated. There was a small car parked outside, too. "Well…yes," he said. "This is Rose Cottage…but I think someone's here."

Meg's wide grin filled her whole face, and she grabbed his arm. "Can we go inside now?"

He opened the driver's door slowly, fighting off the demons that urged him to get back in the truck and drive away.

"Just stay in the truck for a few minutes while I have a look around," he told her firmly, letting Red out the back door. The big dog slipped in behind him as always, silently faithful.

Ross walked slowly down the narrow path toward the cottage, stopping outside the front door and breathing in the heartrendingly familiar smell of wildflowers and gorse. He'd been told that the key was underneath a plant pot on the window ledge—as if he didn't know that; it had always been there.

The plant pot revealed nothing...why wasn't he surprised? Well, whoever was in there could get out right now. Anger rippled inside him. This was Meg's place...and his. No one had any right to be here. He hammered on the door, his fist reverberating with a satisfying thud. The face that peered out at him as the door slowly opened, however, took him totally by surprise. A young woman, probably mid-twenties, stared at him with alarm in her wide eyes. "Can I help you?" she asked.

"What are you doing in my house?" he responded angrily.

They exchanged heated words, but Ross soon understood that this woman wasn't going to budge, no matter what he said. Blood boiling, he turned on his heel and headed back toward the truck.

Red pushed his nose against his master's hand as if in understanding. "What am

I going to tell Meg, boy?" He sighed as he saw his daughter's eager little face pressed against the window.

MADDIE SLEPT FITFULLY despite her medication and woke at dawn with anxiety fluttering inside her. She'd thrived on anxiety once, but it had been offset by the adrenaline that had coursed through her veins as, mounted on a bulging mass of muscle and raw energy, she'd waited for the race to start. Closing her eyes, she allowed her mind to slip back to those giddy days when success had called her at the start of each race, the smell of horses, sweat and fear like a cauldron around her until suddenly the gates opened up and her body took over. And then she'd fly, leaving fear in the stalls, just her and the horse beneath her, battling to win.

A sigh rose in her chest and tears flooded her eyes, making her lids feel heavy. She'd known the risks, the danger. All the jockeys did. And she'd had her fair share of crashing falls from spirited young Thoroughbreds high on life. She'd never expected her career to end in a lonely country lane; that was the worst part. If she'd broken her body on the racetrack, she'd have been a hero, but to lose her hopes and dreams to a cowardly hit-and-run driver as she pedaled to work one morning just felt so wrong.

A sound outside caught her attention, stopping her from dwelling on the past just as her memories were moving on to Alex and his treachery. Some fiancé he'd turned out to be! Maddie crawled out of bed and went to the window. There it was again—a chopping sound accompanied by loud barking.

Her bedroom overlooked the lane, and the window revealed nothing so she went across the landing to the back of the cottage, where the second bedroom looked out into a small copse. She froze, her heart pounding in her ears. A trailer was parked on a patch of grass just beyond the cottage garden, and the man from last night was chopping wood—actually chopping wood—from a fallen tree, top two buttons of his white shirt open and powerful arms raised like some kind of nineteenth century throwback.

He had no right to park there…no right. Then again, she didn't know who owned the land. Maybe he did. Now what was she supposed to do? He was obviously only waiting for her to go out so that he could take over the cottage. Well, she'd see about that. If she locked it up securely and took the key, then he'd never get inside. If he did, she'd call the police because that wouldn't be squatting, it would be breaking and entering. She was angry now, all hint of last night's fear gone. He'd obviously been parked there all night; if he'd wanted to hurt her or break in while she was inside, he would have already done it.

Suddenly, he glanced up at her window as if aware that she was watching him. For an awkward moment their gazes locked, and then he turned away with slow deliberation, swinging his ax with a ferocity that Maddie found disturbing. Well, if he was trying to frighten her out of the cottage, then he had totally underestimated her. If he wanted a fight, then he'd get one.

As soon as she arrived at Sky View to begin her new job, Maddie felt better. She climbed awkwardly out of the car and was immediately greeted by all three of the family dogs: Bess, Jake's black, white and tan Welsh collie; Bess's daughter, Puddle, who belonged to Cass; and Choco, Robbie's brown-and-white terrier cross.

All three dogs eagerly followed her to the house, making her feel totally welcome and pushing any stray thoughts about her unwanted neighbor firmly from her mind. She took a gulp of fresh air. A horse whinnied from somewhere over to the right; the scent of honeysuckle from the hedge that bordered one side of the garden overpowered the pleasant aromas of the stable yard; a brown chicken appeared, clucking as it happily pecked at the earth.

Sky View felt like a happy place, a place to find herself again. She had thought so yesterday, but now she was sure…and knowing that she was at last in a horsey environment again gave her a huge lift. She might not be dealing with the horses directly for a while, but that time would come…because she would make it. Injury wasn't going to stand in her way.

Cass met her at the door with a broad smile. "Right, then," she said. "Let's have a coffee, and then we can discuss what happens around here. All I want from you is to be another pair of hands, to make things a bit easier."

"I get it," Maddie said. "And I'm happy to do anything."

"I see you've met the dogs."

"I was briefly introduced when I stopped by yesterday."

Cass nodded. "Oh, yes, of course. By the way, there's something else I wanted to touch on… You mentioned you had an accident last year…"

Maddie nodded. She had told Cass a little about her injuries, but fearful of not getting the job, she'd played them down. Her new boss had no idea how much she sometimes struggled to do the simplest task, but the last thing Maddie wanted was for anyone to make allowances for her.

"Well, I just wondered if there was anything else I should know. I don't mean to pry, but if there are any jobs that you're not up to, you know, physically, then I'd rather you told me so I don't ask too much of you."

Maddie twisted her hands together in her lap, feeling awkward. She didn't want to lie to Cass, but it was so important to her that she was treated as an equal, not as an invalid. "No," she said determinedly. "I can do most things…or try at least."

"Good," Cass said. "We know where we are, then. Now your first task this morning is to take Robbie to school. I'll come with you, since it's your first time. And here he is," she said as the little boy burst into the room.

"Robbie, this is Maddie. She'll be helping to look after you."

He grinned at her, grabbing a piece of toast and stuffing it into his mouth. "Are you going to take me to school every day?"

"She'll pick you up, too," Cass added.

"Great," he said as they headed to the car. "Dad is always late when he picks me up."

All the way to the school in the village, Robbie chattered on about Choco, his dad and granddad and his pony, filling Maddie in on life at the stables. Her confidence soared at being so readily accepted by the little boy, as if she belonged at Sky View already.

When they reached the school gates, he leaped out eagerly, waving his bag as he raced off with a smile and a wave.

"I always wait until I'm sure he's gone inside," said Cass. "Or I go in with him."

Maddie nodded. "Don't worry. I'll make sure he's safe before I leave. He's such a lovely little boy. He's the image of his dad."

"He's the best," Cass agreed. "And he does look like Jake."

On the drive back to Sky View, Cass did a little gentle probing about Maddie's past experience, asking her again about the accident. Maddie answered all her questions as honestly as she could without going into too much detail, explaining that she was knocked down by a driver while out cycling one morning, but making light of her injuries.

She had good reason not to reveal too much about the aftermath of the collision, but she didn't really know why she was keeping her experience with horses a secret. Was she afraid? Afraid, maybe, that she wouldn't be able to live up to the person she used to be? She just wanted this to be a new start with no expectations from anyone other than herself.

"I'm not Robbie's real mum, you know," Cass said, quite out of the blue. "Now, I love him like my own, but before I came here and fell in love with Jake, I hadn't really had much to do with children. All I wanted out of life was to be a successful vet. That's why I didn't mind that you hadn't had much experience with kids, either. There's something about you, though, that reminds me of myself back then, and I felt that maybe you needed a break… I hope my judgment was right."

"It…it was. Is." Maddie stuttered, surprised by the rush of emotion that Cass's honesty brought out in her. "It's true, I haven't had much experience with kids, but I love Robbie already and I really want to learn.

And…you're right about the break. I just had to get away."

Cass rubbed her stomach absentmindedly. "Well, you don't need to worry—I'm not going to pry about that," she said, smiling. "And hopefully it won't be too long before you'll have to learn about babies, as well."

Maddie smiled back at her, feeling happier than she had in months. "That's a bit more daunting, but I'm sure it can't be that hard."

"To be honest," Cass admitted, "I probably don't know much more than you, but I didn't want some experienced nanny type making me feel inadequate."

"You're safe enough there, then," Maddie responded, finally feeling confident in her decision to come to Sky View. She liked Cass Munro and felt she was up to the job. All she had to do now was build up her strength and—she hoped—gradually start riding again. No one here knew what she was capable of or had been once, so she really did have a whole new start. And it felt good.

THE GOOD FEELING stayed with her right through the day. Doing chores around the house, picking up Robbie in the afternoon and making him some tea—simple everyday tasks that made Maddie feel useful and normal again. Her sense of well-being lasted until she was on her way home.

A curl of wood smoke from behind the cottage brought reality back with a bump. He was still here, then? Well, if he even came near her, then she was calling the cops. Parking as close to the cottage as possible, she jumped out, fumbling with her keys and dropping them before racing down the short pathway to the front door.

The cottage still smelled of burning logs and coffee—comfortable, homey smells that inspired confidence. She'd have some soup for supper, she decided, carrying on the theme.

She was rooting around in the large stack of cans she'd brought with her—cans had seemed like a good idea, but she'd definitely gone over the top, she realized now—when a gentle knock came on the kitchen door. She froze, clutching a can of tomato soup in one hand. It must be him.

But no, men like her unwanted neighbor never knocked gently. Then who could it be? Putting down the can, she headed for the door. Only one way to find out.

The little girl who stood on the doorstep

took Maddie totally by surprise. Long chestnut hair curled down her back, a dusting of freckles across the bridge of her snub little nose stood out against her tanned skin, and unexpectedly dark eyelashes outlined huge, honey-brown eyes. The girl looked cross, thought Maddie, standing back to let her step inside. "Can I help you?" she asked.

The child just lifted her chin. "Why have you taken our house? We've never had a house before, and it's not fair to take someone else's. You should get your own."

"Taken *your* house?" Maddie echoed, confusion slowing her thoughts.

"We've come a long way to get our house," the little girl said, stamping her foot and tossing back her mane of curls. "It's not fair to take it from us."

Clarity slowly dawned on her. "I don't know what's going on here, but I'm guessing you live in the trailer?"

"Yes, with Daddy, Red, Cuckoo and Moneypenny."

Maddie looked at her vaguely. Red must be the huge dog the man had with him yesterday, but who or what were the other two and how could they all live in such a small space?

"And who are Cuckoo and Moneypenny?" she asked.

"They're chickens, of course. And I'm Meg. Daddy calls me Nutmeg, though. I'm six. How old are you?"

"Twenty-six," said Maddie, smiling. "Now why don't I get you a cookie, and you can tell me all about it."

The little girl deliberated for a moment, and then she shook her head determinedly. "No, thanks. Daddy says I have to stay away from you. He says you're mean."

"Well, you can tell your daddy…" Maddie began, but she stopped herself. This was between her and… "What is your daddy's name?"

Meg stared up at her. "Ross. He's called Ross. What's yours?"

Maddie reached out to shake Meg's hand. "I'm Maddie, and I'm pleased to meet you."

Meg pulled her hand away sharply, glancing behind her as if expecting a reprimand. "Well, I don't think we are very pleased to meet you," she said, running off across the yard.

Maddie watched her go, noting with surprise how Ross smiled warmly as his daughter approached. He placed a broad hand on her shoulder, leading her toward their make-shift home. Why were they really here, and why would she have been allowed to rent the cottage if it did belong to them? She needed to find out soon. Standing her ground with this Ross guy was one thing—he could obviously stand up to her—but being here in this warm, comfortable cottage when a little girl lived right next door in a small trailer with her dad and three animals just didn't feel right, especially if they had a right to be here.

Tonight, Maddie decided, hopefully after Meg had gone to bed, she was going to try to find out what this was really all about.

CHAPTER THREE

ROSS SAW MADDIE arrive home, watching with interest as she climbed awkwardly out of her small car and hurried to the front door, dropping her car keys on the way. Was she putting on the slight limp to try to get his sympathy? Well, it wouldn't work on him. Then again, she hadn't actually seen him, so it couldn't be for his benefit. And come to think of it, she didn't exactly look as if she was blooming with health, either. She was quite thin, her expression was strained and there were dark shadows under her eyes. For all he knew, she'd been lying about having paid three months' rent. Perhaps she was a squatter after all—on drugs, even. Judging by her put-together appearance and nearly new car, though, he had to admit that did seem to be a bit of a long shot.

The first thing he'd done that morning was call the solicitor, but that had been a waste of time. As far as they knew, the cottage was empty; probate had been granted and now it was just a matter of waiting for the regulatory period of time before he was actually handed the deeds. When he explained about the woman who appeared to be living there and had insisted that she'd paid rent, they promised to look into it and let him know in due course.

So now it seemed all Ross could do was wait. But he would do whatever was necessary to get his daughter what she was entitled to, that was for sure. And if he found out the woman was lying, then he'd kick her out right away, within the law or not.

Reluctantly, he went back to fixing up the chicken run. "Won't be long now, chucks," he told the tawny brown chicken and her brightly colored cockerel companion. They watched him from their small coop with bright, beady eyes.

It wasn't until later, as he gently placed the chickens into their new enclosure, watching with a satisfied smile as they eagerly pecked at the grass, that he realized he hadn't seen Meg for a while. She appeared suddenly from the direction of the cottage. "She's called Maddie and she's twenty-six," she announced.

"You stay away from her."

Ross's voice sounded loud in his ears, and he placed a hand on Meg's shoulder, surprised at his own reaction. "Sorry, Nutmeg, but we don't know her and you should stay away from strangers."

Totally unperturbed by her dad's outburst, Meg just smiled. "I told her she had to give us our house back."

"Well…good for you," Ross said. "But in the future, stay well away from her. Hopefully she'll be gone soon."

Meg stared at him with her huge, honey-colored eyes… Jenny's eyes. It made his heart hurt.

"She offered me a cookie, but I didn't take it."

Ross ruffled her curly hair. "Good for you, love. Now go and get washed—your supper will be ready soon."

As THE ORANGE sun slipped behind the dark mass of the trees at the edge of the property, Ross sat by Meg's bed, relating his usual bedtime story about elves in the forest that helped injured creatures. Tonight, it was a hedgehog that had become trapped when some silly teenagers had started a campfire. All his stories were aimed at encouraging his daughter to care for animals and learn how to behave in the countryside. As her eyes began to droop, he lowered his tone, eventually leaning down to kiss her forehead before tucking the plaid blanket around her shoulders. She'd had the slightly threadbare blanket since she was a baby, and she wouldn't sleep without it.

Suddenly feeling weary himself, he decided to have a shower and then go through some job leads. He'd saved up enough money to bring Meg back home, but he needed to get work soon or they would be forced to move on. There would always be work for him in Scotland, but moving back there was the last thing he wanted…for Meg, at least.

The small knock on the door came just as he emerged from the shower. "Coming," he called, quickly rubbing himself dry and pulling on jeans and a blue check shirt. He was still rubbing his dark hair with a towel as he opened the door. When he saw the woman from the cottage standing outside, he dropped the towel to his side. "Oh," was all he could manage. "What do you want?"

MADDIE PUSHED PAST HIM, stepping determinedly into the surprisingly tidy trailer. It was small, of course, but it did seem cozy and cared for. There were even flowers on the table.

"Meg's touch," Ross said, following her gaze.

"It seems very…" She looked at him, feeling awkward as she noted his open shirt, revealing a hard, tanned, muscular torso. She cleared her throat. "Comfortable."

He stared down at her, his expression revealing nothing. "What did you expect?"

"Nothing," she said quickly. "I had no expectations."

"Be honest," he urged, his voice deep and slightly harsh. "You expected us to be living in squalor alongside the chickens and the dog. Well, yeah, Red lives here—he deserves to—but as you can see, the chickens have their own place."

At the sound of his name, the huge dog padded into view. Ross dropped a hand to caress his ears. "He likes to sleep near Meg… he adores her."

"Why didn't you tell me you had a daughter?"

Ross shrugged. "Why would I? It has nothing to do with you."

Suddenly, Maddie found it difficult to

breathe. She'd built herself up to this moment, wanting to discuss the situation like two mature adults. But his hostile demeanor was making that seem impossible. It wasn't just about his attitude, though; it was also the raw masculinity he exuded. Was Ross aware how awkward he made her feel? she wondered. She had never met anyone so comfortable in his own skin, so...sure of himself.

Determined not to let him get to her, she tried to ignore her discomfort. "Why did you tell me it was your cottage?" she asked bluntly.

For a second, he stared at her as if she was stupid. "Because it is." He hesitated. "Well, to be honest, technically it belongs to Meg."

"Then how come I've been able to rent it, and you didn't even know?"

He moved toward her, and she forced herself to stand her ground, refusing to take the backward step that would have given her space to breathe. He held her gaze, his dark eyes narrowed. "Perhaps you haven't *paid* any rent. Perhaps it's just a con."

Anger lent Maddie the strength she was losing. "I already told you—I've paid fifteen hundred pounds up front, and if you call the leasing agent, she'll back me up. I think *you're* the con man. You just want somewhere to live for free, and you thought the cottage was empty."

She could tell by his face that she'd gotten through to him. "I think you'd better leave," he said, his voice rising. "And stay away from my daughter."

"Dad?" The tiny voice came from behind them. "What's going on?"

They swung around simultaneously to see Meg standing outside her room, eyes bleary and hair tousled with sleep. One arm was draped across Red's huge back, his head the same height as hers. At the sound of her voice, he gently lapped his tongue across her cheek.

Ross's attitude changed at once. "It's okay, Nutmeg. You go back to bed. This lady has just come to talk to me about the cottage."

"She's called Maddie," Meg said. "And she has cookies. Have you asked her why she's got our house?"

"It's a mistake," Maddie said gently. "Just a silly mix-up. Go back to bed like your daddy said, and we'll try to sort it out."

The little girl did as she was told, putting her hand across her mouth to smother a huge yawn. The big red dog padded along behind her, settling himself down in her bedroom doorway as if keeping guard.

"I'll just make sure she's settled," Ross said, disappearing into her room.

Maddie was just about to leave when he reappeared. "If you pay me back the money I've paid out, then I'll leave," she told him.

Ross's dark eyes glinted. "I'd rather make sure you've actually paid it first."

"I am not a liar, but go ahead," she said coldly. Desperate to get away from him, she pushed open the door and glanced over her shoulder as she stepped outside. "Anyway, as I already said, if it really is your cottage, you should know that."

The door banged shut behind her, and Maddie breathed in the cold night air, suddenly aware of how hot her cheeks were and grateful for the breeze's cooling touch. Well, she'd tried, and if that wasn't enough, then too bad. There was no reasoning with the guy. If it wasn't for Meg, she'd have gone out of her way to make sure she'd never have to speak to him again. She should have realized yesterday that trying to have a civilized conversation would be a waste of time. He'd even let his daughter believe she was a bad person, and that wasn't fair when he didn't know her. She'd had her say, and now the ball was in his court.

It was only much later, in the moments between waking and sleeping, that Maddie remembered the gentleness in Ross's voice when he'd spoken to Meg... The softness he'd shown then had certainly belied the bitterness in his dark eyes and the hard outline of his muscular physique. It was his gentleness that stayed with her, however, as her heavy eyelids finally drooped shut.

CHAPTER FOUR

THAT NIGHT, AS USUAL, Maddie slept restlessly. She always woke up several times if she hadn't taken painkillers, but she hated to depend on them. Some nights, though, the constant ache in her left leg and back was unbearable. The doctors had told her to take things slowly, and she was still supposed to be doing physiotherapy, but to her it was all useless. As far as she was concerned, there was only one thing that would make her whole again, and that was getting her life back.

Going carefully down the stairs in the darkness, she dug around in her bag for her medication, washing down the pills with a glass of water. Through the window she could see a glow in the trailer. She stood for a moment, taking in the scene as the silver moon slid from behind a dark cloud, casting an eerie light that made the trees look like sentinels.

She felt a surge of irritation. Things were tough enough right now without having to put up with Ross's harassment. And what if he was telling the truth—what if the cottage really had been left to Meg? She didn't care where Ross lived, but Meg deserved better. If she saw him around, she'd put her offer to him again, but she certainly wasn't going to seek him out. Hopefully, he'd soon find out she was in the right and go back where he'd come from until the three months were up.

Without meaning to, Maddie found herself wondering where that place was. His accent held a strong Scottish burr, and Meg's voice had a hint of it, too. Well, if he headed back there today, it wouldn't be too soon. Wearily, she headed back up the steep staircase and snuggled into her bed, waiting for her medication to soothe away the pain. She needed a good night's sleep to function properly tomorrow, but at the moment sleep felt a very long way off.

When she woke again, the pale light of dawn was creeping through her window. She had opened the curtains a crack when she went to bed, not liking total darkness; now she could see the Lakeland hills looming into the sky with rugged splendor. For a moment, she was disoriented. Where was she?

Memories flooded into her confusion: Alex when he loved her… Alex when he'd turned away, stony faced. He was such a successful jockey, groomed for stardom by his trainer dad, Josh Andrews. Maddie had been totally over the moon when he'd first asked her out and unable to believe it when he'd asked her to marry him. Theirs was to have been the biggest wedding of the decade, he'd insisted. That was the first time she'd questioned their relationship; he didn't seem to take into account that she just wanted a small wedding, and that had sowed a seed of doubt.

When she'd had her accident, a month or so later, he'd been at her bedside every day at first…until the weeks turned into months. When they'd told her she would never ride again, she'd been distraught, and if she was honest with herself, she might have taken her frustration out on Alex. It was easy to be bubbly and fun when you lived life in a whirl of success…not so easy when your whole future had crumbled and your dreams were shattered. His visits had had become less and less frequent until he admitted that he'd found someone else.

In a way, Alex's betrayal had been a relief. After that, she hadn't needed to try, and she'd been able to wallow in her own self-pity. She wasn't proud of it, the depression that had left her without motivation. Then one day she'd looked out the window at the glorious sun-filled sky and realized there was still so much beauty in the world. That was the day she'd made a promise to herself to get her life back…no matter what.

A cockerel shrieked out its morning call, and Maddie pulled her covers over her head. They had a cockerel for goodness' sake! Oh, well, at least she wouldn't need an alarm clock while Ross and Meg were around. Today, she was off to Sky View again, and she couldn't wait.

After eating a light breakfast of tea and toast, Maddie locked the cottage door and pocketed the key, deliberately not looking at the trailer as she walked up the pathway and opened her car. When something nudged her from behind, she turned with a start to see Red gazing up at her happily, his long pink tongue hanging from the side of his mouth to reveal a set of dangerous-looking fangs. Somehow, though, she felt totally unafraid. "Hello, boy," she said, holding out her hand.

The giant dog nuzzled her gently, belying his fearsome appearance.

Maddie noticed Meg watching solemnly over by the trailer. She waved, but when Meg just wiggled her fingers in return, obviously afraid to show a response because of her dad, Maddie felt a rush of anger at his unfairness. Where was this little girl's mother, and why were they living in a trailer, anyway?

It was none of her business, she decided, so she got in her car and drove off. Besides, she wasn't even interested in Ross's way of life.

At Sky View, Cass Munro was waiting impatiently. "Sorry," she said as Maddie came in through the kitchen door. "I forgot to ask if you could come a bit earlier today. I have a doctor's appointment and I'm running late. Jake brought a client in for breakfast and I haven't even had the chance to load the dishwasher, so if you wouldn't mind taking Robbie to school and clearing up the breakfast dishes after… He's all ready to go."

"Of course." Maddie smiled, placing her hand on Cass's arm. "It's what I'm here for. You just take your time."

As if on cue, Robbie ran in through the back door with Choco at his heels. "We've been right up to the top of the hill," he cried. "I'll just get my school bag."

"And remember to wipe your face," Cass called after him as he raced off up the stairs.

Forty-five minutes later, Robbie duly dropped off at the village school, Maddie surveyed the pile of clean breakfast pots beside the sink with satisfaction. She was needed here, and it felt good to be needed after being unable to do anything useful for so long.

Her mother had called last night, stressing about how she was eating and whether she was doing too much. Maddie had to admit it was nice to know her mum cared. Here at Sky View, no one knew just how badly injured she'd been. For a long time after the accident, she'd been in a vague, formless, pain-filled place. Then the depression had descended, taking over her every thought…until, after eighteen long months, as she watched a swallow skim across the glorious summer sky, she suddenly remembered that she, too, still had a life—*her* life. She needed to live it and not just go through the motions. After that day, she'd let nothing hold her back from her ambition to make enough of a recovery to stand on her own two feet and have a future again.

To her surprise, she was glad that Alex was

no longer around to hold her back. This was her fight, hers alone, and it had finally begun.

Despite her satisfaction, even by midmorning Maddie was finding it tough to keep going. The nagging pain in her leg and back had become a throbbing ache, and she longed to sit down and take a rest.

"Does it hurt a lot?" Cass asked in a casual tone when she got home from her appointment. "Take a break if you like."

"No!" Maddie shook her head. "Thanks, but I'm here to work."

"Then make us a drink and we'll both take a break," she suggested.

As they sat at the kitchen table five minutes later, sipping coffee in companionable silence, Cass looked across at her with a puzzled frown. "So...what happened? The accident, I mean."

Unused to such a direct line of questioning, Maddie hesitated. "I was cycling to work one morning, and someone knocked me off my bike," she eventually began. "To be honest, I can't remember much about it, and I'm okay now...except that my leg sometimes aches."

Cass stirred sugar into her mug then met Maddie's gaze with sympathy in her eyes. "And that's all?"

Unable to bear seeing the same sad expression everyone gave her back home, Maddie gritted her teeth. Before she knew it, the Munros would be talking about her in lowered voices, going quiet the moment she walked into a room. *Poor Madeline, her whole career ruined...and she was doing so well.*

"It's hardly anything, really," she said, forcing a bright smile onto her face. "Just a bit of a nuisance. It doesn't hold me back at all."

She stood and went back to peeling carrots, pretending she hadn't seen the concerned look on Cass's face.

At midday Jake, his dad, Bill Munro— a tall, thin man whose current project was fixing up the holiday cottages—and Jed, the young lad who helped Jake back the youngsters, came in to eat. They sat at the large kitchen table, laughing and joking and talking about their plans. Maddie handed out food and poured tea, desperately trying not to limp as she moved around the large, homey kitchen.

"Sit down and join us, lass," said Bill, smiling in Maddie's direction. "You have to eat, too."

Jake nodded in agreement, pulling out a chair, and she sat, feeling awkward.

"I already told her," Cass told them. She turned to Maddie. "Get your lunch—I can see to dessert."

"It's okay," Maddie insisted, not wanting the fuss.

"Sorry, lass, you're overruled," Bill said, stroking his neat, white beard, his eyes crinkling in a smile. She settled into the chair with a sigh as Jed passed her a plate.

When the talk turned to horses, Maddie found it difficult not to join in. This was so stupid. Maybe she should just come clean and let them all in on the truth, tell them about her ambition to ride again. They'd help her; she knew they would. She didn't want help, though, did she? She didn't want people to make allowances, to see the pity in their eyes as they watched her struggle to be even half of what she used to be. She wanted to be respected for what she'd achieved on her own merit; that was why she'd come here—to be treated like a normal human being again.

"Have you done any riding, Maddie?" Bill asked, right out of the blue. She couldn't lie about that.

"Some," she told him. "Not for a while, though."

"Well, then," Cass said, placing an apple pie and jug of cream on the table. "You can start again while you're here. We're always looking for exercise riders."

"As soon as we get a suitable horse in for you, we'll get you on board," Jake agreed. "At the moment, they're all only half-broken, or too difficult for a novice."

Novice! Something deep in Maddie's chest curled in objection. "I'm not—" she began before biting her tongue, "that bad. Just rusty, I guess."

"I started on Carlotta," Cass said. "She's the best. Unfortunately, she's in foal right now, or you could have tried riding her."

"In foal to Grand Design," Jake added, excitement rising in his voice. "We're going to have one very special foal, I reckon."

"I know that stallion!" Maddie exclaimed without thinking. "Big bay…quite tricky to handle, but so talented…" She trailed off as she realized her mistake.

Jake frowned. "How do you know that?"

Cass hesitated. *Here's another chance to tell the truth*, her conscience told her. "My dad," she blurted.

Jake sat back, hands behind his head. "Ah, into racing, is he?"

"Kind of." Maddie got up to start clearing the table, remembering the elation of riding the big bay stallion out on exercise, when he was one of the three she used to "do." Tears pressed against her eyelids, and she blinked to try to clear them. She had lost so much more than just the riding. She had lost the companionship of her charges, too.

"You okay?" Cass whispered as they bundled pots into the dishwasher.

Maddie nodded. "Yes…thanks."

"Well, you might want to go a bit easy on my crockery," she suggested, and suddenly Maddie was smiling again.

"Sorry," she said. "I wasn't thinking."

When the men had disappeared out into the yard again, Cass eased herself down onto a comfortable chair beside the stove. "My back aches a bit," she groaned. "I'll just sit for a second."

"You need to rest," Maddie said. "How long is it now?"

"Just a matter of weeks," Cass told her dreamily, touching her stomach. "Look, she's kicking."

When Maddie hurried over, Cass grabbed her hand and placed it next to hers. "See?"

"And it's definite…that it's a girl, I mean?"

Cass nodded, puckering her brow. "To be honest, I didn't really want to know, and neither did Jake, but…"

"But what?"

"Well…" Cass let out a big sigh. "Robbie's twin sister was killed in a road accident, along with his grandma. It was before I even came here, but obviously it's had a huge effect on Rob. We wanted him to know what to expect…no surprises."

"And was he pleased to find out it was a girl?"

"He was—is—over the moon about having a sister again."

"And do you have a name for her yet?"

Cass nodded. "We're going to call her Gwen, after Jake's mum."

As the unborn baby's frantic movement slowed, Maddie withdrew her hand. "That's lovely," she said. "Like a brand-new start."

"A brand-new start," Cass echoed, her eyes gently drooping.

Maddie moved quietly away, not wanting to disturb her. There was so much love in this house where once there must have been so much pain. Jake Munro had gotten past his heartache, and that was what she wanted to do. Learn to live with the past and forge a new future. Would hers hold a family one day? She couldn't help but wonder. It might, she decided, but not for a long time yet. She had to straighten herself out before she could include anyone else in her life...and anyway, look what happened the last time she started to dream of a future...with Alex. No, it was definitely just her and her demons, for the next few years at least.

CHAPTER FIVE

ROSS CLICKED OFF his phone with a heavy heart. So Maddie had been telling the truth after all; she *had* paid for the cottage. Seemingly the solicitors hadn't informed the rental agency of Anne Maddox's death, and they'd rented it out, not knowing… So now what?

He'd felt so positive, coming back here to Little Dale, more positive than he had been since Jenny died. In those early years after her death, dealing with the weight of his own guilt and his mother-in-law's accusations, the only thing that had kept him going was Meg.

He should have noticed how ill Jenny was, he realized that now, and he would have if she'd shown physical symptoms, but depression was way beyond his experience. It had been foaling time on the stud where he worked, too, but that was no excuse for all the hours he spent there…hours he should have spent trying to help his young wife overcome her illness and deal with their baby girl.

Later—way too much later—he had read up on postpartum depression and finally begun to understand just how real and painful the condition could be. He continued to keep reading about it to this day, again and again, as if for the first time, asking himself why. That couldn't bring Jenny back, though, couldn't get rid of the guilt that haunted him.

She had taken her own life because he was too selfish to put her before his work. Her mother had known it; Anne Maddox had blackened his name in their community so convincingly that some people had shunned him in the street. That was when he'd decided to take Meg and leave, go back to his native Scotland. And to his surprise, Jenny's mother hadn't even kicked up a fuss when he'd told her he was taking her only granddaughter so very far away. It seemed as if there was nothing left inside her but hatred and blame, and she hated *him* so much she would rather lose Meg than have him around. She'd done the right thing by her granddaughter in the end though, by leaving her the cottage. He would always be grateful to her for that.

He and Meg had been relatively happy in Scotland, even though he'd known that they would need to settle down somewhere eventually. He'd found plenty of part-time work on farms and studs, even working in forestry for a while. He and Meg had traveled wherever he was needed, though never so far away that he couldn't get Meg to Tinytots in Kelso.

He'd tried a few different nurseries, but Tinytots, run by a warmhearted, middle-aged woman named Clare, was the only one that he really trusted with his daughter. When she wasn't there, he looked after her himself, waking with her in the night, caring for her when she was ill or teething, playing with her and introducing her to the countryside he loved...wanting her to love it, too. He'd had no social life of any kind for years, to such an extent that some people nicknamed him the Recluse, but he didn't care. He didn't believe he deserved a social life. His lot in life, he had long ago decided, was to make it up to Jenny by giving their daughter the best that he could.

When Anne Maddox died, leaving her granddaughter the cottage where he and Jenny had lived for the short time they were together, he knew that giving Meg the best meant bringing her home to Little Dale to claim her heritage.

The last thing he'd expected was to find

someone living there; he'd been so angry, truly believing the woman was lying. So now what? Dealing with people had never been one of his best skills, and the lonely years in Scotland had left him even more awkward with strangers, especially those of the opposite sex. There would never be anyone in his life again after Jenny—he was sure of that. He'd failed his wife, and he didn't deserve another chance at that kind of happiness. What right did he have to destroy yet another woman's life?

He wasn't going back to Scotland, though, wasn't going to give up and give in. This Maddie person would just have to put up with them for the next three months; he had no money to give her, even if he wanted to.

Having settled on his course of action, Ross decided to spend the day putting down roots. He laid a row of paving stones up to the trailer door to keep their feet out of the mud. He went to town with Meg and bought a plastic storage container from the local DIY store to put their dirty boots in, and he passed the afternoon building a barbecue area out of bricks just under the shelter of the trees. When their unwanted tenant came back, she would see that he had no intention of moving on. Maybe that would persuade her to move on herself...sooner than she'd planned, at least. It was obvious that she was uncomfortable with his presence, maybe even a little threatened, and he didn't have any intention of trying to change her mind about that. All he wanted was to be settled with Meg in the cottage...and to land a decent job, of course.

That was another thing he packed into his busy day: traveling around to some local farms in the hopes of finding part-time work, at least. Unfortunately, he had no luck, but tomorrow he had an appointment with the principal of Little Dale Primary School. Once Meg was settled in there, he'd have more free time to pursue his job prospects.

Putting on the kettle, he called for Meg, who was sitting at the table drawing. She loved to draw. "You might be going to proper school soon," he told her.

"Will there be lots of kids to play with?" she asked, pencil poised above the paper.

"I guess so," he said.

"Will they be nice?"

For a moment he just stared at her, his small, innocent, beautiful daughter, and the weight of responsibility made him shudder. He'd tried to bring her up to be independent and strong in a hard, tough world, but he knew she could never be tough enough. She had her mother's sweet, soft personality, and that would never change. It was Jenny's own personality that had let her down at the end, the inability to stand up to pressure. She'd needed looking after, and he hadn't seen that.

That was one thing that drew him to Maddie, he supposed. Despite his determination to dislike her, she had that same vulnerability... and yet she'd stood up to him so bravely, holding her ground. That was what he wanted Meg to be able to do.

"I hope so, love," he said finally.

"Are you all right, Daddy?" Meg asked, huge eyes gazing solemnly up at him.

He blinked, smiling. "Why, yes..."

"You look funny...kind of sad. Are you sad?"

"Sometimes," he admitted, holding out his arms. She ran into them, and he held her tightly, twirling her around. "We all get a bit sad sometimes."

"Is it because someone is living in our house?"

"Yes... I guess so."

"Maybe we could live there, too, if there are enough bedrooms."

"I don't think she'd like that," he said. "No...we'll be fine in here until she moves out, and then we'll decorate the whole place. You can choose any color you want for your room."

"Pink and purple," Meg exclaimed, clapping her hands as he put her back down.

Red jumped up, pushing against her, and she wrapped her tiny arms around his huge neck.

"Can Red come to school with me?" she asked. "He'll sit quiet—I know he will."

Ross studied his daughter's bright little face, his heart aching. "I'm sure he'd love to, and I wish he could, too, but I don't think dogs are allowed in school. Don't worry, though—I'm sure you'll make lots of friends really soon."

MADDIE DROVE HOME from Sky View as the day drew to a close, feeling tired and drained but happier than she had in a long while. It was nice to be taken at face value again, and she was glad that she hadn't given in to the temptation to own up about her riding experience.

When Jake had told her she could start riding when they had a "suitably quiet horse," the idea had rankled her. She, Maddie Maguire, the person who used to take pride in being able to ride anything, lowered to novice status? But she'd soon realized she had to think like a novice if she was going to get back on a horse again—which the doctors had told her was impossible. Her balance wasn't what it used to be, and she didn't even know yet how capable her body was. She had to take it one step at a time if she wanted to get anywhere at all. And if that meant being a novice for a while, then she just had to swallow her pride and get on with it.

Her stomach lurched when she spotted the trailer through the trees. Would Ross come over and try to bully her out of the cottage again? There was something very disconcerting about him, a primal ferocity that overrode modern etiquette. How he'd ever managed to father such a lovely little girl was beyond her. Anyway, he was in for a shock if he thought he could frighten her away; she was made of tougher stuff than that. He had turned her offer down, so now she just had to stand her ground for the next three months—which, despite her delicate appearance, she knew was well within her capabilities. You didn't get to ride highly strung young Thoroughbreds, let alone win races, without being able to stand up for yourself.

Trying to stand tall, Maddie walked slowly and determinedly toward the front door of Rose Cottage, staring straight ahead and refusing to even acknowledge the fact that Ross might be watching. She slammed the door and bolted it, giving in to her nerves for a moment by leaning back. From outside, she could hear music and Meg's high-pitched laughter. What was the little girl laughing at? she wondered with a sudden tug of loneliness. Unable to resist the temptation, Maddie went across to peer through the window that looked out on the trailer. Ross was sitting cross-legged on the ground. Smoke curled up from some kind of barbecue, and he was playing a guitar—actually playing a guitar!—as if everything was okay, when he had disrupted her whole life.

Suddenly, as if aware of her gaze, he looked up, meeting her eyes from across the distance. Maddie froze, her heart hammering in her chest, and then she turned abruptly away. It was certainly going to be a long three months if this was what she was going to have to put up with every night.

Maddie made herself a cup of coffee and

sat down, cradling the mug in her hands as she went over the day's events, remembering how the talk had turned to horses. Finding out that Jake Munro's mare, Carlotta, was in foal to Grand Design had brought her past tumbling back and reminded her sharply of Alex.

They'd nicknamed the colt Dennis, though his real name was Grand Design. He had been one of her three charges at Apple Tree Stud, and it was Alex who had persuaded his dad that she would be able to handle him. She'd struggled with Dennis at first and been bitten more than a few times, not to mention the episode when he dumped her on the gallops. But eventually her resilience had paid off. She and Dennis had reached an understanding, a companionship that had lasted until he'd been sold. She'd cried all night when he left, and the stable yard at Apple Tree had felt empty without him.

Suddenly realizing she was sitting in darkness, Maddie got up and headed for the switch, hesitating as she passed the window. She could see lights on in the trailer, and then the door opened, light silhouetting the man's big frame. What was he doing here? Why was he all alone with his little girl, and was this really his cottage? He must have found out that she had every right to be here or else he'd have been over here to give her a hard time again. His demeanor had unnerved her at first, but she didn't feel quite so threatened now. The way he was with Meg…and Red, who never seemed to leave his side, made her believe he couldn't really be a bad person… could he?

The little girl had looked so much like him when she'd questioned Maddie about her taking their house, so fierce and angry. Perhaps tomorrow she should try to talk to her again. If they were going to be living next door for the next three months, then she didn't like the idea that Meg thought she was mean.

She'd have an early night, she decided, to build up her strength for tomorrow. She was so relieved by how well she seemed to be getting along with everyone at Sky View. Then again, they were all so welcoming and easy to talk to…even Jake Munro, who she'd been a bit in awe of.

The memories of Grand Design, and consequently Alex, were harder to deal with. Mostly, nowadays, she was glad he hadn't hung around to see her like this, but she couldn't help but reminisce, back to those amazing days when they were a golden couple in the racing world.

Steeling her mind, she went into the kitchen, forcing herself to concentrate on the basic task of making something to eat. Those times were gone, and reflecting on them would just depress her. At least she had hope in her heart again. That just had to be enough…for now.

CHAPTER SIX

MADDIE WOKE EARLY, discovering immediately that she'd really overdone it the day before. She could hardly manage to climb out of bed, and her left leg refused to do as she told it. Knowing the cause, she fought off the panic attack that threatened, fixating on breathing deep and slow. It was ages until she needed to get ready for work, and experience had taught her that she just had to stay calm and be patient.

Sitting on the side of the bed, she began her exercises, wincing in pain but determined to be ready to leave for Sky View by eight. Slowly, her muscles eased and her coordination improved enough for her to get dressed and go down the steep, narrow staircase.

As she passed through the hallway, she heard a gentle tapping on the door.

"Hello?" she called as she slowly went to open it. Surely, her unwanted neighbor would have made a lot more noise, but who else would be knocking so early in the morning?

Meg stood outside. "No dog?" Maddie asked, smiling.

Meg shook her head. "He's gone with Daddy."

"What!" Maddie frowned. "He left you alone?"

Meg stepped across the threshold. "No, he's just doing the chickens and letting Red go for a run... Do you have any milk?"

Maddie stifled a smile. "Have you run out?"

"Daddy forgot to buy some yesterday. He says it doesn't matter, but he loves to have a cup of coffee with his breakfast. I thought you could let us have some, but don't tell him or he'll be cross."

It obviously hadn't occurred to her that her dad might wonder where the milk came from, but Maddie didn't point that out. Hopefully, Ross would just let it lie.

"What's your full name, Meg?" she asked.

"Megan Noble," Meg said proudly, tossing back her long chestnut curls. "And my dad is called Ross Noble."

"That's a lovely name." Maddie smiled.

"I've got plenty of milk, you can have as much as you like."

"And you won't tell Dad?"

"I won't tell your dad. Here, we'd better hurry if you want to get back before he does."

As they walked into the kitchen, Maddie felt Meg's hand curl around hers, and warmth trickled through her veins. "So we're friends now, are we?"

She was rewarded by a wide, heartfelt smile. "If you want to be," said Meg.

"I want to be," Maddie repeated. "And I won't tell your dad about the milk."

By the time Maddie finally set off for Sky View, having taken her medication and eased her objecting limbs into submission, she felt much more ready for the day. Her previous preoccupation about the man in the trailer seemed less important, and she barely gave him a thought as she headed for her car. She wasn't afraid of him anymore, and as far as she was concerned, his presence at Rose Cottage was just a nuisance she'd have to endure for a while. When he suddenly appeared beside her, however, her heart sped up, pounding in her throat.

"I'd rather you didn't encourage my daughter if you don't mind," he said curtly. "I can't have her disappearing all the time."

Rankled, Maddie stopped in her tracks. "Then maybe you should keep a better eye on her. I haven't 'encouraged' her and don't intend to. If you don't want her around me, then maybe you should go somewhere else and come back when I've moved out."

"In three months, you mean," Ross snapped, his dark eyes narrowing.

Maddie nodded, raising her eyebrows. "Ah, so you've spoken to the rental agency."

"I may have...but I still intend to camp here until you leave."

Maddie set off toward her car again, walking carefully. "Well, that's your prerogative, but if you think you can frighten me off, I'm afraid you're wasting your time. I'm a lot tougher than I look."

Ross paused, and automatically she stopped, too, standing tall and holding his gaze in defiance. A sudden softness in his eyes took her by surprise, but then his mouth set into a grim line. "I don't doubt it," he said quietly.

Maddie turned away abruptly, more uncomfortable with the momentary flash of warmth and perhaps admiration than she was with his more familiar display of anger. "Now if you don't mind," she insisted, "I'm late for work. Oh, and by the way…"

He frowned. "By the way what?"

She stuck out her chin, looking him straight in the face and hoping he didn't notice the slight trembling in her limbs. "Meg only came to ask for milk—*for you*—so maybe you should appreciate her a bit more instead of trying to get at me."

To her relief, Ross stepped away from her without another word, but the expression in his eyes spoke volumes. He didn't like her, and she didn't like him.

"Don't worry," she called after him as he strode away. "I'm quite happy to keep my distance…from you, anyway. If Meg chooses to seek me out, though, I'm not going to turn her away."

MADDIE DROVE TOWARD Sky View, her mind totally taken away from the spat with her unpleasant neighbor by the sheer beauty of her surroundings. The rugged fells loomed against a pale blue sky shot with gray and silver, and rough fell sheep roamed way up toward the skyline, tiny white dots against the greens and browns of grass and bracken on the lower slopes, tucked in cracks and valleys to seek protection from the wild winds that must surely blow here in the winter months. Today, however, it was calm and balmy, both colorful and gray, a stark contrast that made the landscape seem even brighter.

And way, way below her as she climbed toward Sky View, she could see the lake glittering in the morning sun, a paradise for boats and wildlife.

Determined to forget about Ross Noble, Maddie started to hum, feeling happily hopeful as the roofs of Sky View Stables appeared just ahead.

Maddie pulled up at the end of the yard instead of driving right to the house, needing the fix of horse sights and smells she'd get by walking through the stable yard.

A heavily pregnant gray mare appeared through the front gate, led by Jake.

"Morning," he called.

"Morning," she responded. "This must be Carlotta."

When he stopped for a moment, she placed her hand on the elegant arch of the mare's neck, drinking in the feel of her and desperately wanting to press her cheek against the silky softness of her coat. "She's just as beautiful as the painting of her you have in the house," she said.

Jake smiled proudly. "She's going to have a beautiful foal, too, I reckon."

"If it's to Grand Design, then it sure will be," Maddie agreed, already biting her tongue as the words spilled out.

Jake looked at her curiously.

"At least…if his photograph is anything to go by," she managed.

"Yes…he's a handsome horse," he agreed. "I don't reckon the picture you saw will have done him justice. Anyway, I'm off to turn her out. Cass will be waiting for you."

"Of course… I'd better hurry," Maddie cried, glancing at her phone.

After she returned from dropping Robbie off at school, Maddie settled into her daily tasks, enjoying the routine. It gave her confidence to feel that she was actually useful here at Sky View. That had been her worst fear—that she'd find she didn't have enough strength or coordination to do what was required of her. Deep down, she worried that Cass knew more about the extent of her injuries than Maddie had let on and was giving her an easy workload. No, that wasn't possible, she realized as she began setting the table for lunch; there was no way anyone here could know how badly hurt she had really been.

"By the way," Cass said, looking up from the stove. "You'll need to set an extra place. Bob Nelson, who owns the sire of Carlotta's foal, is stopping by. We have another filly that we might put to one of his stallions, and we wanted him to take a look at her."

"Grand Design's owner." Maddie stifled a gasp. The past she'd tried so hard to put behind her sprang into her consciousness.

Cass nodded. "That's right... You have a good memory."

When Bob Nelson came into the kitchen half an hour later, chatting to Jake about his horses, Maddie half expected to recognize him and had a minor panic attack about him recognizing her. To her relief, the small, white-haired man was not familiar, and she heaved a sigh. She was there when Dennis's new owner had come to collect him, but she'd been way too upset to take much notice of anything other than the big bay stallion. Maybe poor Dennis had changed hands yet again, and Bob Nelson was his new owner.

When Jake and Cass insisted she join them for lunch, Maddie was happy to sit down and listen to them chat about horses, although she had to stop herself from joining in on more than one occasion.

They were almost finished the meal when she noticed Bob Nelson eyeing her curiously. "Don't I know you?" he asked.

Maddie froze. "Um…no, I don't think so. You must have mistaken me for someone else."

For a moment, the older man held her gaze. "I could have sworn…" He shrugged. "No matter. As you said, I must have made a mistake."

"Seems you must have a double, Maddie." Cass smiled.

Maddie stood hurriedly, almost losing her balance in her rush to start clearing the table.

"She knows all about Grand Design," Jake remarked. "Through your dad, right, Maddie?"

"Er…yes, kind of," she mumbled, pushing crockery into the dishwasher. "I just know that he's beautiful but cantankerous."

"Well, that is a good description of him," Bob agreed.

As the older man went to leave with Jake ten minutes later, Maddie glanced across at him and caught his gaze again. The puzzled frown on his face unnerved her slightly. She'd never set out to lie to anyone…and she hadn't, not really. She was just keeping some things to herself until the time was right. If Bob Nelson did recognize her, then she would come across to Jake and Cass as deceitful, and that was the last thing she wanted.

When Maddie set off later that afternoon to pick Robbie up from school, she felt positive and lighthearted, absorbing her surroundings with a new awareness. Fell sheep with black faces and wild eyes scattered off the road as she rounded a corner, trotting off through the bracken just as the sun burst from behind a cloud, casting its beam across the fell side so that its greens and grays took on a mantle of gold. Why was it, she wondered, that the sky here seemed so much bigger than anywhere else? A hum bubbled through her lips and she smiled to herself, feeling that she'd somehow turned a corner, and this time it was in the right direction.

She flexed her legs as she drove along. Unbelievably, they felt less tired and painful than they had yesterday, and she was definitely more coordinated. Her back still ached with nagging consistency, but she knew that was something she just had to learn to live with. Balance, stamina and coordination were what she needed if she was going to ride again. Finally it felt as if her goal might be within her grasp.

She arrived at the school way too early and pulled into the parking lot outside the old-fashioned gray stone building, settling back into her seat to wait. With new hope also came the memories of what she'd lost, and for once she allowed them to crowd back into her head. Starting with the morning she tried not to think about, the day her life was turned on its head.

CHAPTER SEVEN

SHE WAS LATE for work, thanks to Alex. They'd had another of their arguments again last night; if it wasn't a disagreement about their wedding plans, then it was usually over what he called her "lack of business sense." Sometimes Maddie felt as if he was trying to groom her for a future as a trainer's partner rather than his wife. Well, she was definitely not going to give up racing or working with the horses hands-on, no matter what he thought.

Last night, she'd still been upset about Dennis, and it had irritated him. It was always hard to let go of a horse you'd cared for constantly, though, and Dennis, aka Grand Design, was extra special. She'd been bitten by him, kicked by him and dumped on the gallops more than once, but then they'd made their breakthrough and suddenly found trust.

She'd insisted on leading him up the ramp when the new owner had come to collect him two days earlier. It had been such a mistake, though, letting Dennis believe, she felt, that she'd broken that precarious trust. That was what she'd been upset about the night before, but Alex could be so cold sometimes. Horses were just a means to an end in the racing industry, he insisted, there to win races and make money. In his eyes, a reflection of his dad's attitude, sentiment had no part to play in the business. You cared for the horses to your best ability, fed them the right food, gave them the best training, helped smooth out their problems, but getting too attached, as Maddie did, was, according to Alex, a mistake.

She'd left him in a temper, she remembered, and woken up the next morning bleary-eyed with the tears she'd shed. They had been hailed as racing's golden couple, both talented jockeys with a bright future. It was expected that Alex would one day take over from his father, and Maddie would be by her husband's side, supporting him as Alex's mum, Joan, had done for his dad. But it hadn't felt like that to her then; it had felt as if he was trying to take control of her, even of her emotions, telling her how to feel and how to think and what to do.

With a gulp of apprehension, Maddie allowed herself to remember what had happened next...

She'd slept in past dawn, waking in a panic because she was late. Pulling on her jodhpurs and a thick, pale blue sweater, she had grabbed a packet of crisps as she passed through the kitchen before jumping on her bike. She was intent on getting to the yard before Scott, the head lad, noticed her absence. Her engagement to the boss's son held no clout with him, and she respected that.

A late February frost had brought a sparkle to the gray surface of the lane. Even the few brave daffodils, whose glorious yellow flowers heralded the approach of spring, had glittered. Maddie could almost feel the sharp, clear morning air on her face as she relived the moment.

Her thighs had ached with effort as she pedaled up the hill from the village, and then she was freewheeling down the other side, her breath coming more easily as her bike increased speed.

It was as she approached the bridge that she saw it. The lane narrowed and she slowed her pace just as the black SUV came roaring into sight over the bridge, traveling way too fast. For a moment, she'd frozen. There was nowhere to go. Pulling on her brakes, she'd veered right, seeing the white face of the driver as he tried to avoid her. Oblivious to the ice, he'd stood on the brakes, but the big vehicle had just carried on, slithering sideways on the slippery road. She would never forget the horror that filled her whole body, the sheer, tortured fear that took away her breath and rendered her helpless.

When the vehicle hit her, strangely there was no pain. She felt a thud, heard the crack of bones unable to withstand the onslaught, felt the fuzziness inside her head that distanced her from the scene…and then came the blackness.

"MADDIE…MADDIE!"

It was only when Robbie pulled the car door open that she heard him. "Sorry," she said, blinking. "I was miles away."

"I won, Maddie!" he cried, jumping up and down.

"Won what?" she asked.

He flashed her a puzzled glance. "The drawing competition—you know, you helped me with it yesterday?"

"Of course… Sorry, Robbie, that's brilliant. Your mum and dad will be so proud of you."

"She is kind of like my mum, isn't she?" he said thoughtfully, climbing into the backseat. "Cass, I mean… It's like I've got two mums."

"You can never have too many mums." Maddie smiled. "Now tell me what they said about your drawing."

Robbie's excited chatter about his teacher's glowing praise for the galloping horse he'd drawn, and his detailed account of the other contestants' entries, took Maddie's mind well away from her memories of the fateful morning that had realigned her hopes and dreams.

When they got back to Sky View, Robbie relayed the whole story again for Cass, who then asked Maddie if she would take him out to the yard to see his dad. Robbie's dog, Choco, followed them, bouncing around in excitement.

They found Jake in the barn, feeding some youngsters. Maddie drank in the sweet aroma of hay, running her eyes over the six yearlings that were diving into buckets of feed. The environment brought such a heavy weight of memories that she felt the sudden rush of tears.

"Are you okay?" Jake asked, noticing her expression.

"Yes," she said, forcing a smile. "Just a bit of hay fever, I think."

"Best get back into the house, then," he suggested. "Cass will have some antihistamines, I'm sure. Rob can stay and help me."

Maddie walked slowly back across the yard, stopping by each stable to gently stroke the head of every inmate. So many beautiful horses—grays and bays and chestnuts, all eager for attention. The horses at Sky View were happy horses, she decided, wondering how long it would take before she felt confident enough to try riding one. It annoyed her that she had to wait until a quiet one came into the yard, but that was something she just had to accept. Planting a determined smile upon her face, she continued to the house. If she had to pretend to be a novice, then that was what she would do.

"You may as well head off," Cass suggested when Maddie stepped into the kitchen. "Thanks for picking Robbie up."

"It's what you pay me for," Maddie said, grinning.

"Yes, but you're so good with him."

Maddie shrugged. "Well…he's a great little boy."

"He certainly is. Oh, and by the way, I forgot to tell you earlier, but you may as well have tomorrow as your day off. I'm at the hospital and Jake is coming with me. We're going out to lunch after, and Bill is away for the day, too, so there's not much point in your coming in. Is that okay?"

"It's fine by me," Maddie said. Truth was, the thought of having a day to rest and build up her strength was very appealing. She'd done more in the past few days than she had in over eighteen months.

"So I guess I'll see you on Friday, then. Can you get here in time to take Robbie to school?"

"Of course," Maddie responded, pulling on her jacket. "And have a nice day tomorrow… I mean, not at the hospital of course, but…"

"I know what you mean." Cass laughed. "Doctors' appointments are never much fun, but we'll have a nice lunch somewhere and then we're going to go and buy a stroller… Wow, I never thought I'd hear myself say that."

"Well, it's a bit too late to change your mind now," Maddie said, glancing meaningfully at Cass's belly. "And you're going to need a stroller pretty soon."

Cass grimaced. "Three weeks tomorrow, actually, and I'm definitely not looking forward to it. I mean, I'm looking forward to being a mum, of course—it's just the birth that worries me."

Maddie placed a reassuring hand on Cass's arm. "Thousands of people have babies every day, so surely it can't be that bad. And if it was, then why would anyone have more than one?"

"Thanks, you're right. I'm just being stupid. I'll see you on Friday, and you can give me your opinion on my beautiful brand-new stroller. I'm thinking of getting something really outrageous."

"Good for you." Maddie smiled again. "And have a nice day tomorrow."

As she walked toward her car, Maddie felt a sudden lurch of regret. If things had been different, she could have been like Cass right now, married to a man she loved, satisfied and secure…maybe even pregnant, too. No… she definitely wouldn't be pregnant; she'd still be riding in races and living her life.

Alex's face came into her head, an image of him on the day he'd told her he had met someone else, and she knew her sense of regret was misplaced. Relief was what she should be feeling, for escaping from a relationship that would only have ended in heartache anyway. If Alex hadn't left her then, he would have done it later when she'd become dependent on him again. Despite her brave words to herself, however, the only feeling that consumed her as she set off for Rose Cottage was despair. Riding a horse again felt so very far away, and that was all that was keeping her going.

CHAPTER EIGHT

EVER SINCE THE ACCIDENT, Maddie had made a conscious effort to keep her memories at bay, trying not to think too much about before, when every day was packed with exhilaration and adrenaline. In fact, she sometimes felt as if her whole life was in two separate parts—before and after. She tried to focus on the after, because before was too painful to bear. Finding out that Grand Design was stabled not too far away, however, had broken down her carefully nurtured barrier. The link with the stallion was just too strong to ignore.

Somehow, she decided, as she climbed awkwardly into her car and started the engine, she was going to try to see him, just to make sure he was happy and well cared for. She didn't yet know how to go about it, but at least she had met his new owner, so that was a start.

As she drove back to Rose Cottage, Dennis was all she could think about. His power when she rode him up the gallops, and the way he used to nuzzle her, putting his nose over her shoulder to draw her back when she tried to leave him…happy memories from another life. She didn't even notice the gorgeous scenery all around her, or think about the man in his dratted trailer, until it came into view. With a heavy lurch, her mind came back into the present.

The little girl, Meg, was outside playing with Red. Her chestnut hair had been braided and tied with brown ribbons, Maddie noticed, and she wore a bright blue dress with flowers on the front. Who could have done her hair? Surely not her dad; he didn't have a sensitive bone in his body. Perhaps he had a girlfriend. Though if he did, then Maddie certainly hadn't seen her around…not that she cared, of course. It just bothered her that he'd been so harsh this morning, ordering her to stay away from his daughter as though she was a bad influence or something. Oh, he had pretended it was just for the little girl's safety, to discourage her from wandering off, but she wasn't stupid. She didn't like him, and he didn't like her—that was the crux of it. Well, it wasn't her fault that she'd paid good money to rent the cottage.

When Meg saw Maddie's car pull up, she ran toward it, waving madly, braids bouncing on her shoulders and skinny legs flying. Red ambled along behind her, keeping guard.

Maddie clambered out into the late-afternoon sunshine, gradually easing her limbs into position as Meg came to a stop, a huge smile on her bright little face. Maddie hesitated, wondering whether she should send the girl back home, but her doubt lasted no more than a second. If Meg wanted to see her, she was only too happy to oblige. Never mind Ross Noble and his irritating arrogance.

"You look nice," she said. "Have you been somewhere special?"

Meg shook her head, and one braid slid from its confines. "We've just been practicing for when I start school after summer."

Maddie nodded. "That's a good idea. You need to look nice and tidy for school."

"They keep falling out, though."

"What, you mean your braids?"

"Daddy says he can't get them tight enough."

"So your dad actually braided your hair and put the ribbons in and everything?"

"Is there something wrong with that?"

The deep voice made her start, and she

spun around to see Ross towering over her. "N-no," she stuttered. "I just mean…"

"Meg and I do just fine, and we don't need anyone to interfere, thanks. Come on, Nutmeg."

He turned away abruptly, motioning for his daughter to follow, but for a moment, she hung back. "I was going to tell her about my school," she began, hopping from foot to foot with excitement. "We went there today to have a look around," she told Maddie.

Ross glanced back, reaching out to take her hand, and his dark, glittering eyes suddenly found Maddie's. She held his gaze, determined not to let him know how daunting she found him.

"I'm not some kind of ogre, you know," she said. "Or a bad influence. Maybe you should let her mingle a bit more if you want her to settle easily into school."

"She's used to day care, so school won't be a problem," he responded curtly, turning away again. This time, Meg followed obediently, but Red still hung back. Maddie scratched the backs of his ears, trying to control her shaking hands. What was it about Ross Noble that made her feel so uncomfortable?

When he let out a low whistle and the dog raced off without a backward glance, loneliness settled over her in a heavy cloud. Was that man friendly with anyone? she wondered, or was it just her he didn't like? Surely, he couldn't still be annoyed that she was in the cottage; she'd offered to move out if he paid her the money back. What more could she do? It was the rental agency he should be angry with.

FORTUNATELY FOR MADDIE, she didn't see either Meg or Ross for the next few days. Red, however, turned up at Rose Cottage several times, scratching at the back door like an old friend eager to come in. Maddie saved him scraps, which he scarfed down gratefully, wagging his tail and accepting her caress before hightailing it back to the trailer, almost as if he knew he was breaking the rules. It surprised her how much she enjoyed his brief visits. In fact, she realized as she saw him trotting toward the back door on one of her days off work, she'd come to look forward to his visits. She'd buy him some dog treats when she went to the village store, she decided, smiling to herself as she imagined what Ross Noble would say if he knew.

The grocery store was near the gray stone church that melted into its surroundings as though it was a part of the earth itself. How many events had it seen? Maddie found herself wondering. Weddings, christenings and funerals, generation after generation, through both happy times and sad. So much emotion must have overflowed from its arched wooden doors, and yet it seemed like such a peaceful place.

The store itself was small, its shelves stacked high with so many goods that it was difficult to find what you were looking for. She grabbed the dog treats and put bread, milk and cereal into her basket, failing to spot the laundry detergent or frozen food. Glancing around for assistance, she realized no one else seemed to be there—no customers and no shopkeeper.

Finally, an elderly woman dressed in a tweed suit and sporting brown brogues appeared through a door at the back. Maddie stared at her. She looked as if she should be out on a country walk rather than working in a grocery shop. "Can I help you?" she asked, fastening a pinafore around her ample middle.

"Yes, I—"

"Are you just passing through the village, or are you here to stay for a while...on holiday or working?"

Her directness took Maddie by surprise. "I...I'm renting a cottage and working for the Munros," Maddie told her. "And you are?"

"Store owner, Nora Ryland. I'm way too old for this job, I know, but when my sister died...well, what else could I do? So...what cottage would that be exactly?" she asked.

"It's about a mile or so from the village, and it's called Rose Cottage."

"But you can't be," Nora insisted. "Anne Maddox owned that cottage, and she recently died, poor thing."

"Oh, I'm sorry to hear that, but it really has nothing to do with me," Maddie said. "I've rented it in good faith through an agency."

"The thing is," Nora went on, warming to her subject, "no one knows yet who she left it to. She does have a granddaughter, but that selfish, unscrupulous son-in-law of hers took her away from here when his wife, her daughter, Jenny, died."

Maddie's ears pricked up. Could it be Ross and Meg she was talking about?

"What do you mean, selfish and unscrupulous?" she asked, unsure if she really wanted to hear the answer.

"Well, put it like this," Nora said in a disgruntled tone. "If he'd been a better husband, Jenny would still be alive today."

"Why is that... What do you mean?" Maddie didn't want to pry but was unable to prevent herself from asking.

Nora rolled her eyes and lowered her voice. "It's common knowledge that, after having the baby, Jenny wasn't well. Postpartum depression, I think they called it. Never heard of it in my day. Of course, he should have stayed home to look after her, but he just kept on going to work, leaving her on her own. One day he came home to find she'd killed herself...slit her wrists in the bath. Tragic affair...most of the villagers shunned him, and after the funeral he just up and went, taking the little girl with him. Well, I hope he doesn't have the gall to come back—he isn't wanted around here."

A flood of rage at the woman's total lack of sensitivity rendered Maddie speechless for a moment. How could anyone speak so coldly about such a terrible tragedy?

"But if the little girl inherited the cottage, then surely he would *have* to bring her back?"

she suggested, her voice flat with contained anger. "He would owe her that, at least."

Nora's lined face crinkled. "Anne was a good friend of mine. She had her quirks, to be sure, but her heart was in the right place. 'Write and tell him that you want to see the child,' I used to tell her, but she'd have none of it. Stubborn woman, Anne Maddox… I do miss her though. If he came back, then it'll be to put the place on the market, I would imagine. He knows he's not welcome in Little Dale."

"What's his name?" asked Maddie tentatively.

Nora snorted. "Ross Noble, and the little girl is Meg. She'll be nearly six years old by now."

Maddie froze. Nora made him sound like a monster. "Surely he can't be that bad," she said, unsure why she suddenly wanted to speak up for her arrogant neighbor.

"Believe you me—there's not a good bone in his body."

"But he must love his little girl."

"Probably locks her in on her own all day when he goes off to work…or maybe he's put her into a home. He's certainly capable of it."

Remembering how Ross had braided Meg's

hair so she would look nice for school—and his tender expression whenever he looked at his daughter—made Maddie bristle in his defense. "Well, I'll admit he's obnoxious," she said. "But I can guarantee that he loves Meg."

"And how would you know that?"

Maddie looked the older woman straight in the eyes. "Because he's currently camped out behind Rose Cottage."

Nora paled. She seemed speechless for a moment...and then began the questions. Within minutes, Maddie felt as if she'd drawn out every fact available about Ross. How he looked, how Meg looked, what they'd said to each other, how long Maddie was staying at the cottage... Feeling awkward but not seeing any harm in giving the inquisitive older lady the facts, Maddie responded as honestly as she could. She figured it wouldn't be long before people noticed Ross was in town, anyway.

It was only when the doorbell jangled and someone else came into the store that Nora's attention wavered. "Right, then," she said abruptly. "So do you want to pay now?"

Realizing she was being dismissed, Maddie smiled to herself. It was obvious that Nora was desperate to relay all her information to the new arrival.

"Deirdre Blunt," announced the smartly dressed, middle-aged woman who now stood beside her at the counter. She held out her hand and Maddie took it. Was everyone in Little Dale so nosy? she wondered.

"Maddie Maguire," she said, dropping her hand to rummage in her bag for her wallet.

Nora pushed her glasses up her nose, staring at the cash register with narrowed eyes. "Twenty-two pounds fifty, please," she announced, hurriedly taking Maddie's two crisp twenty-pound notes and pushing the change into her hand, turning away immediately with a meaningful glance at Deirdre. It was clear that Ross Noble and his daughter were going to be the talk of the village pretty soon.

"Bye…and nice to meet you both," Maddie called, escaping into the street with a surge of relief.

As she wandered along, absentmindedly taking in her surroundings, she couldn't help but dwell on what Nora had told her. If Jenny Noble had taken her own life in Little Dale, then surely she'd be buried here, in this peaceful, tranquil churchyard. On impulse, Maddie went through the open gate, passing between the holly bushes that stood like sentinels on either side of it. She scanned the rows of tombstones, some bright with flowers and some bare, seemingly forgotten. The whole place felt so full of emotion, both happy and sad. Love and life, sadness and sorrow, all buried here in this peaceful, timeless place.

It was as she rounded a corner and came upon some new and well-tended graves that she saw them. Meg was holding a small bunch of flowers, and Ross was stooped down on one knee, head in his hands as he stared at a shiny black marble headstone. The big dog, Red, stood motionless behind them, as if overseeing proceedings.

Maddie's instinct was to hurry off immediately. It wasn't her place to stay and watch them grieve, and she certainly wouldn't want either of them to know she was here. So much for Ross Noble not caring about his wife, she thought. His behavior at her graveside revealed exactly the opposite. She glimpsed his face and saw a depth of emotion that moved her right to the core.

Dispelling her sudden rush of sympathy for the man she was determined to dislike, she tried to run, stumbling awkwardly across the grass, wanting to get far away from the graveyard and all the sad emptiness that lingered there. When something wet and warm pressed against her hand, she almost screamed.

"Red!" she cried as the big dog licked her hand. She stopped to crouch down and cradle his huge head between her palms. When a low whistle floated through the clear, fragrant air, Red looked up at her as if he was saying goodbye before loping off in the direction of his master.

Maddie watched him go, almost wishing she hadn't found out about Ross's past. She didn't want to feel sympathy for him, didn't want him to invade her life by revealing his inner self… Maybe it was simply guilt that had brought out the deep emotion he'd revealed at his wife's graveside. Perhaps he *had* treated her badly, and perhaps he really was everything that Nora Ryland believed him to be. She'd stay well away from him in the future, she decided; it was the only way to stop herself from getting any more involved. Ross and Meg had become too entrenched in her life already; she needed to focus on herself and her own problems.

CHAPTER NINE

ROSS SAW HIS unwelcome neighbor arrive home from work, park her small car and head for the house. He felt a surge of irritation at his lingering admiration for the way she obviously tried to walk without limping. Her attitude about the cottage still bothered him a lot, even though, if he was honest with himself, he knew it wasn't her fault that she happened to be living there. But he'd become so used to his reclusive lifestyle over the past five and a half years that he just didn't want her in his face. The sooner she was gone, the better, and then he and Meg could try to get some normality into their lives…if there was any normality to be had anymore.

When he'd taken her to school the other day, the teacher had been pleasant enough, but as they walked back to his truck, a local woman had crossed the street to avoid him, making a snide remark, its meaning all too clear from the expression on her face.

He followed Maddie's progress as she reached the front door. He was uncomfortably moved, despite his reservations, by her determination. What had happened in her life? Illness, perhaps, or injury; maybe she'd had a car crash. Well, the last thing she needed in her life right now was any input from him. His ability to understand and identify with his own wife's vulnerability had been tried, tested and found desperately lacking. How could he ever hope to help someone he hardly knew fight her demons, when he had so many of his own to overcome?

Shaking his head, he went to feed the chickens and put them away, calling to them in what he hoped was an encouraging tone. As they hurried past him into the shed, clucking loudly as if in response, his phone began vibrating against his hip. Dropping down the hatch to keep the chickens safe from foxes, he pulled it from his pocket. "Hello?"

As always, he made sure he sounded distant and unapproachable.

"You rang about a job?" The man's voice was curt and businesslike; that suited Ross.

"Er, yes…and you are?"

"Robert Cranshaw, Harpers Farm. My regular farmhand is in the hospital, and I need someone experienced to stand in for a month or so. Come and see me tomorrow if you're interested…if you are keen enough, you won't mind it being a Sunday, surely. I'll need to see you work a dog with the sheep and maybe help with the milking for a while. A couple of hours should be enough to see if you are up to it."

Ross's stomach lurched. He really couldn't miss this chance, but what about Meg? He could hardly leave her in the truck. "I'll be there," he heard himself say. When the phone clicked off, he just stood for a moment, holding it in his hand. Now what was he going to do?

ROSS WAS STILL undecided on his course of action the next morning, and by eight fifteen he was toying with the idea of calling this Robert Cranshaw guy and telling him to forget it. He watched with irritation as Red ran off toward the cottage. Did he think Ross didn't know where he was going? No doubt Maddie was encouraging him; perhaps he should tell her that he was perfectly capable of feeding his own dog.

It was as Red came back, slinking low to the ground as though he knew he was in trou-

ble, that Ross realized something: Maddie
had changed her routine. Normally, she left
before eight. Did that mean she was taking
Sunday off, too? A thought circulated inside
his head, circulated and settled into a pos-
sibility. Perhaps she'd look after Meg for a
while. The idea of lowering himself to ask, of
trusting her to take care of his little girl at all,
for that matter, repelled him, but what other
choice did he have? With no work, he'd be
forced to go back to Scotland, and he wasn't
ready for that yet, despite how hostile some
of the locals still seemed.

Calling to Meg to stay inside until he came
back, he set off for Rose Cottage, memories
screaming inside his head. The day he carried Jenny over the threshold…the day she
was carried out again, no longer breathing.

WHEN SHE HEARD the loud knocking, Maddie
knew at once who it must be. She headed toward the door, drawing on her reserves of
strength. What was wrong with her obnoxious neighbor now?

She found him speechless on the doorstep,
his mouth opening to form words that didn't
seem to be coming.

"Can I help you?" she asked, standing as

tall as she could and refusing to waver from his dark gaze. It was the first time she'd seen him looking uncomfortable, she realized. That gave her confidence.

"I've a favor to ask," he blurted.

"What…a favor from me? But I thought you wanted me to keep my distance."

Ignoring her sarcasm, he ploughed resolutely on. He tried to appear pleasant…and failed hopelessly, Maddie thought, hiding a smile.

"I take it it's your day off?"

"You take it right," she said, beginning to enjoy their exchange. It was nice to have the upper hand for once.

He moved from foot to foot. "Thing is… well, I have an interview for a job and…"

"You want me to babysit Meg," she finished for him. "Because you're desperate and there's no one else."

"Something like that," he admitted.

"Of course I will," she said without hesitation, already looking forward to it. "I'll enjoy the company, and I have nothing else to do today. What time do you have to go?"

ROSS WATCHED HIS daughter walk off hand in hand with Maddie, and something stirred inside him. It should have been Jenny holding her hand…would have been if it wasn't for his selfishness.

Their visit to her grave had brought back so many memories and made it all fresh in his mind again. If only he'd understood how desperate she'd been. When they'd come back from the cemetery, he'd opened Google, re-searching postpartum depression all over again and rereleasing a thousand demons. If only he'd known how real a threat it was. If it wasn't for his selfishness, then Jenny would still be alive today to hold her daughter's hand.

Unable to get the thought from his head, he dragged out all the information he'd printed off the computer the other night, torturing himself with the things he had missed.

Persistent sadness and low mood, lack of interest and energy, fatigue, low self-esteem…

The list was endless. He'd known she was tired and irritable, of course, and he couldn't help but wonder if that was partly why he'd stayed at work so much, to avoid another row. It hadn't seemed like that at the time, though; there were just so many mares on the stud ready to foal. They needed care, but his wife had needed it more and he hadn't even seen it. Truth was, he had been completely selfish. If he had insisted she go to the doctor, at least he would have learned about the symptoms and the real danger Jenny's condition posed, as he'd learned when it was too late. He'd have known it could grow worse when the baby was six months old, and known just how badly it could mess with a new mother's head.

Stuffing all the papers into the bin, he called to Red and strode outside; he had to do what was best for Meg now, and that meant getting a job.

The lane that led to Harpers Farm was freshly surfaced with gravel, and even the shoulders were well tended. Ross liked that—it showed Robert Cranshaw was proud of his farm. Hope lifted his spirits and helped him focus on the present. If he could just make a good impression…

He pulled over to the side of the road and buttoned up his collar, glancing into the mirror and running his hand through his thick, dark hair.

"I should have gotten a haircut," he said to Red, who observed his master with disdain.

In Scotland, everyone had known him, and he hadn't had to try to make a good impression. All the farmers and studs were aware that he could turn his hand to anything and was capable and reliable; he'd always taken pride in that. *Pity you weren't capable and reliable with your wife*, an inner voice taunted. He tried to shut it out, needing to concentrate on today.

Driving into the yard, he parked beside a high wall and jumped out, glancing with interest at his surroundings. All was neat and tidy and where it should be. He was going to enjoy working here, he decided, marching toward the middle-aged farmer who had emerged from the large white farmhouse.

"Hi..." He held out his hand. "I'm Ross Noble."

Robert Cranshaw appeared to freeze, his previously pleasant expression marred by an angry frown. "Not Anne Maddox's son-in-law..."

Ross dropped his hand, knowing what was coming; this reaction was what had driven him away from Little Dale over five years ago.

"Get out of my yard. You're not welcome here...and you won't get work anywhere around Little Dale once I've put the word around."

Ross wanted to defend himself, but experience told him just how useless that would be. Instead, he turned on his heel and went back to his truck with his head held high, just trying to breathe. So it seemed that his mother-in-law's poisonous tongue still counted for something around here…how stupid of him to hope the past might be forgiven and forgotten. Desolation descended, hurling him back to the lonely days after Jenny's death when it had seemed as though there was nothing to live for…except Meg. She had seen him through…was still seeing him through. And to think he'd left her with a veritable stranger today. He slammed his truck into gear and roared off up the lane, back to the only person in the world who believed in him.

MADDIE WAS ENJOYING spending time with Meg. It was lonely sometimes, living alone in the cottage, and she appreciated having some company for once. Armed with the cookie jar, she headed back to the trailer, where she had left the little girl coloring. Meg looked up with a smile as she planted the jar on the table in front of her. "May I have one?" she asked politely.

Maddie smiled back, liking her good manners. It seemed to her that Ross Noble was two different people…a truly nice, caring guy when he was with his daughter, but totally ruthless and hard when it came to anyone else. Except for Red, of course; it was evident that he loved that dog.

"I've brought them for you," she replied, taking the lid off the jar. The chocolate cookies were still in their wrapper, and she carefully removed it, taking it across to the bin. She couldn't help but notice the pieces of crumpled paper as she opened the lid. It looked as though someone had stuffed them in there in a hurry, without squashing them down. A heading jumped out at her—Postpartum Depression: A Very Real Problem.

Hurriedly, she ran her eyes across the page before returning to the table and absentmindedly passing a cookie to Meg, who took it eagerly. He must have thrown out the article, but why? Obviously he'd been reading about his wife's condition, perhaps trying to make sense of her suicide. Nora said he'd been selfish and uncaring, but it was clear to Maddie that he must harbor a deep sense of guilt. Had he ever had the opportunity to talk to anyone about it since it happened, living all alone in a trailer with just Meg for company? No wonder he was so angry at the world. Somehow, she couldn't see him ever opening up, not to anyone...

"Can we go for a walk?" Meg broke into Maddie's train of thought. "Me and Daddy go into the woods to see the animals, and he tells me all about things."

"What kind of things?" Maddie asked, surprised to discover yet another side of Ross Noble, a side he obviously showed only to his daughter.

Meg stared at her solemnly through huge, honey-brown eyes. "Just stuff...you know—what wild animals eat and where they live. We saw a badger once."

Maddie couldn't help but smile at the excitement on the little girl's face. "Of course we can go for a walk," she agreed. "Trouble is, I'm not so good at walking."

"Is that why your leg sometimes does funny things? Daddy says you must have had an ask...askid..."

"An accident, you mean," Maddie finished for her. "Well, he's right enough there. I got knocked off my bike, and I hurt my back and my leg and my hip...oh, yes, and my head."

"You're getting better, though?"

"Yes," she said determinedly. "I am getting better every day."

"So can we go now?"

Maddie nodded and took the little girl's hand, leading her outside.

It was peaceful in the small copse behind the trailer. The whisper of a breeze sang through the treetops, rustling the leaves like a sigh, but apart from that, it was eerily quiet. Maddie and Meg walked slowly, hand in hand, stepping carefully through the undergrowth, loath to break the mystical spell that seemed to hover around them.

The sound, when it came, was harsh and shocking, conveying all the agony of a terrified soul. Maddie started to run as best she could, holding her hip as she pushed though the bushes. Meg raced ahead of her, unafraid and eager to help.

"Here!" she called back to Maddie. "It's a rabbit."

Following the sound of Meg's cry, Maddie burst into a clearing and saw the little girl's huge eyes flooded with tears as she cradled the furry brown creature against her chest.

"It's hurt," she said.

Gently taking the small wild rabbit from her, Maddie gave it a cursory examination.

"Its leg is broken," she said, her heart sinking. Now what to do? "It must have been in a trap."

"Or been caught by a fox," Meg suggested. "My dad would either try to make it better or put it out of its misery."

"And what do you think *we* should do?" asked Maddie, noting how alert the tiny creature seemed. It likely hadn't been here long; perhaps they'd startled the fox.

"Always try to help it get better first," Meg advised solemnly, obviously quoting her dad. "Euth…an…asia is always the last option."

Another side to Ross Noble, Maddie thought. What else didn't she know about him? "I tell you what," she said, the vague memory of a sign she'd seen on her way into Little Dale springing into her head. "I think there's an animal sanctuary near here—let's take it there."

"Animal…sanchewry," Meg repeated, as if trying the word on for size.

"It's a place where they help animals," Maddie explained. "Come on, we'd better hurry. We'll have to call your dad, though, or he might be worried."

On the way back to the trailer, Meg insisted on holding the rabbit. At first, Maddie was hesitant, but it became clear that Meg had been well taught; she was gentle and kind and very, very caring. *A credit to you, Ross*, Maddie thought. Was there no end to the man's talents? Oh, yes, of course, she remembered. He was rude and obnoxious, and he had no manners.

"You wait here while I go and get my car keys," she told Meg, who stood motionless, clutching her precious load. Her eyes seemed to fill her whole face. *Just eyes and freckles*, Maddie mused with an impulsive smile. "Don't worry," she said, cupping the little girl's face in her palms. "I'm sure they'll be able to make it better."

"Sometimes things don't get better, though," Meg responded sadly.

Unsure how to answer, Maddie sped off toward the cottage, hoping against hope that the outcome would be good. When she returned, hobbling slightly across the rough ground and trying to ignore the stabbing pain down her leg, Meg was waiting patiently beside the car, still carefully holding the baby rabbit.

"You get in," Maddie said. "I'll just write a note for your dad. I can't seem to get hold of him on the phone, and I don't want him thinking I've kidnapped you."

Ross STEERED HIS truck back toward Rose Cottage, still angry and more than a little hurt by the way Robert Cranshaw had treated him. Well, he wasn't going to give up this easily. The whole community might hate him, but Meg had done nothing wrong. This was her home, and there was no way he was going to let them be chased away from it by some misguided locals. He would be the first to admit he hadn't tried hard enough to understand Jenny's problems, but despite what the nasty rumors suggested, he really had loved her and he would never forgive himself for what had happened.

When he arrived back at the trailer, still stewing with anger, he was surprised to find the place empty and quiet. Perhaps they'd gone for a walk. Going outside again, he called for Meg, his voice fading into the treetops. No response. Red raced to and fro, searching for his little mistress and eventually coming to a halt and looking around in consternation. Ross stiffened, tension quickening his heartbeat. Maddie's car was gone. Where were they? All kinds of crazy thoughts ran through his mind. What had he been thinking? Maddie Maguire was virtually a stranger to him…so why had he thought she was fit to look after his little girl?

"Meg!" he yelled again, knowing he would get no answer.

He raced back inside to grab his phone; he'd taken her number, he was sure of it. Scrolling through his contacts with shaking fingers, he clicked on Maddie's name, but the call went straight to voice mail. Now what? The police?

As he hovered over the emergency number, he spotted a piece of paper on the floor beneath the table. He grabbed it and smoothed it out, reading the hastily scrawled message, already reaching for the keys to his pickup.

Taken injured rabbit to animal sanctuary, won't be long. M.

What was Maddie thinking? She had no right to take his daughter away without speaking to him first; he should never have trusted her.

CHAPTER TEN

MADDIE HEAVED A sigh of relief when she saw the sign for Cravendale swinging in the breeze. Good thing she'd noticed it the other day, she thought, not that you could really miss it.

"What nice animals," remarked Meg, peering at the large, beautifully painted sign. "They're all peeping in and out of the words... What does it say?"

"It says Cravendale Animal Sanctuary," Maddie told her, pulling into the parking lot and cutting the engine. "And I'm hoping it's a place where you can take wild animals if they're lost or hurt. Come on, let's go and take a look around...or better still, you stay here and I'll have a look around. And don't get out of the car until I get back."

"I won't," Meg promised, gently stroking the rabbit, which stared at its surroundings with huge, terrified eyes.

A barn with a sign over the door was sit-

uated at the end of the yard, back-to-back
with some gray stone farm buildings. Maddie
headed toward it, trying to ignore the heavy
throb pulsing down her back.

At what appeared to be the main entrance
to the building, a set of large, freshly painted
double doors, she stopped for a moment before pushing them open. Inside, on her right,
was a door marked Surgery; she supposed
that was where they treated injured animals.
She raised her hand to push the door open
just as a young woman came around the corner. For a moment Maddie just stared at her,
feeling insecure, overshadowed and acutely
aware of her injuries. The woman was so
alive and vibrant, her blue eyes shining out
from a delicate, beautiful face. Although she
was tiny, even smaller than Maddie herself,
she seemed larger than life.

"I thought I heard a car pull up," she said
with the widest smile. "Can I help you?"

Maddie took a breath, trying to pull herself
together. "Yes," she managed. "I hope so. We
found an injured rabbit…is that what you do
here? Help them?"

The woman nodded. "That's exactly what
we do… Well, not actually me personally, but
my fiancé, Andy, is the resident vet and Paula

Carr runs the place. Me and my dad are in a kind of partnership with the center, too. My name is Ellie, by the way. And you are…?"

"Maddie… Maddie Maguire. I'm here with Meg, the little girl I'm looking after."

"Right, well, if you go and get the rabbit, I'll find Andy and hopefully we'll have it better in no time."

WHEN SHE SAW Maddie coming back, Meg clambered out of the small red car, still carefully holding her precious cargo.

"You okay?" asked Maddie.

She nodded. "Are they going to fix the rabbit?"

Maddie smiled gently, rubbing some dirt from the little girl's face with her thumb. "They're going to try. Come on, we have to go through that door over there."

There was a smell of fresh paint inside the building, overpowering the other scents of antiseptic and animals. Meg and Maddie stood in a corridor, indecisive, until eventually Maddie pushed open another door that led into a large airy space lined with pens and cages.

A white-haired man walked toward them, carrying an armful of sweet-smelling hay.

Maddie recognized him at once as Bob Nelson, the stud owner who had joined them for lunch the other day at Sky View. "Hello again," she said.

"Well, if it isn't the young lady from Sky View," he responded, shaking the hay out into a rack in an empty pen. Meg stepped closer, peering through a gap in the fence. "There's a donkey coming in later today," he told her. "It's very thin, so it needs plenty of good food."

"And then will it get better?" she asked, eyes wide.

"We hope so, lass. Is that a rabbit you have there?"

"It needs fixing," she said solemnly.

"You've come to the right place, then. Here's Andy—he does the fixing."

The tall, fair-haired young man who approached from another door marked Private seemed nice, Maddie thought. He had friendly eyes.

"Hi," he said with a broad smile. "You've already met my fiancée, Ellie, I believe. Now, is this the patient?"

"We found it in the woods," Meg told him as he leaned down to take the rabbit from her arms.

"Well, let's get it into the surgery and see

what the problem is," he said, already gently feeling the tiny creature's limbs. "You can wait if you like, or just leave it with us if you'd rather."

"We'll wait if that's all right," said Maddie. "Just until we know whether it's going to be okay."

As Andy strode off toward the surgery, totally absorbed with the injured creature, Maddie turned to Bob Nelson. His thoughtful expression worried her slightly.

"I just can't help thinking I've seen you before," he said. "Before the other day at Jake Munro's, I mean. You look so familiar."

"No," Maddie was quick to respond. "I'm sure we've never met."

"Would you like to see the horses while you wait?" he asked. "I remember you were interested, and they're just over in the other yard."

Maddie's heart sped up…did he mean Dennis? "So your stud is here?" she asked, trying to contain her excitement.

Bob nodded. "This *is* Hope Farm Stud. The animal sanctuary is just a side project dreamed up by my daughter. It only just opened properly—thus the smell of fresh paint."

Maddie listened distractedly, head filling with memories. She longed to see Dennis, the stallion she'd ridden and worked with for so long, but was she really ready to come face-to-face with the life she'd lost? The decision was abruptly taken from her by the reappearance of Ellie Nelson.

"There's someone here looking for you," she said. "He's out in the yard, and he doesn't seem too happy."

"That'll be Meg's dad," Maddie said, her heart sinking. "I'd better go and see him."

When she stepped outside, Maddie saw Ross at once. He was standing by his truck with Red beside him, arms folded and a thunderous expression on his face.

"Well, if it isn't Ross Noble," Bob Nelson announced as he came up behind her. "So you've finally come back home, then."

"This was never home to me," Ross snapped. "But it is home to my Meg, and she has a right to be here."

"Of course she does," Bob agreed. "And don't worry—I'm not one to judge you. Tragedies happen in all walks of life, and blame is negative and pointless, in my book."

Maddie thought she saw Ross's expression soften, but then he flashed her an angry glance before hurrying across to his daughter. "Come on, Meg," he said. "We are going home. She had no right to take you away without my permission."

"But we had to help the rabbit," cried Meg.

He took her hand firmly, ushering her into the truck and glaring at Maddie. "Well, then she should have called me first."

"I take it the interview didn't go so well." She couldn't resist saying it. "And for your information, I tried calling, but you didn't pick up. Don't worry, Meg…I'll let you know how the rabbit is."

Ignoring her, Ross looked over at Bob Nelson. "Sorry about this," he said. "And… thanks. For what you said."

It should be me he's saying sorry to, Maddie thought as his truck disappeared down the lane. Then again, she could understand his panic at finding Meg gone. One thing she could never doubt about him was his love for his little daughter; she admired him for that.

"Who'd have thought it?" Bob said. "Ross Noble, back after all this time."

"So you know him, then?"

Bob nodded. "Oh, yes…he came to Little Dale about nine years ago to work on a farm. He and Jenny Maddox got together right from the first and they were married in a flash. Trouble was Anne Maddox, his mother-in-law, never really took to him—I don't think she would have taken to anyone who might take her precious Jenny away from her, to be honest.

"After the baby came along, Ross got a new job on a stud about twenty miles from Little Dale—just the kind of job he wanted, with horses. There was a cottage with the job, and he wanted to move there with Jenny and the little one, but Anne wouldn't have it. Jenny was so afraid of upsetting her mother that she refused to move. I don't know the details, of course, but it must have been tough for all of them. Him traveling miles at all times of the day and night to see to the mares that were foaling, while she was struggling to cope with a new baby."

"Nora, from the shop in the village, told me that Jenny had postpartum depression," Maddie said, frowning. "Perhaps Ross didn't understand what she was going through, but what I can't understand is why her mother wasn't there for her. Why didn't *she* talk to him? Or maybe she did…and he just didn't listen."

Bob shrugged. "Who knows? Anne Maddox was a bit of a tyrant, and maybe Jenny didn't want her to see just how tough she was finding it, in case it made her turn even more against Ross."

"Nora said she took her own life, and it was all Ross's fault. Do you believe that?"

Bob sighed. "Well, of course I only really know from local gossip, which isn't the best source, but apparently Jenny did suffer severely from postpartum depression and never really told anyone how much she was struggling. She spent a lot of time on her own with the baby, and that didn't help. Depression can have a strange effect on people—it's a serious illness that can make a person suicidal. Nora was right about Jenny's suicide, but in my opinion, for her to put all the blame onto Ross is downright cruel. Whatever his failings, he did love his wife. I'm sure about that. Anyway, one afternoon when he was at work, Jenny left Meg with her mother, went home and cut her wrists in the bath. Ross found her when he came home about six."

A stifling rush of emotion cut Maddie's questions short. "That must have been so horrific," she eventually murmured, fending off the images Bob's story evoked. "That poor, poor girl...to be feeling so low when she should have been enjoying the new life she'd brought into the world."

"Trouble was," Bob went on, shaking his white head sadly, "not only did Anne Maddox blame Ross—she turned all the villagers against him, too. She was so bitter in fact that she didn't even take any notice of her granddaughter, and with a baby to look after, he was forced to leave the job he loved. One day he just took off with little Meg, and no one has seen him since."

"Until now," Maddie reminded him.

"Until now," he repeated. "Anne Maddox died a few months ago, and she must have left Rose Cottage to her granddaughter. It has been rented out since he left."

"Actually, that's how I met Ross and Meg. They have a trailer parked in the copse behind the cottage. It was a big mix-up with the rental agency. To be honest, I'd love to just leave and let them have it, but I've paid three months' rent up front and I can't afford to rent anywhere else."

Bob nodded knowingly. "So I'll guess you're not so popular with Ross Noble, then?"

Suddenly, Maddie smiled. She really liked this kind older man. "Well, I'm certainly not his favorite person."

"Come on, then," he said, changing the subject. "Let's go and see these horses."

Ross's anger faded to the back of Maddie's mind as she followed Bob across the yard. She tried desperately to walk sure and even, gritting her teeth.

"Are you okay, lass?" he asked, gesturing toward her slightly shambling gait.

"Just tired," she told him, trying to increase her speed.

"Well, there's no need to rush. Dennis isn't going anywhere."

"So he really is here," she cried, unable to contain her excitement for a moment longer.

Bob frowned. "As I remember, you said you knew about him through your father... is that right?"

"Kind of," she said, hurrying over to where the stallion stared out over his half door.

"Hey, Dennis!" she murmured, ignoring the hot tears that ran unchecked down her cheeks. She wrapped her arms around his beautiful, familiar head. Bob Nelson handed her a tissue, saying nothing.

Without thinking, she slid the bolt on the stall door, but at the last second she held herself back.

"You don't mind, do you?" she asked, before opening it.

Bob shook his head. "Feel free," he told her, a bemused expression on his face. "Just be careful…"

Maddie slipped inside the stable, murmuring the endearments she always used to use around the stallion. Her heart raced as she relived memories too painful to bear. How could she have lost all this—not just this special horse, who had meant everything to her, but her future, her career and her whole way of life? She breathed in his aroma, pressing her face against the silky softness of his coat, unable to believe that fate had finally turned in her favor… Or had it? How could she try to cover up her past, when Grand Design, the horse of her dreams, lived so close by?

She was so absorbed in greeting Dennis, she barely heard Bob Nelson step into the stall behind her.

"You were engaged to Alex Lyall," he said abruptly. "I knew you were familiar. I saw the pictures in the racing papers. Racing's golden couple… Okay, so what's the big secret? What are you doing way up North, pretending you have limited experience with horses?"

She felt the color drain from her face. "I'm so sorry," she said, "I feel like a cheat and a liar."

"Well, your secret is out, so why don't you come back to the house and tell me all about it."

IT WAS A RELIEF, Maddie thought, as she sat in the kitchen at Hope Farm, sipping a cup of strong coffee, to finally tell the truth. But what would everyone else think? Would she have to leave her job at Sky View in disgrace? She imagined the disappointment on Cass's face when she learned that her employee had been less than honest...and probably the anger on Jake's. They had been so kind to her. At least it wouldn't affect Ross. He couldn't stand her anyway; he'd just be glad she was leaving.

"Right, then," Bob said, sitting down across from her. "Ellie and Andy will be out in the center for at least another half hour, so why don't you tell me what this is all about?"

Maddie took a gulp of her coffee, wincing as it scalded her mouth. "I didn't intend to deceive anyone, but you're right. I was engaged to Alex Lyall, and we were hailed as racing's golden couple. It was only because

Alex's dad is a huge trainer and Alex himself is such a successful young jockey, not to mention being pretty good-looking, too. I was doing okay, too, though—I'd won a few races and was getting better and better rides."

"Had you worked with racehorses for a long time, then?"

"Since I was seventeen."

"And I'll guess that you worked with Grand Design."

Maddie hesitated, remembering. "I looked after him for two years," she eventually responded. "He was so special."

"It must have been tough, giving it all up."

Tears welled in Maddie's eyes at the older man's understanding tone. "Tough doesn't even come close." She sighed. "I didn't have much choice, though. A driver knocked me off my bike when I was cycling to work one morning. If he'd stayed around to help, it might have made a bit of difference. Anyway, my injuries were bad. Head injuries, broken back and hip, plus other less obvious problems. They told me I was lucky to be alive, and that was enough for a while. I just focused on recovering enough to get out of the hospital. Then they told me I'd struggle even to walk again, let alone ride a horse.

And it wasn't just the physical injuries that held me back…

"I went into a depression for a while. There just seemed to be nothing to live for anymore. Alex gradually stopped coming by so often, and then he admitted that he'd found someone else. It felt like a relief, in a way, because then I didn't even have to try. My poor parents were so worried. Anyway, about a year later, when winter faded out, I woke up one morning and took in all the glory of spring— the fresh green of the grass and bright yellow daffodils—and realized that I still had a life. It felt as if the world was waking up…and so was I. As spring turned into summer and my determination grew, I decided to focus on proving them all wrong and finding some kind of life with horses again. I worked at my exercises, pushing myself to the limit…and then I saw the job at Sky View advertised. I couldn't resist it."

Silence fell as Bob digested her information. "And that's why you're here," he said. "To infiltrate Sky View's stables and get yourself back into the life you loved."

"That's why I'm here. I didn't intend to trick anyone—I just wanted to be somewhere I could gradually get myself back into riding with no pressure and no expectations from anyone but myself. Jake has already told me that when a quiet horse comes in, I can try riding, and I did tell him that I have some experience…"

"But just not exactly how much," remarked Bob. "I'll tell you something here, lass—I don't think you're lying or cheating, and I admire your determination…although I do think maybe it's time to tell the truth. No one will judge you, you know."

"Thanks," Maddie said, swallowing the lump of emotion in her throat. "And I was going to come clean eventually…when I'd proven myself, to me as well as to everyone else."

Bob nodded. "Well, your secret's safe with me for now. I won't tell a soul, even if you do decide to keep it to yourself for a bit longer. But…you will be careful, won't you?"

Maddie looked up at him, her stomach fluttering with surprise and excitement. "And you really won't tell anyone?"

He shook his white head. "I still think you should be honest, but no, I won't say anything. Anyway, we'd best go and see how your rabbit's doing. The little lass will want a full report, I'm guessing."

As they walked back across to Cravendale, Maddie's mind slid back to Ross. "Did you know Ross Noble well when he used to live here?" she asked.

Bob shrugged. "Well enough. He did some work for me."

"And did people around here really hate him so much?"

"A lot of them did. Anne Maddox was a big churchgoer and a pillar of the community. She told everyone she could that Ross had as good as killed her daughter...frightened her into suicide, almost."

"And do you believe that?" asked Maddie.

He shook his head. "I try to take people at face value. As I told you earlier, I think it was a tough time for both of them, and I don't think for a minute that Ross realized how ill Jenny really was. One thing is for sure—I know they loved each other. He was never a talker, though, even then. Always kept himself to himself. I guess all the bitterness will have made him worse now."

It sounded to Maddie as if the sooner she could get away from Rose Cottage, the better it would be. She had enough problems of her own without getting involved in someone else's. Still, she needed to report to Meg about the rabbit, no matter what Ross said… and, unlike his poor wife it seemed, she definitely was not afraid of him.

While she waited in the parking lot for Bob to get a progress report on the rabbit, Maddie remembered the discarded article she'd seen in Ross's bin. Despite her resolution not to get involved, she couldn't help the pang of emotion that hit her as she imagined big, fierce Ross Noble searching for information on postpartum depression after his Jenny died and finding out way too late just how ill she had been. He must have been so traumatized, finding her like that and then realizing he could have been there for her if only he'd understood what she was going through. And to have his mother-in-law turn the whole village on him… He must have felt so guilty and so very alone.

"Good news!" called Bob, breaking her train of thought. He was walking eagerly toward her from the door marked Surgery with a wide smile on his weather-beaten face. "Andy fixed the leg and it's going to be fine. Your rabbit is currently happily settled in an enclosure and will be set free as soon as it's healed."

Maddie felt a warm glow spread through

her whole body. At least this would prove to Ross that she had done the right thing in bringing the baby rabbit here. Meg would be delighted; that was the main thing.

"That's brilliant," she said. "I'd better get home and tell Meg."

Bob followed her to her car. "I meant what I said," he told her. "I will keep your secret… for now, at least. Take it slowly, though, won't you?"

"One step at a time," she told him, smiling.

"Of course, you can come and visit the horses here if you want," he suggested.

She laughed. "Thanks. Now that I've found Dennis again, I definitely don't want to lose touch. I need to prove to myself that I really can do it, though…the riding, I mean. With no expectations and no allowances from anyone."

CHAPTER ELEVEN

MADDIE HEADED BACK to Rose Cottage feeling physically and mentally drained. So much had happened today. Taking the rabbit to the animal sanctuary and Ross's anger at what was supposed to have been a good deed; seeing Grand Design again and then the shock of Bob Nelson's realization. Could she trust him with her secret? Remembering his expression, she was sure that she could, and it gave her confidence to know she had an ally who understood her reasons for being so secretive about her intentions, even if he didn't totally agree.

As she pulled up outside the cottage, she realized that the most important thing was to go and see Meg, no matter what Ross said. She must be longing to know how the rabbit was.

Maddie approached the trailer on tired legs, but it was more her reluctance to see Ross that slowed her steps. Dusk was settling down over the majestic Lakeland hills, turning the horizon to flame. She stood for a moment, watching the huge golden orb of the sun slipping down behind their rugged mass. She imagined Jenny standing here, struggling with the demons that had clawed at her common sense, dragging her down into that desperate place. And if those thoughts made Maddie feel sad, then she could only guess how much they must affect Ross. Despite her irritation with the man, she couldn't help but feel his pain; perhaps his bitterness and aggression were justified, but she knew from experience they were not the way to healing. To heal, he had to learn to let go and forgive himself.

Maddie turned back to the trailer nestled in the woodland. She found Ross's aggressive behavior hard to take, and yet, if she was honest with herself, there was something about him that drew her, something that wasn't only about sympathy for his plight, although that did play a part. Her reclusive neighbor had an excuse for his hostility, even though it really frustrated her, but the other feelings he evoked in her were evasive and difficult to understand. There was just something about the dark glitter in his eyes and the way he moved in that raw and physical way.

Her cheeks flushed, and she pushed her crazy thoughts into the back of her mind. She should stay well out of his way. Ross Noble was no good; everyone thought so...except for Bob Nelson, apparently.

To her surprise, he appeared in the doorway just as she reached the steps. Had he been watching out for her? No, she decided, definitely not.

"You'd better come in," he said, his tone gruff and strangely awkward. "Meg is in the bath... She was pretty filthy."

Maddie couldn't help a small smile from escaping, despite her apprehension. She had prepared herself for a show of aggression and had decided to insist on seeing Meg. This neutral, almost approachable attitude was throwing her off, and she felt way out of her comfort zone. "She got muddy trying to rescue the rabbit," she explained. "But there was no stopping her."

He nodded. "Kindhearted, my Meg—she loves all animals. About today..."

Maddie held her breath. Was he going to set off on one of his rants? She looked him straight in the eye, refusing to be daunted...

and met only softness. To her dismay, her heart began thumping loudly in her chest.

"Meg explained what happened," he went on. "And I...I..."

"Yes?" Maddie's tone was encouraging. She found herself enjoying the moment.

He lowered his eyes, concentrating on his bare feet. His toes were long and finely formed, she noted, with broad flat nails and a dusting of dark hair above the knuckle joints; they made him suddenly seem vulnerable, those bare feet.

Looking up with a surge of embarrassment, she met his dark gaze again; there was a hint of amusement in face. "I'm sorry, that's all," he said. "Sorry for being angry with you, especially in front of Bob Nelson."

"Well, he didn't have a bad word to say about you," she remarked.

"He is one of the few who didn't judge me after..."

"I know what you went through," she told him. "And for what it's worth, I wouldn't judge you, either."

"Wouldn't you?" he said, holding her gaze.

He took a step toward her, and suddenly, somehow, she was in his arms, close against his chest. Heat coursed through Maddie's body. She felt helpless, ecstatically helpless, as his arms tightened around her like bands of steel. There was nothing in her consciousness but the man who held her, and when his lips came down over hers, warm, demanding and all-consuming, she gave in to her senses and the whole world stood still.

The big dog, Red, broke the moment, pushing eagerly against them, wanting attention from his master. Common sense suddenly prevailed, jolting her like a gunshot. What was she doing? What was *he* doing?

Bracing her hands against Ross's chest, Maddie pushed back, her face scarlet with embarrassment at the depth of her own reaction to his kiss. He dropped his arms to his sides, his expression going blank.

Meg's voice brought them both back to reality. "Daddy!" she called. "Who's there?"

"It's just me, Meg," Maddie responded, trying to loosen the tension in her taut muscles as the little girl appeared in the doorway, wrapped in a towel. "I've come to report on the rabbit."

Ross tucked the clean white towel more tightly around his daughter's small frame, avoiding Maddie's eyes.

"It's going to be fine," she said. "It has a

cast on its leg, and when it's better, they're going to set it free."

"Free..." Meg repeated with a broad grin. "Rabbits like being free."

Maddie nodded, smiling back at her. "I think we all like to be free sometimes," she said.

"Freedom can be overrated," Ross cut in. "Off to your room, Meg. I'll be there to dry you in a minute."

"Will I be able to go and see it?" she pleaded.

He hesitated. "We'll see," he said finally, and she raced happily off to her room, leaving Maddie and Ross alone with a yawning space between them.

Maddie quivered as he turned back toward her. "It seems I need to say sorry yet again," he said, staring at a point just over her shoulder. "I don't know what came over me."

Maddie shrugged, trying to make light of it. "Maybe we were just two lonely people who needed a moment. It was just a kiss."

His eyes darkened. "Was it?"

She nodded, backing away. "Tell Meg I'll keep her posted about the rabbit."

Despite her show of bravado, as she returned to the cottage, Maddie knew that despite her bold words, the feel of his lips on hers was so much more than just a fleeting, meaningless kiss. Ross Noble was a dangerously attractive man, and she needed to stay well away from him. She had enough complications in her life already.

NEXT MORNING, TO Maddie's relief, there was no sign of either Ross or Meg; Red didn't even come scratching on her door, and she missed his early-morning greeting. When she arrived at Sky View at exactly eight thirty, Robbie was watching for her from the window. When he saw her car draw up, he ran out into the gray, misty morning, swinging his school bag.

"We're doing sports today," he exclaimed, climbing into the car.

"And I take it you like sports?"

"Too right I do." He grinned. "Especially rugby."

He waved at Cass, who was standing in the doorway, and she blew him a kiss. Maddie pressed the gas and felt a warm rush of contentment. She liked the comfortable normality of the routine at Sky View, and she was needed here…that was enough for now.

The morning passed quickly once Maddie

returned from the school run. When Cass suggested she take a break, she headed off across the yard, eager to get a glimpse of the horses and wondering how soon she could start trying to persuade Jake to let her spend some time with them.

Jake's mare, Carlotta, leaned over her half door, eager for attention. Maddie was only too happy to oblige. As she stroked the gentle horse's sleek, silvery neck, she tried to imagine what the foal might be like, desperately hoping she'd still be here to see it in the spring.

"I can see that you're fond of horses," remarked Jake's dad, Bill, stopping for a moment to put down the bag of feed he was carrying on his shoulder.

"I love them," said Maddie.

"Do you have much experience with them?"

She nodded. "Some…before my accident."

Bill pushed his cap back on his head and drew it forward again. "Oh, yes… Cass mentioned that. Got knocked off your bike, didn't you?"

"Yes…it was a while ago now."

"Were you badly hurt?"

Seeing the beginnings of sympathy in his

eyes, Maddie shook her head. "Not too bad—I'm fine now."

"Glad to hear it," he said. "You'll have to spend a bit of time on the yard, then. When Cass doesn't need you, that is."

"I'd like that," Maddie said with a rush of excitement. She'd been right to come here, she decided. Everything seemed to be starting to work out right already.

When Maddie returned to the house, Cass was sitting in her chair beside the stove, taking a break herself.

"Sorry for being so long," she said. "I got a bit waylaid."

"With Bill I'm guessing." Cass smiled. "I saw him heading in that direction, and he does love to chat."

"He wanted to know about my accident."

Cass frowned. "I can see that you still sometimes have trouble walking, but you're generally okay, aren't you?"

"Yes, definitely," insisted Maddie. "My leg still aches when I'm tired, but my headaches have about gone since I came here."

"Well, that's good. By the way, I heard you have unwelcome neighbors at Rose Cottage. Are they a problem?"

Heat flooded Maddie's face. "No, not really… How did you know?"

"Oh, nothing stays a secret for long in a small place like this. I met Nora in the shop earlier, and she was ranting on about Ross Noble being back, camping beside Rose Cottage. They all seem to think he's bad news, so I was a bit worried about you. He was long gone when I arrived at Sky View, of course, but Jake and Bill knew him. Ross left, I believe, after his wife died."

"It was a tragedy," said Maddie, blushing even deeper at the mention of his name.

"What…he's talked to you about it?"

"No, not really." She looked away, feeling awkward. "To be honest, all he's done, mostly, is complain about me being in his daughter's cottage." *Oh, and he kissed me.*

Cass took hold of her arm. "You should have told me," she said. "About Ross Noble bothering you, I mean."

Maddie smiled, alarmed at how much the very sound of his name affected her, and determinedly took control of her emotions. "It's okay. He doesn't bother me too much, and to be honest, as I said, I have heard about what happened with his wife and I think he has a point. Meg, his little girl, inherited the cottage from her grandmother, and he just wants to claim what is rightly hers. The fact that I've paid to rent it annoys him, but it's not my fault and I can't do anything about it yet."

"And it doesn't worry you…him being there?"

Did it worry her? She remembered the ferocity she had found so daunting when he first came banging on her door. "He did at first," she admitted. "But I think he's all bluff and bluster. I'll have to find somewhere else to live soon, anyway."

"I have an idea," Cass said suddenly. "I'll have to run it past Bill and Jake first, but…"

"What kind of idea?"

Cass smiled, barely containing her excitement. "A good one."

CHAPTER TWELVE

"YOU AWAKE, NUTMEG?" called Ross, peering around Meg's bedroom door. She smiled sleepily, and he smiled back. "Don't forget to clean your teeth."

The little girl ran into the small bathroom, splashed some water onto her face and rubbed at her teeth with her new pink toothbrush before going to find her dad. "I've done it," she said proudly. "Now can we go and get my school clothes?"

"You don't start for another two weeks," he told her. "But we can go today if you eat up all your breakfast."

"It's nearly still night," she said, tucking into the scrambled eggs on toast he placed in front of her. "Why did we have to get up so soon, when it's not school and you aren't going to work?"

Ignoring her question, Ross pushed her hair back from her face, securing it clumsily with a bobble to keep it out of her breakfast.

"We'll have to have another go at braiding your hair before school starts," he said.

Meg nodded. "I could ask Maddie to show you how to make them really tight," she suggested.

His response was immediate. "No! We don't need her help...or anyone else's, for that matter."

"Can we go and see the rabbit today?"

"Maybe after we've been to town."

Meg looked up at him, her mouth stuffed full of eggs and toast. "Why *do* we have to go so early, anyway?"

Ross hesitated. He could hardly tell her that it was because he didn't want to risk bumping into Maddie. Kissing her had been such a huge and stupid mistake; he'd stayed awake half the night thinking about it, and he still couldn't come up with a valid reason for his behavior. He'd felt bad for being angry with her, especially in front of Bob Nelson, and he had wanted to apologize. Trouble was, apologies didn't come easily to him. Frankly, no kind of communication, other than with animals or Meg, came easily. Guilt clawed at his insides. If it had, then maybe Jenny would have been able to talk to him about what she'd been going through, and she'd still be alive today, to be a mum to Meg. She'd been vulnerable, and he had been unapproachable. He saw that now, years too late. Maybe that was it, then—maybe Maddie's vulnerability had momentarily reminded him of Jenny.

One thing was for sure: he had made a total idiot of himself. The last thing he needed was any kind of romantic relationship. And he didn't see that changing any time soon. Anyway, he would probably only let her down when she needed him most. Maddie deserved someone a lot more reliable than he was. An image of her slid into his mind; she looked kind of delicate, and she obviously struggled with her walking sometimes but the determined flash of green in her hazel eyes when she'd faced up to him hadn't escaped him, either. She deserved someone who could care for her properly and help her grow strong.

For a moment, he was overwhelmed with memories of the night before; the feel of her in his arms, the sweetness of her lips. One minute, they had been a mile apart and then suddenly, inexplicably, they had come together as if drawn by a magic, invisible cord.

With a snort of derision, he pushed the thoughts aside. He didn't even *like* Maddie... did he? He certainly hadn't when they'd first met. He smiled, remembering the ferocity in her huge eyes as she stood her ground when he confronted her about the cottage. She might appear vulnerable, but she could certainly give as good as she got when she needed to. And he had to admit that she did have a kind of beauty…not that she was his type, of course. Anyway, as she'd said, it must have been a mad moment of loneliness. He'd just rather not have to face her today, that's all.

"Come on, Meg," he urged. "Let's get you ready and go to town for those school clothes. What did the teacher say you needed?"

"A red sweater from the school with a badge on it and a red checked summer dress and new white socks and black shoes…oh, and—" She jumped up and down in excitement. "A coat! I need a coat. Then can we go to see the rabbit?"

Ross smiled at his daughter's enthusiasm. "Yes," he said. "We can go and see the rabbit."

To his relief, Ross noted that the cottage curtains were still drawn. Light shone from behind them, glowing through the fabric; when one twitched, he increased his pace, dragging an objecting Meg by the hand.

"Slow down, Daddy," she cried. "I want to say goodbye to Maddie."

"Maddie is busy," he told her, bundling her hurriedly into her car seat and strapping her in before calling for Red. The big dog appeared from the pathway that led to the cottage, jumping obediently into the back with a lingering glance at the cottage. Ross cursed inwardly. She had even gotten to the dog! The farther he stayed away from her, the better. Nothing was more sure.

Revving the engine, he roared off up the lane. Meg did need school clothes, but it was work he should really be looking for. If he didn't get something soon, then he wouldn't be able to afford any clothes.

"We are going to see the rabbit, aren't we?" asked Meg.

Ross nodded, smiling to himself as an idea formed in his head. "Yes, love, we sure are."

Maybe by taking Meg to see the rabbit, he would kill two birds with one stone, so to speak. Bob Nelson did seem to be on his side, so perhaps he'd have some work for him. At least he knew that when he arrived at Hope Farm, he wouldn't be immediately ordered off the premises.

Their visit to the store proved to be anything but successful. For a start, they arrived before it opened and had to wait around for half an hour. Then Ross discovered he'd left the list behind, there didn't seem to be any dresses in Meg's size and when he started to look for a coat, he realized he didn't have a clue how it was supposed to fit. In the end, he'd just bought two school dresses, a V-neck sweater and some white socks before deciding to come back another day.

With a sigh of relief, he fastened Meg into her car seat again and started the engine. He should be used to this by now—after all the disasters he'd been through trying to buy baby and then toddler clothes. Sometimes he wondered how they'd managed to get even this far in one piece. "Come on then, Meg," he said. "Let's go see the rabbit. We can shop another day."

The journey to Hope Farm, which was set way up on the fell, took Ross's memories racing back to when he'd first arrived in the Lake District. He loved Scotland first and foremost, always would, but there was a different kind of beauty here, with glorious colors and glittering lakes, all set against gray stone and everywhere the tough fell sheep, running free.

The yard at Hope Farm stud seemed abnormally quiet, he thought, as he drove in and parked near the house. Hoping to see Bob Nelson, he'd elected to drive into the main yard rather than going immediately to the animal sanctuary.

"This isn't where we came last time," Meg objected as she climbed out of the truck.

"Yes, it is," Ross insisted. "Just a different part. I have to see someone first, before we go to find your rabbit."

When he knocked on the house door, Bob's daughter, Ellie, opened it. "Hi," she said. "Are you looking for my dad?"

"Yes…is he around?"

"He's just in the meadow past the stone barn, fixing a fence. The rabbit is doing well, by the way. I can take this young lady to see it if you want to go find him. You can catch up with us later."

Ross nodded. "Thanks, I'd appreciate that."

Meg went off with Ellie Nelson happily enough, holding her hand tightly and skipping with excitement. Ross watched them for a moment before striding off to find Bob, reciting his request inside his head. *I was wondering if you had any work going. I'm good with horses, but I can turn my hand to most things and I'm reliable and honest.*

Just as Ellie had told him, he found the older man in the small meadow beyond the barn. The smooth green grass, dotted with brown chickens all pecking and clucking, sloped up toward the fell where bracken and twisted trees took over, nature held at bay by a gray stone wall.

Bob was leaning forward, holding a fence post with one hand and trying to wield a big hammer with the other. "Let me help you with that," said Ross, reaching for the hammer. Bob looked at him with surprise and nodded, yielding to Ross's youth.

Three big swings and the post sank into the earth. Bob pushed against it. "Thanks," he said. "That'll do."

Ross dropped the hammer and turned his attention to a black-and-white border collie that jumped up against him, begging for attention. Ross scratched the backs of his ears.

"Well," Bob declared. "I see you're in a better mood today. That's Jack, by the way."

Ross frowned, hesitating, his carefully rehearsed speech completely gone from his head. "I'd had a bad day," he explained, feeling awkward. "No one around here seems prepared to give me the time of day...much less work of any kind."

"So it's work you're looking for, is it?" asked Bob.

"I'd be glad of anything."

"We don't have much right now, but I'll bear you in mind," the older man told him.

Ross felt bitter disappointment settle over him.

"Why don't you try Jake Munro at Sky View, though?" Bob continued. "They have a lot of building work going on there, if you're up for it, not to mention the stable work, of course. They get a lot of horses in and out—it might suit you there."

Ross hesitated, not wanting a repeat of his experience at Harpers Farm.

"And you don't need to worry about him turning you away," Bob said. "I can't see Jake being bothered about something that happened all that time ago. He'll be a hard taskmaster, mind."

"I don't mind hard work," Ross told him, hope creeping in. "And thanks for the suggestion."

Bob nodded. "I will bear you in mind if anything comes up here."

"I really appreciate it. And now I'd better

go and see the rabbit that caused all the trouble yesterday."

"It was kind of Maddie Maguire to bring it in. She's a good sort."

"If that's a reprimand, then I deserve it. I've already apologized for my bad temper."

"Glad to hear it," said Bob, going back to the fence.

"Do you want me to stay and help you… for free of course?"

"Thanks, but that post was the last one. It's hard trying to get any posts in around here, and with the fence down, that darned fox would have a field day with the chickens."

Ross walked back down into the yard feeling better than he had in a while. Perhaps Jake Munro and his dad would have some work for him…anything would do. As he passed his truck, Red, who was tied up nearby in the shelter of a large oak tree, whined his objection at being left behind.

"Won't be long, lad," he promised.

He headed over to the door marked Surgery and then opened another that led into a large airy space; it smelled of hay and animals and fresh paint.

"Here, Dad!" called Meg, her bright little

face shining with excitement as she peered into the baby rabbit's enclosure.

Ellie Nelson was crouched down beside her; her big blue eyes held the same expression as Meg's, he noted. "It's doing fine," Ellie said. "Eating well and everything... thanks to Meg here. She saved its life."

"It wasn't just me," Meg said. "Maddie brought me here...she's kind."

"Come on, then." Ross's voice sounded rougher than he'd intended, and he saw Ellie's brightness fade just a little so he attempted an awkward smile. "We'll be back to see it before you set it free...if that's all right?"

"Anytime," Ellie said.

CHAPTER THIRTEEN

WHEN MADDIE ARRIVED back at Sky View with Robbie, having picked him up from school, Cass was nowhere to be seen. A niggle of worry made her heart race. What if she'd gone into labor?

To her relief, Cass marched in through the kitchen doorway ten minutes later, a secretive smile on her face.

"Ah, Maddie!" she cried. "There's a load of laundry in my car. Please would you go and get it for me and put it in the machine? I've overdone it a bit, I'm afraid, and I'm going to lie down."

Noting how pale and strained she looked, Maddie hurried over to her. "Are you sure you're okay? You're not in pain or anything, are you?"

"No…" Cass placed a hand on her arm. "It's nothing like that. I literally have just done too much. I went to the cottage to tidy it up a bit and brought some cushion covers and other bits and pieces back with me. There might be someone coming to stay in it soon, and I wanted it to look nice."

"You should have let me do that," Maddie said. "It is what I'm here for. So…you're renting it out?"

Cass nodded, heading for the stairs. "Perhaps."

By five o'clock, when Cass still hadn't reappeared, Maddie went to the foot of the stairs. She didn't want to disturb her boss's rest, but a dull pain throbbed in her back and her head ached unbearably. "Hello?" she called. "Are you okay?"

To her relief, Cass's voice came floating back. "Yes… I'll be down in a minute.

"Sorry, I fell asleep," she said, making her way awkwardly down the steep staircase. "You should have called me sooner."

"Are you sure you're okay?"

"Of course I am. I might be the size of a house, but I've actually got a while to go yet. You head off—you look a bit tired yourself."

"I'm fine," Maddie insisted, but she couldn't quite hide the drag in her left leg as she stepped forward.

Cass placed a concerned hand on her arm. "Never mind me," she said. "But…I can't help thinking sometimes that your injuries from the accident were far worse than you've led us to believe. You can tell me, you know—I just want to help."

Maddie shook her head determinedly. "And you have helped me…by giving me this job, and a future. I really appreciate it. My leg does bother me a bit at the end of the day, and my back still aches sometimes, but it's nothing. It's you who needs to look after yourself."

"I'm just pregnant." Cass smiled. "A natural phenomenon."

Maddie decided to take a detour through the stable yard before leaving, wanting to tell Jake to keep an eye on Cass. The oh-so-familiar atmosphere hit her as she rounded the corner: horses banging their doors at feed time, their heads tossing in excitement; the aromas of hay and dung and saddle soap, so immediate and yet so very far away, sensations from her other life. Memories assailed her, and she stopped in her tracks, fighting off a rush of emotion as she realized anew how much she had lost. Her future and the way of life she had believed to be hers were gone. She had been reduced to being a home help with a broken body and a broken heart. Sometimes she just couldn't bear it.

"Maddie!" Jake called, appearing from one of the stables. "Is everything okay?"

She gulped, trying to regain some composure. "I came out to tell you to keep an eye on Cass," she eventually managed. He rushed over, his face clouded with concern.

"What happened?"

"No, don't worry. I just wanted to tell you she went to the cottage this afternoon and came back exhausted. She had a nap, though, and she seems fine now."

"You're sure?"

"Yes, I'm sure. But it's not up to me to tell her to take it easy, so I thought you might want to have a word."

His worried frown gave way to a smile. "Thanks," he said. "I must admit that when Cass wanted to hire you, I wasn't too keen. I told her she should get someone local, someone we knew. She was adamant, though. 'She just seems so desperate, Jake' she said. She wanted to give you a chance."

Maddie laughed. "You make me sound like a charity case."

"No," he insisted. "It wasn't like that. Cass always wants to help both people and animals—that's why she became a vet. What I meant is that I'm sorry for my doubts. You've turned out to be a real asset, and I'm glad you came here."

"Thanks," said Maddie. "I'll see you tomorrow."

As she walked slowly off across the yard, a warm glow filled a void inside her. She was needed and appreciated, and that felt good.

"By the way," Jake called after her. "I haven't forgotten that I said you could start riding as soon as we get something suitable in."

"I'll hold you to that," Maddie responded, the warm glow spreading through her whole body.

WHEN MADDIE GOT back to Rose Cottage, she saw Ross's truck right away, haphazardly parked next to the trailer. Her heart sank; all day she'd kept herself busy and pushed any thoughts of him right out of her head. Now they came bouncing back with a vengeance. After last night, she didn't trust herself anywhere near the man. She still didn't know exactly how the kiss had happened. One moment, he was apologizing to her for his outburst at the animal sanctuary—she'd enjoyed that, seeing the usually unapproachable and angry man reveal another side of his

character. He'd looked kind of awkward...
almost vulnerable. A rush of blood burned
her cheeks; there had been nothing vulnerable about that kiss.

Hurrying into the cottage, she deliberately
did not look in the direction of the trailer.
What would she do if he came to the door?
Then again, why would he? He was probably
just as embarrassed as she was...if not more
so. She turned the bolt and tried to focus on
what Jake had said about her riding. Meeting
Grand Design again yesterday, her favorite
horse ever, had strengthened her resolve, and
then seeing the horses and talking to Jake
at Sky View today had made her goal feel
within her grasp.

With a satisfied sigh, she rummaged
through the cupboard for something to eat,
settling on a tin of beans. She was just pouring them into a pan when she heard a sound
outside the back door. She stopped dead, tin
raised aloft and heart pounding. What if it
was Ross? What should she do? The answer
came at once: she would act cool and let him
know she'd already put the kiss right out of
her head.

The sound came again, more a scratching than a knock. Relieved, she hurried to

open the door, holding out her arms to the big red-brown shape that gamboled like a puppy into her small kitchen. "Well, hello, boy," she cried. "And where were you this morning?"

Red wagged his plumed tail, and she scratched behind his ears, enjoying his display of affection. "Better get you some treats, then," she said. "Before your master comes looking for you. We don't want that, do we?"

Glancing uneasily out the window, Maddie saw Ross in the trailer. She narrowed her eyes, trying to pull her gaze away but was unable to stop herself from staring. He was trying to braid Meg's hair again. She must be starting school soon. It would be hard for Ross, sending his little girl to proper school… or perhaps it would be a relief. Somehow, though, she didn't think so.

After Red ate his treats, she let him out, and he trotted off with a smile on his face, leaving Maddie feeling strangely lonely. Maybe she should get a dog of her own, she thought, one like Robbie's dog, Choco… or like sweet gentle Bess, mother to Cass's dog, Puddle. Bob Nelson had one of her pups, too. Tomorrow, she decided, she'd ask Cass if Bess was likely to be having another litter, and whether she could buy a pup…if they didn't mind her bringing it to work with her, of course.

Maddie glanced out the window once more before going back to her supper. A golden orange sun was slipping toward the dark line of the horizon, so beautiful and silent and totally isolated from the rest of the world. Suddenly, she noticed Ross was standing out in the yard, looking across at her, his huge frame outlined by the setting sun. When her eyes met his, a sudden shiver ran through her, and she turned away abruptly, afraid of the way he made her feel.

Ross saw Red come loping back from the cottage, licking his lips. "Traitor," he told him as he opened the door.

"What's a traitor?" asked Meg.

"Nothing for you to worry about, Nutmeg. I see your braids are already coming loose."

"I told you," Meg said. "We should get Maddie to give you a lesson."

"And I told *you*, Nutmeg…we don't need anybody or anything."

"We do need Red," she reminded him.

"Okay, I agree. We do need Red, but that's it. Your friend Maddie will be leaving the cottage soon, and then we probably won't see her again. I just need a bit more practice at doing your braids, that's all."

"I could just have a ponytail," Meg offered.

Ross smiled. "Well, that's always an option. Now, come on…get yourself ready for bed while I go and feed the chickens."

As he stepped outside into the deep golden light of the setting sun, Ross glanced automatically at the cottage that held so many memories, both good and bad. Suddenly, he realized Maddie was staring out at him, her pale face lit up by the sun's warm glow. For what felt like an endless moment, their eyes met and held, and a long-forgotten emotion stirred inside him, a heavy, sweet longing in his chest. When she turned away brusquely, disappointment took him by surprise, closely followed by a rush of irritation. It felt as if she had squeezed past the carefully guarded barriers around his heart. It frightened him, that loss of control. The sooner she moved on, the better, he decided.

As he tossed and turned in his bed that night, drifting in and out of sleep, all the memories he had shut out crowded back in again. His eyes flickered open in the darkness. Maybe coming back here had been a mistake. So much of Jenny still lingered in this place, reawakening emotions he'd believed to be long gone. Was that what had happened with Maddie? he wondered. Had their sudden, crazy kiss been the result of the past barraging his senses? He needed to rekindle the anger that had carried him though the bad times, he realized…and stay well away from Maddie Maguire. To fall in love again was not on his agenda… not after what happened last time.

CHAPTER FOURTEEN

On Friday, Maddie woke early and climbed reluctantly out of bed, not wanting to bump into Ross on her way to work.

When an unexpected knock came on the kitchen door as she was about to leave, she opened it cautiously and was surprised to see Meg, bright eyed and cheery faced, standing on the doorstep.

"Hello," she said with a broad grin, stepping inside. "Do you have any cookies… please?"

"Of course," Maddie said. "Don't tell your dad, though. I don't think he'd approve of cookies before breakfast. Where is he, anyway?"

"He's chopping some wood and feeding the chickens… I sneaked off."

"That was a bit naughty, Meg—he'll be worried about you. Here, I'll give you a cookie— I've got chocolate chip or oatmeal—and then you'd better go back before he misses you."

"Oatmeal, please," said Meg. "Can I eat it here?"

Maddie glanced at the door, almost expecting Ross to appear, guns blazing. "Okay, but only if you're quick."

"I'll be quick," Meg promised.

The little girl sat down in a chair, swinging her legs and nibbling on the biscuit with tiny bites to try to make it last as long as she could. "We went to see the rabbit again." Her voice was high-pitched with excitement. "And guess what? It's nearly better, and soon they're going to set it free so it can go back to its family."

"And it's all thanks to you," said Maddie with a smile, ruffling the little girl's chestnut curls.

Meg beamed with pride. "They said I can go and watch. If Daddy can't take me, will you?"

Maddie's response was instant. "Of course I will—just let me know when it is. But I'm sure your dad will want to go."

Meg shook her head slowly. "He might have a job by then. It makes him sad not having any work to do."

"Everyone has to work," Maddie told her.

"It's how we get money for food and all the other things we need."

"In one week I'm going to be starting proper school," Meg boasted.

"Well, lucky old you," Maddie said just as Ross's deep voice floated across the yard.

"Meg!" he called. "Where are you?"

The little girl jumped off the chair, holding her finger against her pursed lips. "He'll be cross with me for not telling him where I was going," she whispered.

"Go on, then," Maddie urged. "If you're quick, he'll hardly know you've been gone." Meg ran out the kitchen door, heading off around the side of the cottage with a small wave. Red trotted past her, long pink tongue hanging from the side of his mouth. The big dog paused at the door, looking appealingly at Maddie.

"Meg!" Ross's voice came again, more urgent now, and Red bounded off after his small mistress, knowing where his duties lay.

When Maddie walked into the kitchen at Sky View half an hour later, Robbie and Jake were still having breakfast.

"There's tea in the pot if you want a cup," called Cass from the comfortable chair beside the stove. "Or get yourself a coffee if you like—I've just brewed one for Bill."

"Thanks. I'll have a coffee if that's okay." Maddie savored the unexpected sense of belonging. It gave her a surge of confidence. She turned to Robbie. "Last day of school for a week, isn't it? What are you going to do on your holidays?"

"He's going to help on the yard and ride his pony," Jake answered for him, jumping up and pouring the last of his tea down the sink before rinsing out his mug.

"And ride my bike, watch TV and play my computer games," Robbie added.

"We'll see about that," Jake said, but there was a smile behind his frown. "Let's see how you do for the first couple of days. You have to earn time off, you know."

"Give him a break, Jake," Cass pleaded. "He's only eight."

Jake laughed. "Okay, then, I guess you know best. He'll have to do some work on the yard, though. It's never too soon in life to start learning your craft."

Cass raised her eyebrows, smiling at Maddie. "Ah, but what if he wants to do something else?"

"Like what?" asked Jake.

"Go to university, maybe, and train to be a doctor or lawyer… What do you think, Maddie?"

"Well, he's bright enough," she answered, pleased to be included in the lighthearted conversation.

Jake nodded, pulling on his jacket with a twinkle in his eyes. "Must take after his dad, then…and if you get a really good job, Rob, then you can look after us all in our old age."

"Trust you to think of that," Cass groaned, laughing. "Anyway, that's a long way off yet. Come on, Robbie, you're going to be late for school if you don't hurry."

"I'll go and start the car," Maddie said. "It looks like you have a lot of studying to do."

MADDIE ARRIVED BACK from the school run to find Cass waiting eagerly by the door. "Oh, good, you're back," she said. "I want to show you something."

"What is it?" asked Maddie with a puzzled frown.

"It's a secret, so just come with me. I don't think you'll regret it. You'll need your car keys."

Excitement bubbled up unexpectedly. It had been a long time since Maddie had felt excited about anything much…except for coming here, of course, but that had been more apprehension than excitement. Taking her keys from her pocket, she followed Cass out to the car, waiting until her boss was settled into the passenger seat before starting the engine. "Now," she said, "just tell me where to go."

To Maddie's surprise, they drove only a few hundred yards before Cass directed her down a narrow grassy lane and told her to pull up outside a small, stone cottage. It looked nice, she thought as she climbed out of the car, square and strongly built with evenly placed windows that sparkled in the sun, overlooking a view that took her breath away.

"Pretty spectacular, eh?" remarked Cass, rubbing her stomach.

"Is the baby kicking?" Maddie asked, immediately aware of the other woman's discomfort.

"You might say that." Cass smiled. "Now, don't you think this is the best view ever?"

Maddie stood still, entranced. Her heart lifted. "There are so many spectacular views around here…but yes, this is one of the best. The sky looks so wide and wild…you can see the storm clouds gathering in the distance, even though the sun is shining here. And the colors on the fell are so vibrant, like an oil painting."

"And you like the cottage?"

Maddie shot Cass a confused glance. "Yes," she said slowly. "I presume this is Sky View Cottage, where you tired yourself out yesterday? Do you want me to do some cleaning or something? Do you have visitors coming in?"

"No!" Cass exclaimed. "It's for you…to live in."

"What do you mean, to live in?"

"Well, what do you think I mean?" Cass laughed. "I've run it past Bill—technically it belongs to him—and he's agreed that you can have it rent free, as a part of your job, at least until you're done with your lease on Rose Cottage. You can move out of there right now, get away from Ross Noble and be closer to the stables for when the baby comes." Suddenly, her face fell. "Of course, if you'd rather be more independent…"

"No." Maddie placed a hand on Cass's arm. "It's just…"

"Just what?"

The tears she'd fought to hold back fell from her eyes. She blinked hard, almost blurting out the truth. *You've already given me my life back...or the chance to get it back, at least.* "It's just so generous of you," she managed. "Thank you...from the bottom of my heart."

"Just the top will do," said Cass, lightening the moment, and suddenly both women were laughing.

"I can't wait to tell Ross Noble that he can have his precious cottage back," Maddie said. Suddenly, his face slid into her mind's eye, his dark eyes smoldering as she pushed him away. She touched her fingers to her lips, remembering the way they'd tingled from the warmth of his. And Meg, bright faced, sitting at Maddie's kitchen table eating cookies. She was going to miss them, she realized. Red, too—she'd come to expect his visits and displays of affection. Still, it would make Ross happy if he didn't have to see her again. Since that kiss, he'd gone to such lengths to avoid her that she had no doubt about *his* feelings. She regretted it, too—of course she did, but at least she was adult enough not to attach any importance to it. She was looking forward to telling him she was moving out of his life.

"So when do you want to move in?" asked Cass, breaking into her thoughts.

Maddie's face lit up. "The sooner the better for me, but are you really sure about it? I mean, just think how much rent you'd get if it was a holiday let."

"And just think how much better I'll feel when I know you're only minutes away," Cass said. "You might end up wishing you'd kept your independence."

"It's just good to feel that I'm some use again."

A slight shadow crossed Cass's face, but the moment passed. "Well, then, what about tomorrow?" she suggested.

Maddie hesitated, overwhelmed by the speed at which her life was suddenly changing. "Well, it is my day off," she said. "So yes, I guess I'll move in tomorrow. But you're really sure it's okay?"

Cass nodded. "I wouldn't have asked you if it wasn't."

MADDIE WAS HALFWAY home when her car died. One minute, it was purring up the hill on the other side of Little Dale, and the next the engine was chuffing and spluttering. When it finally stopped, blocking the lane, Maddie couldn't believe it. This little car had brought her safely all the way from Devon without missing a beat, and her dad had made sure it was in good condition before she left. She tried to restart it, turning the engine over. It wow-wowed each time but refused to spark. If she wasn't careful, she'd kill the battery. She looked around in desperation, hoping to see someone who might be able to help.

She had been late leaving work, and the sun was already sinking, turning the sky to flame as it slowly slid behind the dark mass of the fell that loomed ahead of her, stark and beautiful but oh-so-isolated. Now what to do? Her back ached and her head was throbbing, but she was going to have to get help. Pulling her phone from her pocket, she dialed Sky View, wishing she didn't have to drag them into this but not knowing who else to ask. The phone bleeped and disconnected. Great. No signal.

Climbing out of the car, she set off up the lane, unsure whether to carry on toward Rose Cottage, which was closer, or head back down to the village. The garage would be closed by now, and she didn't really know anyone else around here…except for Ross, she realized. She sighed. He was the last person she wanted to have to depend on.

For a few hundred yards she walked stoically onward, trying to ignore the warning bells that told her she was pushing herself too hard...until a wave of dizziness made her unsteady on her legs. With the beginnings of panic, she sank down onto the shoulder, knowing she had no other option than to rest awhile. The beauty of her surroundings held no solace as she tried to get comfortable on the grass.

She heard the loud roar of a vehicle five minutes later. Recognizing the sound, she tried to struggle to her feet just as Ross's truck appeared around the corner. As he pulled up beside her and jumped out, to her dismay, her legs finally let her down completely.

"Maddie!" she heard Meg cry in horror as she rolled down the bank and into a ditch. A rush of embarrassment turned her face fiery red as Ross scrambled down to help her.

"I just tripped," she mumbled when Ross scooped her up like a child.

"It didn't look like a trip to me," he said in a cold, hard voice. "Perhaps it's time you started taking better care of yourself. I mean, what do you think you're doing, out all alone in the middle of nowhere in your condition?"

"I don't have a…condition," she insisted, feeling awkward in his firm grip.

"Oh, so you just fall down banks when you think no one is looking for fun, do you?"

Maddie wriggled, trying to free herself from his arms. "I just tripped," she declared, all embarrassment washed away by a surge of anger.

"That's not how it looks to me," he said, setting her down at the edge of the lane.

"You do have a really bad limp." Meg was studying her with a worried frown.

"It's just when I'm tired," Maddie told her, trying to make light of the situation.

"And why have you abandoned your car in the middle of the road?" Ross asked. "I wouldn't have been able to get past it if I hadn't been in a four-wheel drive."

"It abandoned me," Maddie groaned. Annoying Ross Noble was not the best course of action right now, and she hated having to plead. "It…it just stopped, and I have no phone signal. Is there any chance… I mean, would you…"

When he held her eyes with his, she felt powerless, unable to let go of the intensity in his gaze…which softened suddenly into tenderness, stripping away her defenses and making her feel like a needy child—a child who just wanted to cry on the broad width of his shoulder. He moved closer, and she panicked, disturbed by the depth of her own emotions and unsure how to handle her sudden longing for him to hold her.

"Don't worry, if you're on your way somewhere," she said, determinedly flicking back her shoulder length hair and standing as tall as she could, trying to appear confident and self-assured. "I'll get help from someone else."

"Don't be such a fool," he told her. "Too much pride will get you nowhere... I'm testament to that. And you do limp when you think no one's watching."

"Plus you fall down banks," Meg added in a serious tone.

Seeing the expression on the little girl's face, Maddie couldn't help but smile. "I might have a bit of a limp," she admitted.

"Look," Ross said. "I know you had an accident. Don't be ashamed to admit that you're still struggling."

Maddie's face fell. "How do you know that?"

Ross shrugged. "Bob Nelson told me."

Alarm bells rang inside her head. He'd

promised to keep her secret. "What else did he tell you?"

"That you were injured in an accident and…and…"

Maddie's heartbeat doubled. "And what?"

He looked her straight in the eye. "And that you are brave and proud and don't want to be judged by it. Come on, I'll take you and Nutmeg home and then come back for your car."

"Thanks," Maddie said, embarrassed by the sudden rush of heat flooding her face. When Ross's fingers clasped her arm, holding her back for a second, her whole body tingled.

"For what it's worth…I agree with him," he said. "Now come on, let's sort out this car of yours."

CHAPTER FIFTEEN

"IF YOU WATCH MEG, I'll go and see if I can do anything with your car," Ross suggested when they got home.

"Meg can come to the cottage with me if she wants," Maddie offered. "I could make you both something to eat…in thanks, you know, for your help."

A brief smile flitted across Ross's face. "I wouldn't be too quick to be grateful. I haven't actually managed to do anything with your car yet. Anyway, as I said, it seems to me that it would be more sensible for you to rest."

After Ross left, Maddie's brave face slipped. She sat down, wrestling with a wave of hopelessness. Was it always going to be like this, struggling every day just to do the things that normal people took for granted?

Meg stared at her, noting her expression. "Does your leg hurt?" she asked, a small frown puckering her usually bright face.

Maddie nodded. "Just a little."

"But it will get better soon, won't it?"

"I hope so…if I try very hard to do my exercises."

Meg's face clouded over. "You are very lucky, then," she said. "My mummy had an a…a…a…"

"Accident," Maddie repeated with a sudden lurch of sympathy for the woman she would never meet.

"My mummy had one of those, and they couldn't make her better. My dad says she was too hurt to ever get better, so she went to heaven."

"I guess she'll be happy now, then…in heaven," Maddie said.

Meg nodded. "Daddy said it's where she wanted to be, so I shouldn't be sad."

"I guess that's true, then. Do you miss her?"

The little girl went silent, her face twisting as if she was wrestling with her answer. "Not really," she eventually admitted. "Because I can't really remember what she was like. I do miss not having a mummy, though. All the kids at nursery had them. Do you think they all have mummies at proper school? I've got a uniform and everything, you know… Well, not quite everything, because Daddy forgot the list."

"It doesn't matter if you have a mummy or just a daddy—" Maddie told her, trying to control the emotion in her voice "—as long as you have someone to love you and look after you."

Meg stared at her solemnly. "But you don't have anyone to love you and look after you."

"Not here, maybe, but I have parents back at home who love me."

"And I've got Daddy," the little girl announced.

"You've got your daddy," Maddie agreed. "Now, would you like the TV on?"

AFTER ALMOST AN hour with her feet up, Maddie felt her bodily strength beginning to seep back in, and with it came her strength of mind. It was humbling, she thought, to realize what other people went through. Jenny Noble must have been in a very low place to leave behind her husband and baby girl. At least Maddie only had herself to think about, and that was how she intended to keep it…at least until she got her life back.

The sound of an engine brought her out of her reverie. "Sounds like your dad's back, Meg."

The little girl ran to look out the window.

"He's in your car...and poor Red is squashed in the back."

Maddie pulled herself into a sitting position. "Where's his truck?"

Meg pressed her nose against the glass, peering into the gloomy evening light. "It's just over there, where he always parks it."

"How is that possible?" Maddie said. "He can't drive two vehicles at once."

The door burst open then, and Red bounded in ahead of Ross's tall figure. He dropped a bag onto the table and an enticing smell filled the trailer. "Fish and chips, anyone?" he asked.

"Oh, yes," Meg squealed.

"Thanks, Ross," Maddie said. "You didn't need to bother, but I must admit I'm starving. Come on, Meg, help me get plates and cutlery while your dad takes his jacket off."

"No," Ross cut in. "Let's go and eat outside. It's a lovely evening, and it's stifling in here." He hesitated, studying Maddie closely. "Unless you're still a bit..."

"I'm fine now, really," she insisted. "And I'd love to eat outside." She smiled at him, noting warmth in his eyes that she hadn't seen before.

The air was clear and warm, softened by a

summer breeze. Ross started lifting the take-out containers out of the bag.

"Do you want plates?" Maddie asked.

Meg stared at her in horror. "They're fish and chips, Maddie! You eat them out of the trays with your fingers."

"Of course you do." Maddie laughed. "What was I thinking?"

"These are the best chips ever," Meg cried as they all tucked in, looking happily from one adult to the other as she stuck a fry into the ketchup she had brought outside with them. Red stood beside her, wagging his tail and eagerly waiting for scraps.

"Thanks for this," said Maddie when they'd finished. "And for getting my car back. What was wrong with it, anyway?"

Ross raised his eyebrows, trying to hide a smile. "To be honest, I just turned the key in the ignition and it started. I think there must be some dirt in the gas, though, because it kept spluttering all the way back. You probably flooded the engine trying to start it after it cut out. You'll have to go to the garage in the morning."

"Well, thanks again," Maddie said. "Anyway, how did you manage to get your truck back, too?"

Ross shrugged. "It wasn't far, so I walked."

"He ran," Meg explained. "I saw him from the window. He likes running."

"So do—" Maddie paused. "I mean, I used to love running, too, when I was trying to get fit."

"Fit for anything special?" Ross asked.

"I know," Meg said, interrupting.

"What do you know?" Maddie was eager to avoid the question; she didn't want to lie, but she could hardly say "to get fit for racing" without explaining herself. For a moment, she considered telling him the truth. After all, why did it matter if he knew about her past? But she held her tongue, realizing Ross would then also know about both the collapse of her successful career and the end of her high-profile engagement. He'd see her in a totally different light…as a failure. Anonymity was still way too important to lose.

"I've got an idea," Meg went on, jumping up and down with excitement.

"Well, come on, then," Ross said. "What is it?"

"When your leg gets better, Maddie, you and Daddy can run together."

Ross glanced across at Maddie, his eyes narrowed. "Now there's a goal for you."

Suddenly, Maddie felt happier than she had in over eighteen long months. "What, me being able to run again or persuading you to go with me?"

Ross just shook his head. "I have no doubt that you'll be able to run again. I've seen your determination firsthand."

Maddie would never have believed when she first arrived at Rose Cottage and met the wrath of Ross Noble that a couple of weeks later, they'd be eating fish and chips together on a balmy summer's evening.

"Meg and I will clean everything up," she offered, holding the table top firmly to try to get to her feet without stumbling.

"No need," said Ross. "I'll do it when you're gone."

Was that a dismissal? she wondered, noting how his face had suddenly closed up.

"Well, if you're sure."

"I'm sure…let's just sit awhile."

"Daddy likes to listen to the night noises," Meg said. "He listens and then tells me stories about what they all are."

"Go on, then." Maddie smiled. "We'll all just sit quietly, and he can tell us what's going on."

Ross shook his head. "I don't think Maddie would really be interested in our silly games."

"Try me," she said.

Darkness was slowly beginning to close in, and the creatures of the night were unfurling themselves from the safety of their lairs. An owl hooted close by, and a small scratching sound came from under the trees.

Ross looked at Meg. "Can you hear Mrs. Mouse scratching? She's peeping out to see if it's safe to come out." For a moment they were all silent, listening to the tiny sound. "She needs to go and find food, but there's a great big red fox sitting right outside the hole where she lives."

"Is it Friday Fox?" Meg asked, twisting her hands together in excitement.

Ross nodded. "That's right. And what do you think Friday is doing?"

"Well…" She squirmed in her seat. "I suppose she's looking for food, too, and Mrs. Mouse definitely does not want to be a fox's dinner."

"There, did you hear that rustle in the undergrowth?" he asked Maddie. She smiled in surprise, as entranced as Meg. "Well, that's Friday going about her nocturnal business—"

"Which is catching rabbits to feed her family," Meg blurted out.

"Exactly. That's what any wild thing tries to do…find food for its family."

"Where do you think Friday is going?" Meg asked.

Ross sat quite still, listening. "She's heading off toward the village. Let's hope it's rabbits she's after and not someone's chickens."

After a few more minutes, during which they all quietly took in the night sounds, he stood. "Now," he said. "I don't really think Maddie wants to stay and listen to any more of our wildlife stories, does she? Anyway, Meg, it's time you were in bed. I'll go and get your bag, Maddie…"

"Thanks." Maddie rose to her feet awkwardly, acutely aware of him watching her. Hearing him tell his daughter stories to teach her about the wildlife around them had shown her a side of him she wouldn't have believed could exist, a side she found herself longing to learn more about. Was that why he had so abruptly dismissed her, then? Because he was afraid of how close they were getting?

Maybe it was just as well that she was moving away tomorrow, she decided. Neither of them wanted a repeat of the last time they got too close for comfort. She'd come here to prove something to herself, and that didn't include having any kind of relationship, especially with a man as confusing as Ross Noble.

"Thanks again for the help—I really appreciate it," she said stiffly, suddenly remembering she hadn't told them she was moving out. "By the way…" she began, but her words faded out. Now just didn't seem like the right time.

"I'll walk you over to the cottage," Ross offered. His smile was back, but it was distant now and superficial.

She fumbled with her jacket. "No need, really, I'm fine now."

"Better safe than sorry," he insisted.

There was no point in arguing, so she nodded and he walked beside her, saying nothing. She tried to make her steps sure and bold, matching his, while he slowed his pace. Despite her pride, she appreciated the thoughtful gesture.

The sun was down behind the hills, casting a deep crimson glow across the rapidly darkening horizon, and for a moment Maddie stopped, entranced.

"It is just so beautiful." She sighed, wrapping her arms about herself as she realized just how much she was going to miss this place.

As they approached the front door, Ross hung back. This was the nearest he'd actually been to the cottage in over five years, apart from the day he and Meg arrived to find it occupied. But he'd been fueled by anger then, and without the diversion, memories flooded in, making his heart beat faster. He stopped dead in his tracks. How could he have ever believed that he and Meg could be happy here...where Jenny had breathed her last breath?

Suddenly, he felt as if he were in a time warp, so clear and stark were the memories, as if it had happened only yesterday. He'd come home late after dealing with a difficult foaling, racked by guilt for being away so long. He'd hurried through the house, calling her name...and had been met by silence, a silence that was never to end... And when he found her...

"I've got to go," he mumbled, turning hurriedly away.

"There's just one thing," Maddie said, reaching out to take his sleeve, restraining him.

He hesitated, looking back at her. "What? What is it?"

"I'm sorry, I should have told you earlier... I have some good news for you..."

"What news?"

"Come inside for a minute, and I'll tell you," she said, turning the key in the lock and opening the door to Ross's past.

He froze, not wanting to look but unable to stop himself. The hallway appeared exactly the same as it had on his wedding day, when he'd carried Jenny over the threshold.

"No," he insisted, panic rising. "I need to get back to Meg."

She hung on to his sleeve as he tried to turn away. "I'm moving out," she said. "Tomorrow. You can have the cottage back."

His response came by instinct, from the heart. "I don't want it. You've paid for it, and you need to stay here."

"No," she told him. "You don't understand. It won't cost me anything, because I'm going to live at Sky View rent free."

"I don't want it," he said, his voice tight and fierce. "You've paid for it, and you have to stay."

He strode off toward the trailer, wanting to look back to where he knew Maddie would be standing, watching him go with dismay in her eyes. But he was determined not to turn around. Why wasn't he happy she was leaving? And why had he told her he didn't want the cottage, when it was all he had thought about since finding out that it had been left to Meg? Was it fear of the past…or of the future?

SURPRISINGLY, MADDIE SLEPT WELL. She woke to the sound of scratching and ran downstairs to let Red into the kitchen. "I'm going to miss you, boy," she told him, placing treats into a bowl. He wagged his tail slowly from side to side, looking into her eyes as if understanding every word.

Today she was going to get one step closer to achieving her goal. At Sky View Cottage, she'd be able to wander down to the stable yard whenever she liked; she'd be a part of the place, and that would open up a whole host of opportunities.

Riding, to her, had always been so natural, so much a part of her life, that she didn't feel any fear of the horses themselves. It was her own body that she feared—that it would let her down…that she wouldn't be able to balance well enough or maintain control of her limbs. She feared failure.

Remembering Ross's response to her news, she wondered what she should do. Hopefully, he would have thought it through by now and controlled his fear of facing demons from the past …because that was what it had been, she was sure of it. He'd been fine until they were actually at the cottage door, and then he'd freaked out. Must have been all the memories the place brought back, she realized. Suddenly she felt glad to be moving out of a house that had held so much misery. But there must have been love and laughter here, too… when he and Jenny were first married and when Meg was born. Those were the memories he needed to cling to. It was frustrating, though, that after trying so hard to get rid of her, he seemed to have changed his mind just as she was going to give him what he wanted. He really was the most confusing man she'd ever met…another reason why she needed to keep her distance.

When she was ready to leave, she'd go and see him, she decided, to give him the keys, say her goodbyes and maybe try and talk to him. Despite her determination not to get too involved, she couldn't deny that she would miss Ross Noble. Touching her fingers to her lips, she remembered their kiss with a strange sense of loss… One thing was for sure: moving out was a good decision.

While Maddie packed her things, she couldn't help thinking about Jenny. There was a picture in the hall that she thought might be of her; the young woman in it had huge eyes like Meg's, and she looked so happy…a pretty girl with a sweet smile and her future stretching out before her. Poor Ross, to have taken all the blame… But had it been his fault? Perhaps Jenny hadn't let him know how down she was feeling. And why hadn't her mother noticed? Anne Maddox supposedly poisoned Ross's name with the locals, but maybe she was the one who had been guilty of insensitivity… Maybe she'd known how bad Jenny was feeling and done nothing, and that was why she'd denounced her son-in-law.

With a heavy sigh, she boxed up the food she'd bought since she got here, surprised at how much stuff she'd managed to accumulate in such a short time. She'd only been here for a couple of weeks, but Rose Cottage already felt like home.

When she had loaded all her belongings into the car, Maddie took a last look around, trying not to think of poor Jenny, struggling with her newborn baby while fighting the demons of depression. Why hadn't she turned to her mum for help? Perhaps it was her mother who had been unapproachable, not Ross? Perhaps she just hadn't wanted her new husband to believe she was anything less than perfect. He needed to know that, to realize that perhaps it hadn't all been his fault. He wasn't the kind of man to neglect his wife; her own observations confirmed that beyond a shadow of a doubt. Ross Noble loved deeply. She had seen it in the way he was with Meg, and it was so obvious that he'd loved Jenny. He loved animals, too, and surely that proved something about him. The guilt he had carried for almost six years may have made him bitter, but beneath his tough exterior was a sensitive, caring man.

A man who might have won her heart in different circumstances.

Jerking herself from her reverie, Maddie went back to packing. She had to laugh. A bit of interest from an attractive man and she was acting like a teenager. But look what had happened to her last relationship; she had really believed that was love, yet she couldn't have been more wrong in her judgment of Alex's character.

It was almost noon when Maddie turned the key in the cottage door for the very last time and headed for the trailer. Ross was out back, throwing a stick for Red. She stood and watched him for a moment, noting the strong, lithe lines of his body as he lifted his arm and the way the muscles bunched beneath the thin cotton of his shirt. Suddenly, the memory of his lips on hers rushed in, as if it had happened only minutes ago, so warm and firm and sweet that she'd felt as if she was drowning. Alex's kisses had never felt like that.

Afraid of the intensity of her own feelings, she called out to him. "Hi! I've brought you the keys."

When he swung around, glaring at her, she understood that it was his very ferocity that attracted her to him.

"The keys," she repeated, holding them out. "Where's Meg?"

The tension in his body revealed his hostility as he turned to look at her. "I told you, I don't want the keys. I'm thinking of moving on. I'll just put the cottage up for sale and keep the money for Meg when she grows up."

Maddie dropped her hand to her side. "But you can't," she objected.

Ross approached her and stopped only inches away, his imposing figure towering over her. "I can do whatever the hell I like."

She tipped back her head to look up at him, holding his eyes with hers, totally unafraid. "No, you can't," she repeated. "This is Meg's cottage, and she has a right to know her background. You would be selfish to walk away."

Something wrenched inside her as she saw his face crumple behind the mask of anger. "It wasn't your fault, you know," she told him, her voice softer now. "And you have to try to focus on the happy memories the cottage holds. You must have been happy when you first got married…and when Meg was born."

His whole body appeared to deflate, and his head fell forward. Maddie had to stop herself from reaching out to stroke his cheek.

"It *was* my fault," he murmured. "I let her down when she needed me."

"No…" Now she did reach out to him, just to touch her fingers to his skin. "Maybe you were too busy to notice that your wife was struggling, and that's unfortunate, but what if she never let you know? How could you have helped her if she wouldn't let you in? Perhaps she didn't want to seem less than perfect to you."

He looked up at her, the beginnings of a new softness in his eyes. "You think?"

"It's possible…" She hesitated. "And I should know since that's how I felt after… after my accident. Yesterday, in the lane, I was ashamed that you'd seen *me* the way I was. To be honest, I've been playing down my injuries because I didn't want to be judged by my inadequacies. I obviously needed your help yesterday, but even then I tried to pretend that I didn't."

Ross kept hold of her eyes, reaching out to her. "You don't ever need to feel inadequate with me."

"No, not now, but how would you know I felt like that if I never let you in…like Jenny?"

He dropped his hand to his side. "You're right. She didn't let me in. I never realized…"

"If she'd opened up, you would have been there for her, Ross. I know that.

"And anyway, what about her mother—

where was she in all this? Her mother was around more—shouldn't she have noticed her daughter wasn't herself? Perhaps it was her own guilt that made her turn against you… and maybe giving Meg the cottage was her way of showing she was sorry for that."

"It's not fair to Jenny to try and make me feel less guilty," said Ross. "I deserve to be blamed."

"What Jenny would have wanted is for you to be the best dad to Meg you can be. Make some new memories for her in Rose Cottage… some happy memories. Here."

When she held out the keys again, he took them and slipped them into his pocket. "I'll think about it," he said, his expression hardening again, shutting her out. "You'd better say goodbye to Meg, or she'll be upset. I'll go and get her."

When he stepped inside, Maddie felt a sudden pang of loss. The pain sharpened as Meg came running toward her with Red close behind. "Daddy says you're leaving," she cried.

"Only to the other side of the village," Maddie told her, crouching down to take hold of her small hands. They felt so soft and chubby, reminding her just how young the little girl was. "I can still see you whenever you want."

"And you'll take me to see them set the rabbit free if Daddy can't?"

"Of course I will, but that's up to your dad. He's got my number and he knows where I'll be. Anyway, you don't need to be sad—" for a moment, Maddie glanced up at Ross, lifting her chin with defiance in her eyes, refusing to be daunted by the dark anger in his "—because you're going to be busy making your new home nice."

"What?" The little girl's face lit up with excitement. "We can have the cottage? We really can have the cottage and I'll have my very own big bedroom and a proper garden to play in?"

"We'll see," Ross said as Maddie held Meg close, fighting back tears. She was going to miss the little girl so much…and Red, too. And what about Ross? she found herself wondering. Was she going to miss him, too?

Oh, yes, she realized. She was going to miss Ross. Just seeing him made her heart beat faster…and that was exactly why she had to distance herself. She needed to get her own life straight before she could even think about becoming involved with anyone…

especially after Alex. Anyway, Ross definitely didn't need another vulnerable woman in his life, and at the moment she felt very vulnerable. Maybe when she was stronger things would seem different.

CHAPTER SIXTEEN

WHEN MADDIE PULLED up outside Sky View Cottage, her head was overflowing with thoughts. The episode this morning with Ross and Meg had tugged at her heartstrings, but deep down she was glad to have moved away from them. She didn't want anything to distract her from her goal of getting her life back to where it used to be...or somewhere close, at least. She needed to stay focused, and her focus had slipped. Now it was time to toughen up, to work harder on her exercises and get her unwilling body back to full strength in order to start doing some work with horses again. On her next day off, she decided, she would go to Hope Farm and see Dennis, if that was okay with Bob Nelson. It was nice to know that at least one person around here knew who she really was...or had been.

The front door opened just as she raised her key to the lock. Cass stepped out into the sunshine, a broad, welcoming smile on her face.

"I hope you don't mind," she said. "But I have another key, and I wanted to put some flowers and things in, you know, try to make it a bit like home."

Maddie stared at her, choked up with emotion. "Thank you," she eventually managed. "It means a lot."

Cass shrugged. "We just want you to be happy here."

"And I will be happy... I'm sure I will."

"Good," said Cass, smiling. "I'll be off, then, and let you settle in. I guess I'll see you tomorrow."

"You'll see me tomorrow," Maddie promised.

"And Ross Noble didn't give you too hard a time? I suppose he was glad to have you gone."

"Funnily enough, he didn't seem too pleased when I gave him the keys. I think maybe he was afraid of the memories he might face in the cottage."

Cass nodded. "Well, that's understandable. I've never met him, of course, but Jake said his mother-in-law made his life a nightmare before he finally left the village. A lot of people around here do say he's a bit strange, though."

"I think he's just screwed up because of his own guilt," Maddie said sadly. "But I believe he genuinely wants what's best for Meg. She starts school after the holiday, you know."

Cass frowned slightly and put a reassuring hand on Maddie's arm. "That's good—you'll be able see how she's doing when you take Robbie in next week. It's obvious you've taken quite a shine to her. But…you haven't taken a shine to her dad, too, have you? That might not be wise."

Maddie shook her head decisively. "You must be joking. He has far too many issues, and there's no room in my life for a man at the moment."

As Cass walked off along the pathway that led through the small copse toward the stables, Maddie went into the house, wondering why it was that when people found out you were single, they always thought you were looking for love. Well, she'd gotten this far on her own after her life was turned upside down, and she would stay on her own for some time yet. One day, when she had her life back, she could maybe give love another chance, but that was a long way off yet.

Tomorrow, she decided, after she finished work, she would spend some time on the yard at Sky View, familiarizing herself with the horses there...that was where her future lay. For now, though, she would just get settled here in her new home.

The scent of the flowers that Cass had so generously placed in the cottage drifted into Maddie's nostrils as she went from room to room. Their sweet scent made her feel good inside, as did the freshly baked cake that sat in the center of the small kitchen table. Making a mental note to remember to thank Cass again tomorrow, she unpacked the box of groceries she'd brought from Rose Cottage and brewed a pot of tea. Then she sat down with a generous slice of cake and ate in silence, looking out the window at the Lakeland hills. Peace, solitude and the chance to sit and dream of her future—what more could she want?

When an image of Ross's face came into her mind, she immediately pushed it away. She was really going to miss Meg's bright little face, but she was well rid of her dad and his problems.

AFTER MADDIE LEFT, Ross had tried to cling to his idea of selling Rose Cottage, despite her words of wisdom. But she had tweaked his conscience too strongly. *Make happy memories here for Meg,* she'd told him, and he knew deep down that she was right. Meg needed to learn about her mother, and although Rose Cottage was in trust to him, it was really she who owned it. Even if he couldn't hack it here, if he decided to go back to Scotland, he had no right to sell the cottage; that was his daughter's decision when she was old enough to know her own mind. He'd even toyed with the idea of renting it out for now, but common sense had prevailed, shored up by Maddie's unwanted advice. In the cottage, they could live cheaply—as long as he found work—and Meg could have a relationship with the place her mother had loved…her heritage.

He knew he needed to look around the cottage on his own, to face his past and all the demons that came with it, before he took Meg there. Thinking it was one thing; actually doing it was quite another. He stood in front of the cottage, considering its honest shape, foursquare and evenly proportioned. It seemed to smile at him, and the windows sparkled in the late-morning sun.

Jenny used to say that it was a happy

place…so why had she chosen to die here? Perhaps she'd been happy in her final moments; perhaps she'd been released from her demons…the ones no one else seemed to have noticed.

Maddie's words had stayed with him after she drove away. She had a way of making him see things in a totally different light. He didn't want to be absolved of any of the blame over Jenny's death, but what Maddie had said made a kind of sense—he couldn't deny that.

Shored up by his new determination to make a go of things in Little Dale, he took Meg to the village that afternoon, walking boldly into the shop and ignoring Nora Ryland's meaningful stare as he took his time picking out groceries.

Totally oblivious to the taut atmosphere, Meg studied the brightly colored wrappers on the candy shelves, choosing a large chocolate bar and turning to him with a pleading smile. "Please can I have this, Daddy?"

Nora tut-tutted loudly, but Ross gave his daughter a broad smile and handed her some money. "Here," he said. "You can pay for it. Choose something else, too, if you want."

After Meg hurried off to his truck, clutching her purchases, he walked to the counter and put down his loaded basket, boldly holding Nora's condemning eyes in his. "I'm here to stay," he told her, "so you may as well get used to it. Oh, and another thought for you—I don't care if nobody around here approves of me, but to punish a child who will be dealing with the loss of her mother for the rest of her life—by shunning her father—is downright shameful."

When Nora looked away, hot color rising in her pale face, he realized that maybe things could change for him here. She rang his goods through in silence and handed him a bag. "Fifteen pounds sixty-five," she said in a tight, clamped tone.

"Thanks." He turned on his heel and left the store with a lighter step than he'd had in a long time.

CHAPTER SEVENTEEN

ROSS ARRIVED BACK at the trailer, unpacked their groceries and told Meg to play outside under Red's watchful eye until he returned from checking out the cottage.

He stood on the doorstep, faltering, wondering how he was going to do this. Glancing over his shoulder, he doubted his decision; there was still time to walk away. Then he remembered the earnest expression on Maddie's face when she had pleaded with him to do what was best for his daughter…and when she had given him a way to see through all the guilt.

Meg was watching him, hopping excitedly from foot to foot, her hand on Red's broad head. He raised his hand, and she waved back ecstatically. He took a deep breath and turned the key, pushing the front door open. It was too late to walk away now.

The first time he and Jenny came here sprang into his mind as if it was just yesterday. Jenny's bright face, so like Meg's, her sweet, naive smile as he scooped her up into his arms to carry her over the doorstep. The feel of her skin against his…

They had been ecstatic when Jenny's mother handed them the keys to the cottage on the day they got married. "Here," she'd said to Jenny. "I think your grandmother would want you to have it." Their first night in their new home had rounded off a perfect day; how could anyone have guessed then that it was doomed to end in tragedy?

He pressed the keys against his palm, his heart racing so hard it felt as if it was about to burst from his chest. For a moment, panic loomed, and he glanced back again, acutely aware of Meg's eyes on him. He'd told her that he just wanted to check the cottage out, make sure everything was ready for her. Truth was, he didn't want to break down in front of his little girl.

He took a step forward, moving backward in time. The hallway smelled of flowers and polish and something else…something sweet and exotic. He'd forgotten how steep the stairs were.

The kitchen was bright and sunny, filled with light. He picked up the faint scent of food.

The whole place felt lived in and cared for, he realized…that must be Maddie's doing. His mind was crowded with unsettling images and memories he was desperately trying to siphon out, only wanting the good ones to linger. There were plenty of those, too: Jenny's smile when he came home from work, her joy when she told him she was pregnant. Their whole future together would have been in this house. The pain in his heart was oppressive, but he knew Maddie had been right. The future *was* here, now, for him and Meg. Hopefully, Jenny would be watching over her daughter as she grew into a healthy, normal girl.

Remembering Jenny's sweetness and innocence, he understood what Maddie had been trying to tell him. Perhaps the blame really wasn't *all* on his shoulders. Anne Maddox had failed her daughter, too, by treating her like a child and turning a blind eye to her daughter's illness. Had Anne's treatment of Jenny dissuaded her from reaching out for help? He had loved his wife's sweet innocence back then, but now he could see so plainly that it had contributed to her downfall. Tears pressed against his eyelids, and for the first time since she'd died, he let them fall. "I am so sorry, Jenny," he groaned, dropping his head into his hands.

Make happy memories here for Meg, Maddie had told him. He took a breath and wiped away the tears, resolved to do just that. The final hurdle still loomed ahead of him—the room where he had found her cold, still body that day. He had to face it and come to terms with it…for Meg's sake. Then he could bring his daughter here, to see the first real home she had ever known. Steeling himself, he headed up the stairs.

GAZING OUT THE KITCHEN window at her glorious surroundings, Maddie felt a surge of enthusiasm that had been missing from her life. There was a time when her whole world had been filled with enthusiasm and adrenaline… and not always for big things like the next race or taking an unknown youngster up the gallops. Back then, she got joy and energy from simple, everyday things like the sun sparkling on the grass in the early mist of morning or suddenly bonding with one of her animal charges.

Horses were humbling, too; they felt their rider's mood and emotions and didn't suffer fools gladly. The wonderful, beautiful stallion

Grand Design was one of her greatest successes. It had taken a while, but he had eventually come to trust her to such an extent that she could do anything with him…and now she was going to be able to spend time with him all over again. Maddie felt as if fate was giving her another chance. On her next day off, she decided, she would go to Hope Farm Stud again. For now, though, she was going to concentrate on making Sky View Cottage feel like home.

All Maddie's belongings had fit easily into two boxes and her small suitcase, which she carefully carried in from the car. It was quite sad really, she thought, to have so few belongings. Of course, she'd left plenty of odds and ends in Devon, but she had brought everything she needed: clothes, some food her mother had packed and a few more precious items, like her favorite ornaments, pictures of the horses that had once filled her life along with one of her parents and Fudge, the dog she'd had as a child. As she unpacked that frame, the idea she'd had of maybe getting her own dog resurfaced.

While she put everything away, Maddie's thoughts kept wandering back to Rose Cottage. Had Ross decided to stay? she won-

dered, or was he already on his way back to
Scotland? If he was, did she care? She cared
about Meg's future, that was for sure, and she
hoped she'd made a difference by daring to
offer him advice…but as for Ross himself?
Hot color warmed her cheeks as she admitted to herself that she really didn't want him
to go. The timing for them was wrong right
now, but she couldn't imagine never seeing
him again.

By midafternoon, the cottage was already
feeling more like home. Wanting to feel she
belonged here, Maddie had wasted no time
in hanging her pictures, and she'd thoroughly
cleaned both the downstairs windows and the
bathroom, even though they looked pretty
clean already. By three o'clock her whole
body ached with the effort, so she sat down
for a while on the floral linen sofa in the cozy
living room, resisting the temptation to take
some painkillers. She had to try to get her
unwilling body back to some kind of normality, and she didn't want to rely on drugs.

Flicking on the TV, she scrolled through
the channels and clicked on a romantic movie.
Its dark-eyed hero reminded her sharply of
Ross, and she flicked it off again, needing

to know if he and Meg were still here…for Meg's sake, not his.

She'd drive by, she decided. If his truck was still there, then so were they.

"MADDIE CAME TO see us," announced Meg when Ross went outside to check on her. "I saw her slow down, but she didn't stop."

"Just as well," he remarked with a frown. "We don't need any busybodies in our life, do we, Nutmeg?"

Meg frowned. "Is Maddie a busybody, then?"

"Sure is," he said, turning away to hide his confusion. Why hadn't she dropped in?

Today had been tough, confronting the memories the cottage held, both good and bad. First, he'd gone into the bedroom he and Jenny had shared and broken down as he remembered their love; a love that had gone so wrong. And then…and then he'd faced the room where she'd ended her own life. He'd screamed silently at the images that had filled his head, as fresh and raw as on the day he found her.

Maddie had held out a lifeline to him yesterday and shown him a way through. He longed to talk to her again and maybe even share some of the pain that he had always kept strictly to himself. But perhaps it was just as well, then, that she hadn't stopped by, because to burden her with his problems would be selfish; she had enough troubles of her own to work on. Anyway, he didn't want her sympathy, and he definitely wasn't ready for her love. She was out of his life now, and he and Meg could move on. School for her began a week Monday, and for him that meant having the freedom to look harder for work; he'd try Sky View as Bob Nelson had suggested, he decided.

"WELL," BILL ASKED Maddie at lunch the next day, "are you all settled in, then?"

She nodded enthusiastically. "I can't thank you enough for letting me stay there... I know you could make a lot of money if it was a holiday rental, but I really will look after the place."

"Just make sure you look after Cass and Robbie," Bill told her. "And the new baby, of course. That'll be reward enough for me."

"You know I will," she promised.

The old man smiled, placing a hand on her arm. "I have no doubt about it. Anyway, life isn't all about money, and I've never rented the cottage out to tourists before. In fact, you'd better watch out, because it has become quite a home for romance lately. Cass rented it when she first came to Little Dale to be a vet at Fell Close, and then Andy Montgomery rented it for a while and he ended up engaged to Ellie Nelson, Bob's daughter. Have you met them?"

"Yes," Maddie said eagerly. "We took an injured rabbit there, to the animal sanctuary, and they took care of us. I'm afraid the cottage's romantic history will have a gap in it, though. I'm perfectly happy on my own."

"That's what I used to think," said Cass, glancing across at Jake. "Everyone needs love in their life, though."

"Not me," Maddie insisted. "So...are Ellie and Andy getting married soon?"

"In the spring, I think," Cass said. "They've already asked Robbie to be the ring bearer."

Robbie jumped up from the table at that, rolling his eyes. "Come on, boy," he called to Choco, and the little dog trotted faithfully behind him.

"Where are you going?" called Cass as he ran out the door.

"Dad is taking Rollo out, and he said I could go with him. I'm going to tack up Splodge."

"Remember to put a head collar on and tie him up when you're grooming him," Jake said. "I'll be out shortly. And his name is Chief, by the way."

Robbie glanced back with a broad grin. "Looks more like a Splodge to me."

"And what will clients think when I tell them I have a lovely pony for sale…named Splodge?"

"Not a problem," Robbie responded, disappearing out the door. "Because he isn't for sale."

"He really has taken to that pony, hasn't he?" Cass remarked.

Jake nodded. "I'm going to let him keep him for a while, I just like to wind him up about selling him. Anyway, he has to realize that everything around here has its price."

"Even me?" Cass giggled.

Jake laughed. "Mmm…two for one. It would be a good deal. I think you just might be a keeper, though."

"You think or you know?" Cass said playfully. "Now go check on Rob."

By three o'clock, when all the chores were done, Cass let out a sigh, holding the small of her back. "I'm going to have a lie down," she told Maddie. "Since I went on maternity leave, it feels as if I've gone downhill. Maybe I should have carried on working for longer… at least then I didn't have time to be tired. Anyway, since there's no school pick up and everything else seems to be done, you may as well head off if you like."

"Thanks," Maddie said. "And you're bound to feel tired, you know—it's only natural. I might just stop by the yard on my way home and see what's going on."

Cass nodded. "Good idea…you need to start spending some time with the horses if you really do want to start riding again. And you might just catch the new arrivals—they should be here anytime. I'm going to take a look myself in a bit."

Maddie's ears pricked up. "What, new horses you mean?"

Cass nodded. "Yes, Don Birchall, a friend of Jake's from Ireland, is sending him some dealing horses today. They can be anything from Thoroughbred youngsters to Irish cobs, competition horses or even ponies…anything he's come across that he feels has potential. Jake schools them and when they're sold, he and Don split the profits. It works well. Any that turn out to be unsalable just go back, which is useful. Jake has a good reputation, and he can't risk selling anyone a horse that's not 100 percent."

"Right, then," Maddie said, suddenly feeling excited at the prospect. "I'll go and see if they've arrived."

The Sky View stable yard was oblong with both wood- and stone-built stables and a large stone barn with double doors. Maddie took in her surroundings, appreciating the tidiness and peaceful atmosphere. The importance of keeping things neat on the yard had been drilled into her from an early age. The horses that peered over their stable doors appeared happy, and she noticed a small pony at the very end of the row. It had to be Splodge, with markings like that. He was all white with one big, brown…splodge…on his hind quarters. She headed over to take a look at him.

Robbie was inside the stable, tying up a hay net. "Hello," he said, smiling at her. "Have you come to see the horse box arrive?"

"If I'm allowed. Is this Splodge? I can see why you called him that."

"Chief!" Robbie exclaimed, rolling his eyes. "My dad has no imagination."

"Did you ride out together this afternoon?"

Robbie patted Splodge on the shoulder, letting him nuzzle his cheek. "Yeah. And I'm not going to let him be sold, you know." He opened the stable door and bolted it carefully behind him.

"I think your dad is just teasing you," Maddie told him. "So I wouldn't worry about it too much."

Robbie nodded, crouching down to stroke Choco, who was waiting patiently. The little brown-and-white dog jumped up in excitement, and Robbie took hold of his front paws, dancing him around in a circle. "I'm not worried, anyway, because I know Cass wouldn't let him. Come on, let's go and see if the truck is coming."

Warmed by the boy's easy acceptance, Maddie followed him across the yard. She tried to ignore the fiery pain that spread from her back into her left leg and force it to move in conjunction with her right. "Mind over matter, Mad," she murmured to herself, repeating the words that had carried her through some pretty rough times in the past year and a half. If she wanted to get her life back, she just had to find a way to get past her disabilities.

"It's here!" Robbie yelled, waving at her to hurry.

She caught up with him just as Jake appeared from the direction of the house. "Right," he said. "Now let's see what Don has sent us this time."

The small, wiry man who emerged from the huge silver horse box looked anything but happy.

"I've had a devil of a journey," he groaned. "The crossing was rough, and one horse in particular has been kicking off all the way here, upsetting the others."

"We'd better get the ramp down and make sure they're all okay, then," Jake suggested.

Maddie watched in fascination as, one by one, the horses were walked down the ramp and into the boxes Jake had already prepared. The first three were young Irish sports horses, two gray geldings and a smaller bay mare. Then came a friendly-looking purebred Irish draught mare. "I already have a home for this one," said Jake. "There's a breeder just a few miles away who wants her."

The driver, who had introduced himself as Dermot, nodded. "The others should sell well, too. They're a classy bunch."

The fifth horse was another mare. She appeared useful—up to weight with a plain head. "This must be the hunt horse Don told me about," Jake remarked, as Dermot stood her up in the yard. "I think I have a buyer for her, too, so she shouldn't be staying around for long. I'll give her a try tomorrow and then give the buyer a call."

Jake walked the mare off to her stable, and Dermot gave Maddie a wink. "I don't know what he's going to think of this last one," he said. "Don told me to just take it home again if he kicks off."

"But it already traveled all the way from Ireland," Maddie objected.

Dermot shrugged and ran back up the ramp. "I just do as I'm told."

He reappeared just as Jake came back from settling the hunter. "What am I supposed to do with that?" he roared as his sixth acquisition appeared.

"Don said that you wanted something quiet and not too big… Well, this is it."

"I didn't say I wanted something ugly, though," Jake groaned.

"I reckon he'll grow into his head."

"He is very thin," Maddie added tentatively. There was something about the little bay horse that appealed to her. He was a million miles away from the Thoroughbreds that had once been her lifeblood…but *she* was a million miles away from the person she'd been back then, too.

"He's only just four years old, and he had a bout of strangles a couple of months ago. It took a lot out of him," said Dermot. He laughed at the shocked expression on Jake's face. "You don't need to worry...he's well clear of it now and definitely not carrying any infection."

"I'll look after him," Maddie blurted out. "You know... help to build him up. He needs a load of weight on."

Jake looked at her, his shock returning. "You?" he said.

"You did say I could try riding when you had something suitable for me. I could just care for him until he's fitter, you know, to save you the bother."

"To be honest, I was seriously thinking of sending him straight back...and are you sure you're up to it?"

Maddie fixed him with what she hoped was a pleading expression. Suddenly, this seemed so important—as though it might be her only chance to work so closely with a horse again. "I won't know until I try."

For a moment, she thought Jake was going to say no. He didn't keep hangers-on, she knew that and this horse was definitely going to be a hanger-on.

"Let her try, Jake…please." Jake turned around sharply at the sound of Cass's voice. "It will be good for Maddie to have something to focus on, and it will get her used to being around horses. Who knows, we might need her help on the yard sometime. Obviously you'd have to show her what needs to be done, but he looks like a good-natured sort."

"Until he gets fit and his personality comes back," grumbled Jake. "I tell you what…"

Maddie held her breath.

"He needs to be turned out for a while anyway, so we'll put him in Copse meadow—that's the long field past the copse that runs across the back of Sky View Cottage. That way you can keep an eye on him from home and get to know him. After that, we'll see."

"You won't regret it," Maddie promised, walking eagerly across to say hello to the sad-looking youngster. His ribs jutted out beneath his dull coat, and he stood with his head lowered but his eyes brightened as he saw her approach.

"Hey, boy," she murmured, scratching his neck; the skin felt tight beneath her touch, as if he was slightly dehydrated. "Everything's going to be fine now...you'll see."

"It's only temporary," Jake warned. "If he doesn't shape up, then I'm afraid he'll soon be gone. I'll put him in a stable for tonight, and tomorrow you can come with me to turn him out." He took the lead rope and began to walk away.

"Thanks," Maddie said. "And thank you, too, Cass, for persuading him."

"Anytime." Cass smiled and turned in the opposite direction, heading back to the house.

"Maybe one day we can go for a ride together," Robbie suggested as they followed Jake to the stable.

Maddie smiled. "I'd like that, Rob."

The little boy looked around for Cass, who was already heading back to the house. "And you, too, Mum," he called after her. "We could all go...after the baby is born."

Cass stopped and glanced back, shielding her eyes from the late-afternoon sun. "Sounds great, Rob. Tell your dad not to be too long, won't you? Tea will be ready soon."

As Maddie reached the stable and watched the scrawny little bay gelding get settled into his new home, she suddenly realized that she hadn't thought about her back or her leg for over half an hour. Hope flooded in; she'd always known that spending time with horses again would help her to heal. It would be a while before she actually rode, but at least she was on her way back.

CHAPTER EIGHTEEN

ON THE DAY Meg started proper school, Ross felt strangely nervous. He'd been looking forward to having more time to job hunt, and Meg had been excited about it for weeks, but now that the day was here, it just seemed too big a leap. His little girl was growing up, and it scared him.

They arrived at Little Dale Primary School early, and Meg held his hand tightly as they walked through the playground and into the building. She skipped along beside him as they went down the corridor toward her classroom.

"You okay?" he asked, and she grinned, nodding eagerly.

"Maddie said that Robbie, the little boy she looks after, would be here."

Something tightened inside Ross as he glanced around, searching for Maddie's slight figure; despite himself, he wanted to see her.

"You'd have thought that they'd be here by now," he said.

He couldn't help looking around for her again after Meg settled in with her teacher, Miss Mills. There might not be room for a relationship in his or Maddie's lives right now, but that didn't stop him from wanting to know how she was doing. Well, he was going to Sky View today to see if they had any work for him, so maybe he'd run into her then. She'd been right about Rose Cottage being good for Meg: it was exactly what his daughter needed—a home of her own. And he'd fallen in love with the cottage all over again as his happy memories came flooding in, leaving no space in his head for the bad ones…except late at night when his imagination invited those difficult memories back in. But he reckoned he deserved that.

Jumping into his truck, he nosed his way through the clutter of hastily parked cars and then headed out on the road to Sky View.

Ross leaned forward over the wheel as the lane rose steeply, climbing toward the wide expanse of wild, moody sky. Today the sun was trying to shine through a tapestry of clouds ranging from pure white, tinged with gold, to gray and almost purple. There was no doubt about it—this was a beautiful place. Unchanged, he'd guess, for thousands of years, overseeing so many lives, births and deaths and a myriad of emotions…all gone now. Like his Jenny.

Not wanting to go down that dark path, he tried to focus on what he could say to Bill and Jake Munro to convince them he would be an asset. They had a stud, after all, and he was experienced with horses…especially foaling mares.

The place appeared deserted when Ross pulled into the yard beside the house. Telling Red to stay, he jumped out into the sunshine, wondering whether to go and knock on the door or walk around to the stable yard. Deciding on the latter, he turned away from the house… He stopped in his tracks as he heard a sound. Was that an animal in distress? The sound came again, breaking the silence that made him feel as if the whole world was standing still.

"Help…someone help!"

It was human…the cry was human. Panic hit as he ran to the house; was it Maddie? He burst in without knocking as a piercing scream shattered the silence.

When he saw the young woman on the

floor, he struggled to take in what he was seeing. Panic clawed at him for a second, and then instinct took over and he was on his knees beside her. She was pregnant and in distress, and it didn't look like there was anyone here to help but him. "Don't worry," he said. "I'm here now to help you. People have babies every day, you know. Is the ambulance on its way?"

The woman panted loudly, trying to control her breathing as her contraction abated. "No phone," she groaned.

Ross pulled his own from his pocket. "We need an ambulance…now, to Sky View Stables near Little Dale. There's a woman in labor…" He turned to the mother-to-be. "What's your name?"

"Cass," she ground out. Ross relayed the rest of the information to the dispatcher and put down the phone.

He reached for her hand as the next contraction took Cass in its grip. This baby was coming, and nothing was going to stop it. His thoughts raced: they needed hot water, towels…

"Just breathe," he told her. "You can do this."

It was there, he realized, the baby was already making its way out into the world. The miracle of birth, new life, here in this kitchen, was not going to wait any longer. "Okay," he said, drawing desperately on all his experience foaling mares, "now push."

MADDIE DROPPED ROBBIE off at school and headed back to her car. The dentist appointment had taken longer than she'd expected, as an emergency came in just before it was Robbie's turn. Taking her phone from her pocket, she dialed Cass to give her an update and make sure everything was okay at home. The call clicked straight to voice mail. She was probably fine, Maddie told herself, trying to stay calm. She remembered how she'd lost service on the road to Rose Cottage—cell phones could be unreliable around here.

Still, Maddie drove too fast, alarm bells sounding in her head. She fought to ignore them. There was no reason why anything should be wrong, and she'd be back soon anyway...

Suddenly, a large tractor came into view, barreling toward her and taking up most of the width of the road. Maddie stood on the brakes, and her car slithered to a halt as the burly farmer shook his fist at her through his window. When the tractor didn't immediately start moving again, she climbed out of her car. "What's wrong?" she cried, reaching up to bang on the window of the big vehicle.

The farmer threw open his door. "I think that's obvious," he shouted. "Blasted thing's cut out, thanks to your crazy driving making me stop so fast, and it won't start again."

"But you have to move," Maddie insisted. "I need to get past. It's an emergency."

"Can't do the impossible," he grumbled. "You'll just have to turn round and go back the other way...through the village and over the fell. Either that or wait until I've rung someone for help. I've been having trouble with the darned thing for a while."

She had no other choice, so Maddie hurried back to her car, slammed it into Reverse and backed into a driveway to turn around before heading back the way she'd come with her pulse pounding inside her head. It would be fine, she told herself. Of course it would.

The first thing Maddie saw when she finally arrived at Sky View was Ross's truck. What was it about the man that made her feel like this, she wondered, uncomfortable and irritated but still so drawn to him? And what was he doing here, anyway?

Red wagged his tail when he saw her, and

she stopped for a moment to reach in through the window and scratch the backs of his ears. "I've missed you, boy."

She heard the cry as she stepped into the house. A basic, primal scream that made the hairs on the back of her neck stand up, followed almost immediately by a baby's wail.

"Cass!" she yelled. "Cass! Where are you?"

"Here," Ross said. "She's here…and she's fine."

When Maddie entered the kitchen, she felt as if her heart had simply stopped. There was Ross, down on his knees on the floor…next to Cass, her face pink with exertion and damp with sweat but lit up by an almost ethereal glow. "Maddie," she murmured, smiling now. "Come and meet Gwen."

Ross was wrapping a squirming, whimpering infant in a towel. He placed the tiny slip of new life carefully into her mother's arms before turning to look at Maddie, his eyes alight with joy. "Better ring Jake," he said. "I haven't had the chance, I'm afraid. The ambulance is on its way."

Maddie froze, unable to take in what she was seeing.

"And then you might want to find some

hot water and cloths," Ross suggested. "So we can get tidied up."

"You've had the baby." Maddie gasped. "But…how?"

"With Ross's help," Cass told her. "I don't know what would have happened if he hadn't come along when he did. I'd lost my phone and…"

"And I got held up," cried Maddie. "I am so, so sorry. Jake will be livid."

"Jake will be thrilled," Cass said, clutching her precious burden with the light of love in her eyes.

A siren broke the moment, and suddenly Maddie was rushing around to get the items Ross had asked for. By the time the paramedics came rushing into the room, Cass was sitting in a chair with the baby on her breast and the worst of the mess was washed away.

"Well, well," commented a smiling paramedic. "It seems you've done our job for us. Better get the two of you to the hospital, though, just to get checked out."

Cass became weepy. "Have you spoken to Jake?" she asked.

Maddie nodded. "I'll get him on the phone again, and you can talk to him yourself. He must be worried sick."

AFTER THE AMBULANCE drove away, Ross and Maddie stood in silence, totally overcome by what had happened.

"So you actually delivered it," Maddie, said, her voice filled with awe. "I mean, delivered *her*...Gwen."

"I didn't really have much choice," Ross admitted. "Anyone would have done the same."

"But how did you know what to do?"

Ross grinned. "I didn't, but I have foaled a lot of mares...the principle is the same, I guess. Stay calm and get them out with as little stress as possible. And of course Cass is a vet, so she knew what to do, as well... she's pretty amazing."

"She is," Maddie agreed. "So is Jake. Do you know he's letting me look after one of his horses? It's a skinny youngster with an ugly head, but there's just something about him... One day I hope to be able to ride him."

Ross took in the excitement on her face, and his heart lurched. Suddenly he wanted to reach out, take her in his arms and feel the sweetness of her lips against his again. She was just so brave and strong and yet vulnerable at the same time. "Have you done much riding?" he asked, trying to crush his crazy feelings. There was no place in his life for a woman…especially not another one whose needs he couldn't possibly meet.

She hesitated. "A bit…but not since I got injured. It might take a while, but I'm determined to do it again."

"Good for you," he told her, meaning it.

BILL CAME HOME from the hospital just as Jake finished singing his praises for his beautiful wife and amazing new daughter. "Well, congratulations to you both, and give Cass my best," Maddie told him over the phone. "And don't worry about Robbie. Your dad is back now, so one of us will pick him up."

"Tell him I'll take Robbie to the hospital to see his new sister as soon as he's done school," urged Bill.

She relayed the message and hung up, turning to the older man with a broad smile. "And congratulations to you, too, Granddad. She is a very lucky baby to have all of you to love her."

Bill's eyes lit up, sparkling with unshed tears. "And oh, how my Gwen would have loved her."

"And now you have another Gwen to remember her by."

After tidying up and preparing a casserole for the Munro men to heat up for their supper, Maddie headed home, reflecting on the day's events and the family Gwen had been born into.

Maddie had had her share of troubles, that was for sure, but her problems weren't really in the same league as Bill's and Jake's. Bill had lost both his wife and granddaughter, and Jake had lost his mother and his daughter. He'd almost lost Robbie, too, when his ex-wife had taken him to America after the accident. Thankfully, she'd come to her senses, but Jake still had deep wounds to bear. All Maddie had lost was her confidence, her pride and a fiancé, who obviously hadn't been worth having in the first place. She'd lost some physical ability, too, but she hadn't lost her whole life, as she'd believed. Somehow, it felt as if she was slowly getting it back.

On her way past the stables, she stopped to collect feed for her new charge, savoring the aroma that filled the feed room and sharply reminded her of her life before the accident. The bay gelding had been turned out into Copse field, and she fed him every night now, noting how much happier he seemed after just a week at Sky View.

As usual, he was waiting for her by the bottom gate that led into the yard. She called out to him but carried on walking until she reached the other end of the meadow, near to the cottage. The gawky gelding cantered along on the other side of the dry stone wall, like a half-grown, playful puppy. "Bert," she said, trying his name on for size. It didn't fit; he needed something better, no matter what Jake said. If he didn't like it, then it would be just for her to use.

Leaving the feed by the cottage, she went through the top gate into the field and slipped on the gelding's head collar, talking to him in a low, crooning voice before leading him out into the grassy lane to tie him to a ring on the cottage wall. When she brought his feed over, he snorted and snuffled, pawing the ground before diving into it as if he hadn't seen food for weeks.

"It hasn't taken you long to learn the routine," she remarked, wondering what Jake would say if he knew she was actually bringing the youngster out of the field to feed him and brush him off. At first, she'd been worried, well aware that, if he pulled or got too full of himself, he could knock her off balance, but he'd proven himself to be quite obliging.

As long as she was careful and didn't get into a dangerous position, then everything would be fine, she told herself, pleased with her prowess. She had once been used to dealing with high-strung, fit young Thoroughbreds, so surely she could manage a half-starved, out-of-shape, crossbred gelding.

"Bert," she repeated disdainfully, and the little gelding lifted his head and looked at her before raising it higher to stare at the hills. He was more handsome already, she thought... and something else, something almost regal. Ideas buzzed through her head, and suddenly she hit on the perfect name. "Pride," she said. "I'll call you Pride, and then hopefully I'll get mine back."

Maddie's phone rang as she returned to the cottage after leading Pride back into the field. When Jake's name flashed out at her, her heart sank. "Hello? Is everything okay?"

"Don't worry," he said. "It's not bad news. Everything's fine and they'll be coming home in a day or two. I just wanted to ask you if you knew why Ross Noble happened to be at Sky View this afternoon. I wasn't expecting him or anything, and it's hardly the kind of place you just happen to be passing."

Maddie remembered her disappointment when she'd asked him the same question after Cass and the baby were taken away in the ambulance. He'd just looked at her and then looked away, muttering something about having to get off. "He didn't say anything to me about it," she told Jake. "Perhaps you should go and ask him?"

"Yes…that's what I thought; I might call in tonight to thank him. It's the least I can do. But…I wondered if you'd like to come with me. To be honest, it feels a bit awkward and you know him quite well, don't you?"

Maddie smiled to herself, surprised by Jake's discomfiture; he always seemed so sure of himself. "Of course I'll come," she said. "I suppose it is a bit strange to think that a stranger delivered your wife's baby."

Jake laughed. "You might say that. I'll be there to pick you up in an hour or so if that's okay."

CHAPTER NINETEEN

MADDIE WALKED ALONG the grassy lane that led to Sky View Cottage to wait for Jake by the road. She leaned against the wall, looking out over the awe-inspiring mass of the Lakeland hills, breathing in the sweet thin air with a rush of well-being. She was getting stronger every day—she could feel it—and she was actually handling a horse again, albeit in a very basic way.

Her life as one half of racing's golden couple seemed a million miles away; she felt kind of guilty for being so secretive about her past, but this was her life now, and she didn't want to dwell on what was gone. She would tell everyone one day, she decided, when she'd proved to herself that she could do some of the things she used to and be accepted for what she was now. And at least one person around here knew her story; that comforted her. She remembered Bob Nelson's offer to let her come by Hope Farm to visit Dennis.

In fact, she'd intended to go on her next day off, but with the baby arriving, who knew now when she'd get a chance?

The sound of Jake's 4x4 brought her out of her reverie. She stepped out into the lane with a smile as he pulled up beside her, but when she went to step forward, her bad leg stayed put. Mortified, she dragged it behind her, acutely aware of the pity on Jake's face. Disappointment clouded her good mood— just when she really believed she was getting back to some semblance of normality, her injuries always seemed to rear up and put her right back down again.

"You okay?" asked Jake, rolling down his window.

She nodded determinedly. "Yes, I'm fine. It's been a long day, that's all."

He laughed. "You might say that. Come on, then, get in and we'll go and face your misunderstood friend."

"He's not really my friend," Maddie retorted. "But I suppose he has been misunderstood. He isn't as bad as they say, you know."

"Well, after what he did for Cass, I guess I owe him a chance at least. I wasn't even around when everything happened with his wife, so I'll try to take him at face value. But are you sure you're up for this? Is your back bothering you?"

Maddie's response was instant. "Of course I'm up to it. It aches a bit when I'm tired, that's all."

Jake glanced across at her, his curiosity evident. "Must be some accident you had."

"At the time it was bad, but it's fine now. I'm almost completely recovered."

Maddie knew the *almost* stretched a bit wider than she was admitting to, but luckily Jake didn't remark on it.

Jake drove just like he did everything else—with quiet determination. Obviously deep in thought, he spoke little, but Maddie was glad about that. She didn't want to have to make polite conversation.

"What do you think I ought to say to him?" he eventually asked.

"Who, you mean Ross?"

"Do you think I should offer him something for what he did?"

"You mean…like a reward?"

He scowled. "No. I just…"

"Just say thank-you and then go with your gut," she told him. "See what happens. I'm sure he's wondering how they both are, so he'll appreciate your visit no matter what."

"It was Cass who told me to bring you along. She said you'd know what to say."

"Well, I'll do my best to chip in, but it's you who has to say thanks."

His knuckles paled as he gripped the steering wheel tighter, and Maddie realized just how apprehensive he was.

"I'm not really bothered about meeting him," Jake said. "Not really. I've never been good at small talk, that's all, and it's a bit of a weird situation. If it was someone I knew, it would be better, but they say this Ross guy can be a bit strange and unpredictable."

"He's just been through a tough time," Maddie insisted. "He doesn't really let anyone in, but he loves his daughter and that must mean something."

Jake sighed, relaxing his shoulders. "So I guess we do have something in common then," he said. "We both have daughters."

"Sure do," Maddie agreed. "Thanks to him."

The sun was just beginning to sink in the sky as Jake pulled up in the lane outside Rose Cottage. A red glow reflected off the neat square windows, and Maddie felt a sudden sense of loss. She'd been happy here for a little while...except for her obnoxious neighbor, of course. Her next thought came unbidden. Perhaps she'd been happy here because of him.

"Come on," she said, noting that Jake was hanging back. "Just say thank-you and then talk horses."

He opened the door, jumping out. "Oh, right! I forgot we had that in common, too."

The door opened before Jake could knock. "If you've come to say thanks, it's fine," Ross said. "I'd have done the same for anyone. And if you're here to complain about my interfering, well, I'm sorry but I'd have done the same no matter what."

He was standing square in front of them, holding firmly onto the sides of the door frame as if to create a barrier.

"You took care of my wife when she needed help," Jake responded, his voice choked with emotion. "And I want to tell you how grateful I am. I know folks around here have treated you badly, but I have no preconceptions. I take people as I find them, and you may have saved my new daughter's life."

Ross stood speechless, seeming unsure how to react to Jake's honesty.

"Ask them to come in for a coffee, Dad," Meg said from behind him. Her chestnut head poked past his legs, and she grinned. "Hello, Maddie."

"Hello, Meg." Maddie was surprised at just how pleased she was to see the little girl.

Ross's shoulders softened, and he stepped back. "I'm sorry for my reaction," he said. "I guess I always think the worst. Come in—I'll put the kettle on."

By the time they'd finished their coffee, Jake and Ross were avidly talking horses while Maddie helped Meg color in some pictures at the kitchen table.

"I wish you still lived here," Meg said, looking up at Maddie with huge, shining eyes.

"Ah, but then you would still be living in the trailer," Maddie reminded her.

Meg shook her head. "No, I wouldn't, because there's enough room here for all three of us…you, me and Daddy."

Maddie's cheeks grew hot, and she glanced across to make sure Ross wasn't paying attention to them. "I don't think your daddy would be too keen on that idea."

"Well, then, will you come and see me lots?"

Maddie smiled. "Oh, definitely…if your dad doesn't mind."

"I'm just tired," she responded. "You must be so happy."

"I'm thrilled," he said, his dark eyes softening. "About the baby, obviously, but also about Cass. You worry, you know…things can go wrong in childbirth, even in this day and age."

"It's a good thing Ross came over when he did…and I'm so sorry for letting you down." There, her apology was out; she'd been worrying about it all day.

Jake shook his head. "It's just circumstance. It wasn't your fault that the tractor broke down or that Robbie had a dentist's appointment. Anyway, it all worked out very well. By a stroke of good luck and some level-headed, quick thinking, Ross saved the day. Plus, he needed a job and I really was hoping to find someone experienced to help me out. He is trustworthy, isn't he?"

Maddie shrugged. "Well, I don't really know him that well—" an image of him carefully braiding Meg's hair sprang to mind, his dark eyes narrowed in concentration "—but from what I've seen, he's a good, solid person. I guess you'll just have to see how he does." Suddenly, she felt a flutter of anticipation…or was it apprehension? It was going to be strange having Ross Noble around again.

"How is the gelding, by the way?" asked Jake, changing the subject.

"Great… He's let me brush him off, and he seems to have really settled down. I've nicknamed him Pride, in the hope that one day you'll be proud of him. Do you mind?"

"A name is just a name as far as I'm concerned. Be careful, though. Don't run before you can walk."

"Shouldn't that be ride?" Maddie laughed.

Jake's face turned a deep shade of crimson. "I'm so sorry," he began awkwardly.

"Don't worry about it," she told him. "I know what you mean."

"Perhaps Ross will be able to give you a hand with him," he suggested. "I'll have a word."

That night, Maddie found sleep elusive. Every time she closed her eyes, images of Alex and her life before her accident burst into her head. Had she loved him? She really believed she did back then. But had she actually just loved the life they had and the future they'd mapped out? Ross's dark eyes burned into her memory, so intense…so dangerous. He was nothing like Alex, and nothing like the kind of man she would maybe hope to meet one day in the distant future. For now, she just wanted her own space to prove to herself that she could be independent and whole again.

WHEN HER ALARM rang the next morning, Maddie felt as if she'd hardly closed her eyes. Six fifteen, just enough time to grab some breakfast before work. No doubt she would be expected to take care of Meg the minute she and Ross arrived. The thought of spending time with the little girl brought a warm glow to her heart, and she jumped out of bed, disappointed at the way her leg let her down... again. If her balance didn't start improving soon, she'd never be able to ride.

Going to the wardrobe, Maddie dug out the jodhpurs she'd brought with her, holding them against her longingly. Would she ever wear them, she wondered, or was she living in hope of the impossible? Closing her eyes tightly, she tried to imagine herself riding Pride, cantering easily across the hills, and suddenly she knew. She was going to do it... or die trying.

Ross's vehicle was already parked in the yard when Maddie drove up to the house.

She parked beside it, glancing at her watch. It wasn't even seven thirty yet; he was keen. From across the yard she could hear the sound of horses, eager to be fed, and the excited clucking of the happy red hens. Catching their enthusiasm, she headed into the house, wondering where Meg was.

Jake was waiting impatiently in the kitchen. "Ah, you're here," he said. "You'll be okay getting Robbie and this young lady some breakfast and taking them to school, won't you? I need to go and show Ross the ropes right away, since I have to go into town this morning. Don't want to be late for visiting hours at the hospital this afternoon."

Maddie nodded. "That's what I'm here for—to help. Give my best wishes to Gwen and Cass. Oh, and will you be back for lunch?"

He shook his head, already reaching for his jacket. "No, you can make some for Dad and Ross, though, if you don't mind. Just soup and sandwiches will do."

After Jake left, Maddie went to talk to Meg, who was sitting in a large chair, eyes like saucers. She smiled when she saw Maddie. "Can I have cereal, please?" she asked.

Maddie ruffled her hair. "Of course you can. I'll just go and shout for Robbie."

The little girl looked suddenly worried. "Is he nice?" she asked.

"He's lovely. You'll like him, I promise."

TWENTY MINUTES LATER, Meg and Robbie were sitting side by side at the kitchen table, happily tucking into bowls of cereal. Taking care of the children was satisfying, Maddie decided.

"Is she okay?"

Ross's deep voice took her by surprise, and she turned to see him in the doorway. Swept up in his gaze, she temporarily lost the power of speech. How was it that he always seemed to have this effect on her?

Her voice when she responded was harsher than she intended. "What does it look like?" she said.

"Just asking." His jaw tightened.

"Sorry... I didn't sleep well, but that's no excuse. Do you want a coffee?"

"If you don't mind. I'll take it with me."

She felt self-conscious as she poured scalding water into the coffee pot, as if he was judging her every move. She reached for the milk, and suddenly her hand slipped.

"You were lucky there," he said, rushing

across to grab the jug. "It could easily have broken. You carry on—I'll mop the milk up."

Feeling awkward and more than a little stupid, Maddie did as he told her. "Has Jake left you loads of work to do?" she asked, determined to pull herself together.

Ross laughed. "If mucking out ten horses' stables and grooming their occupants is work, then yes. To me, though, it's pleasure."

"I know what you mean. There's nothing more satisfying." Ross gazed curiously at her, and she backtracked. "Or at least I would *imagine* there isn't anything more satisfying… than caring for horses as a job, I mean."

"How much experience with horses have you actually had?" asked Ross with a puzzled frown. "Jake said something about me helping you with a youngster you've befriended, but now I'm wondering how much help you really need…"

Maddie froze. This was her moment to tell him the truth, to let him know who she really was. The words stuck in her mouth. So that he could look at her with sympathy in his eyes instead of taking her at face value? No way.

"Enough to be okay around them," she told him. "I'd like to start riding again, though."

Ross held her gaze again, and this time his eyes held a hint of softness. "Are you sure you'll be up to it?"

Maddie bristled. "Of course. Why wouldn't I be?"

He shrugged. "Okay, we'll have to see what we can do, then. Now I'd better get back to work before I get the sack on my first day."

Impulsively, she reached out and touched his arm. "Thanks. I appreciate that. Pride, the horse I've befriended, is in the meadow that backs onto the yard. He's nothing to look at, mind."

"Beauty is in the eye of the beholder." Ross smiled, looking across at the children. "See you later, Nutmeg."

"Bye, Daddy," called Meg, looking up from her breakfast with milk dripping off her chin.

Maddie set off for school half an hour later with a warm glow inside her. Everything around her brimmed with promise: the children's happy banter from the backseat, the way the morning sun crept across the fell, bringing the world to life…and Ross's attempt at friendship.

Cass and the baby would be home in the next couple of days, and she would have so much more work to do, but she didn't mind. Sky View was slowly filling the gaping hole in her life. She just needed her body not to let her down again, like it had on the day her car broke down. No wonder Ross seemed surprised at her intention to ride; he probably thought she was being stupid, that she wasn't up to it. Doubt crept in…what if she wasn't?

CHAPTER TWENTY

OVER THE NEXT few days, Maddie and Ross slipped into new territory. On his second morning at Sky View, after she came back from taking the children to school, he appeared in the kitchen around coffee time.

"Just wondered if you wanted to show me your gelding," he said. "I've run it past Jake."

When she hesitated, he turned away abruptly, heading back out into the yard.

"Yes…please," she called after him. "I'd like that."

He stopped then without looking back, waiting for her to make the next move.

As she approached his broad, formidable back, Maddie's mouth went dry, but when he spun around and smiled at her, her heart began to race. "Come on, then," he said, grabbing hold of her hand. Her skin tingled under his touch, and her heart thumped faster.

"Don't expect too much," she told him.

When they arrived at the meadow, Pride

trotted up to greet them, glad of the company. "Well, you're right about one thing," Ross remarked from behind a smile. "He certainly is no looker…"

Maddie jumped immediately to the horse's defense. "Looks aren't everything. You should see him move."

Ross regarded her with that same puzzled frown again, as if he couldn't quite work her out. "And what would you know about a horse's movement?" he asked. "Anyway, that's what I was just coming to—he has lovely conformation, and he's a very good mover. That's worth way more than a pretty head."

Maddie felt a smile creeping to the surface. "That's what I thought," she agreed.

"We can try lunging him if you like, on your next day off," he offered. "If Jake doesn't mind."

Maddie nodded eagerly, glowing inside. "Thanks, I'll hold you to that. It will have to be after Cass comes home, though. I can't really take a day off yet."

They walked back to the yard in an easy silence, both deep in thought until Ross stopped abruptly. "Hear that?"

Maddie listened to the birdsong and the

distant bleating of sheep being herded in from
the field, wondering what Ross meant. "The
sheep?"

"No…" He took hold of her shoulders, staring up into the bright summer sky. She followed his gaze, not knowing what she was
looking for; snow-white, fluffy clouds made
patterns against a background of clearest
blue.

"There," he said. "Look. It's a peregrine
falcon being barraged by the crows."

The high-pitched call of the bird of prey,
annoyed at being pestered by a pair of crows,
filled her ears. "Why are they doing that?"
she asked.

"Trying to protect their young, I guess,"
he murmured against her ear. "It's the most
natural instinct in the world."

Only too aware of his hot breath against her
cheek and his fingers firm upon her shoulders, she tried to think of something to say,
anything to diffuse the moment. "You know
a lot about nature, don't you?" she managed.

He let her go, and she moved away, widen-
ing the gap between them. "Not really," he
said. "When you work with animals and nature a lot you just see things, I guess."

"I…I like the way you teach Meg about

wildlife with the stories and all," Maddie blurted. She blushed at her own awkwardness. Sometimes she felt as if Ross was two different people, one distant and aloof and the other warm and kind and caring...but she didn't know which was the real Ross. Or maybe they both were.

Ross crossed his arms over his chest. "You can learn a lot from wildlife. Unlike us, creatures follow their instincts to survive...no preconceptions and no expectations."

IT RAINED ON the day Cass and the baby came home, but nothing could dampen the enthusiasm at Sky View. Robbie was allowed to stay home from school, and he proudly went with his dad to collect them while Maddie waited in anticipation.

Last night she'd walked Pride up and down the lane on a head collar after she'd fed him and brushed him off. He had been an absolute gentleman, which was fortunate, because if she was totally honest with herself, she knew that one good yank would have had her on the ground. She had to calculate and prepare for every movement she made in order to control her unruly limbs; a surprise pull could throw her coordination way off, and she couldn't afford to injure herself again—or worse.

Taking hold of the counter for support, she stretched out one leg and then the other, flexing her muscles and trying to decide if they felt stronger. When she first came home from the hospital, she had hardly been able to walk, and it had been a long, hard road to get this far. She mustn't start doubting herself now.

When Ross suddenly appeared in the doorway, she jumped, embarrassed that he'd caught her in such an intimate moment. Why did she always feel like that when he was around? "Just exercising," she mumbled.

"Don't stop on my account," Ross said. "I guess you have to exercise because of your accident. What did happen, exactly?"

"Just one of those freak things...cycling to work, ice on the road and a vehicle came out of nowhere."

Ross frowned. "You must have been badly hurt."

"I'm better now. Well, almost. That's all that really counts."

"Where did you work?"

Maddie froze, unable to tell a direct lie but determined to stick to her story, for a while at least. "It was miles away from here. I lived in Devon. Um…would you like a coffee? Jake will be back soon."

Even as she spoke, she heard a vehicle drive into the yard. "They are back," she cried. "Come on!"

FOR ROSS, WATCHING the proud new mum from afar was bittersweet. After all the congratulations were over, he went back to work with a heavy heart, remembering the day Jenny had come home with Meg in her arms. Her mother had insisted she be the one to pick her up; why hadn't he seen how wrong that was?

Picking up his grooming box, he headed off to Carlotta's stable and started work on her muddy coat. She nuzzled him gently, and he rubbed the backs of her ears. Horses were complicated creatures, he thought, but they were much easier to understand than women. Take Maddie, for instance—there were times when he felt close to her, but then she'd draw away. And then there were times when her eyes locked on his, and all he wanted to do was take her in his arms. When they'd kissed, it had seemed so right; she'd wanted it as much as he had. Or at least that's what he'd thought. How wrong could he have been?

Then again, perhaps she was doing him a favor. He didn't need a relationship right now, and she was better off without him, anyway.

MADDIE HAD EXPECTED things to be a bit hectic, but life with a baby in the house proved to be even more time-consuming than she had imagined. Every day felt like a whirlwind; taking the children to school, clearing the breakfast pots and laundry—so much laundry. Even answering the phone seemed to be her job now that Cass was so busy with little Gwen.

Babies had never been high on Maddie's wish list, but she fell in love with Gwen at once, looking forward to the times Cass asked her to feed her or play with her or rock her to sleep.

"Do you think you'll ever want to have kids?" Cass asked one day when Maddie was singing the baby a lullaby.

Maddie looked up in surprise. "I hadn't really thought as far as that. Getting myself right is my main priority at the moment, but after that...who knows?"

Cass's face clouded over. "But what if you never really 'get right,' Maddie? I've watched you struggle, and I know how tough it is for you sometimes just to walk."

"Only on a bad day," Maddie insisted. "But you didn't see how I was before. The thing is, Cass…as far as I'm concerned, there is no such thing as *if*…it's just *when*."

Cass nodded, gently taking the baby from her and cradling her in her arms. "With your determination, I'm sure it will be soon. Now, why don't you take the afternoon off to spend some time with Pride? You haven't had a day to yourself since before I had Gwen, and I know you're itching to start doing more with him. I'll have to ask Jake if he can spare Ross, though. I don't think you're ready to do it on your own just yet, and he can show you the ropes."

"You really don't have to," said Maddie. "I have done a bit with horses before."

A rush of color burned her cheeks as guilt flooded in; it felt so wrong to be less than truthful with everyone, but she needed this. Soon, she promised herself, when she was able to handle a horse and ride again, she would get everyone from Sky View together, including Ross, and tell them all the truth about being a jockey and exactly why she had kept it a secret. She hoped they would understand. She just didn't want them to see her as a failure, as something less than she once was. She wanted to be judged on her merits now, not as an injured, dumped jockey whose once-golden future had been ripped away.

"I really can manage on my own," she continued. "You don't need to bother Ross—I'm sure he has enough to do."

"Nonsense," Cass exclaimed, already picking up her phone.

WHEN ROSS ENTERED the stable, he found Maddie brushing Pride with rhythmic strokes, completely absorbed by her task. He stood watching for a moment, until she turned around, startled by his presence.

"Well, you've certainly done that before," he said.

Putting down her brush, she gave him a smile and pushed her unruly, golden brown hair back from her face, tying it up into a ponytail. She looked so slight and vulnerable that for one crazy second Ross felt like taking her in his arms and protecting her from the world...except he knew the last thing she wanted was to be protected, even though she obviously needed it. Still, there was a hidden strength behind her eyes that he couldn't help but admire.

"I told you I'd had some experience with horses," she said.

"Right, well…how about we try lunging him," he suggested. "That will give us some idea of just how much schooling he's had. Jake did say he's supposed to be broken, but we won't take any chances. He probably hasn't even had a saddle on for weeks."

Maddie's whole face lit up. "If you've got time, that would be great. I've been dying to see what he can do."

"I'll go and get some tack and lunging equipment, then," Ross said, turning to leave. "You can watch me for a bit, and if he's okay, maybe you could have a try."

"I'd love to," she said, but he noted the quiver in her determined response.

PRIDE TOOK THE saddle and bridle that Jake produced happily enough, standing quietly while Ross girthed him up. "So far so good," he announced, glancing at Maddie with a conspiratorial smile. When she smiled back, he remembered the day they met and realized how far they had come. "Who would have thought it," he said.

"Who would have thought it," she agreed.

Maddie insisted on leading Pride across the yard and into the school herself. "If I can't even do this, then I'm wasting my time," she said, and Ross nodded, seeming to understand.

While she closed the gate, he took the lunge line, tucking the lunge whip around under his arm before coiling up the line on his left hand and holding it close by Pride's head. She stood by the fence and watched him bring the whip quietly around toward the horse's hocks with his right hand. He gave the command to walk on in a firm, decisive tone. Pride walked obediently forward, out onto a large circle, and Ross smiled. "So far so good," he called to Maddie. "He certainly does seem to know what to do."

Within a matter of minutes, Ross had Pride trotting around him in an elevated rhythmic pace that made Maddie catch her breath. "Wow," she cried. "You're right—he really can move."

"They can be as ugly as sin and still look good if they've got the movement," said Ross, giving a long, low command to walk. Pride dropped his pace immediately, and Ross coiled up the line to change the rein. "I'll just try him the other way, and then you can try, if you like," he suggested. Maddie's panic must have shown, because his brow creased into a frown. "You okay?"

She nodded determinedly. "Of course."

After a few more minutes, Ross gave the command to halt and walked toward Pride, murmuring to him in a soothing tone. "Hey, there's a good lad. Now are you going to be good for your mistress, too?"

The scrawny bay gelding looked at him eagerly, pricking up his ears. "He has a good attitude—I like that," Ross said, glancing at Maddie. "Come on, then…your turn."

Maddie was very aware of Ross standing close behind her as he placed the lunge line and whip into her hands and positioned her in the right place. She felt like a fraud, letting him think she didn't know what she was doing, when in reality she'd done it a hundred times before. His hand on her arm burned her flesh; she could feel his warm breath against her ear, and she had to resist the urge to turn around and fall into his arms.

"There," he said, stepping back suddenly. "You can manage on your own now. He'll be fine."

Taking a deep breath, Maddie focused on

the job at hand, and from the moment she loosely wrapped the line around her left hand and tucked the whip under her arm, she was home.

ROSS NARROWED HIS eyes as Maddie stepped forward to rub behind Pride's ears, bonding with him before moving back into position. She gave him the command to walk on with an authority Ross hadn't expected her to have, using her body language in a totally natural way as the horse went out onto a circle.

"I guess you've done more of this than I thought," he said, watching with interest. There was something about her that made him think there was more going on with her than she admitted to. Then she flashed him a wide smile, and he cast the idea aside.

"Like I said, I've had some experience," she told him. "If he was strong, I'd be struggling, but he's just so willing."

"First hurdle over, then," said Ross. "Give him a few more minutes, and I'll have a sit on him."

When Maddie finally coiled up her line and walked over to take hold of Pride's head, she was smiling from ear to ear. "I haven't forgotten how to do it," she cried.

"You don't forget skills like that," Ross told her. "Where did you learn to lunge, anyway? Did you once have your own horse?"

"No," she said, a hint of wistfulness in her voice. "I just helped people with theirs."

He frowned. "Friends, you mean?"

She hesitated. "Something like that... Now, how are you going to get on?"

Ross glanced around. "Hmm. I'd better not mount from the stirrup just yet—there doesn't seem to be a mounting block and you definitely can't give me a leg up. I'll just vault on."

Even as he said it, he was already positioning himself, and with one smooth motion, he was lying across the saddle. Pride seemed totally relaxed, so Ross swung a leg over his back. After leaning forward for a moment, he sat up slowly, talking to the horse all the time as he gathered up the reins. "Okay," he said. "Let's see what he can do."

MADDIE WATCHED, ENTHRALLED, as Ross put the gelding through his paces. Walk and trot seemed fine, but Pride's back went up when Ross asked for canter and he did a succession of bunny hops across the school. Ross gathered up his reins, smiling. "Probably best not to put you on today," he called to Maddie. "A couple more sessions, though, and I think he'll be fine. Someone has certainly spent time working with him, and the rough patches are really just lack of practice."

Remembering the horses she used to ride, Maddie felt suddenly hopeless. Just seeing those few halfhearted bucks had unnerved her, and she found that embarrassing; she used to laugh out loud when horses leaped into the air beneath her. Yes, she decided, she was right not to have told anyone about her past; this way, if she couldn't do it, then she could bow out gracefully without losing face. "I'll take him back to the stable and untack him," she offered.

Ross seemed uncertain about handing over the reins. "You sure?"

She nodded determinedly. "Yes, of course. You get off back to work."

Maddie untacked Pride and brushed him off, enjoying the oh-so-familiar task and the way his coat began to gleam. "We're going to be okay, aren't we, boy?" she murmured. He nuzzled her cheek, reminding her of all the other horses she had looked after...so long ago, it seemed. The two geldings in her care at the time of her accident, Sunshine Bay and Metamorphosis, had been preparing for races at Haydock, and she didn't even know how they'd done. For over a year and a half, she had tried to keep her thoughts firmly away from her old life, but this new association with horses seemed to be bringing back more memories than she could handle. Perhaps facing up to them was the way forward; she would go and see Dennis, she decided, just as soon as she had the chance.

Taking off Pride's head collar, she turned him loose, bolted his door and picked up his tack. It was heavy, threatening her balance, but she determinedly heaved the saddle onto her arm and hooked the bridle over her shoulder—simple things that were once so easy. Now every task seemed like a huge effort.

With relief, she placed the saddle on the rack and hooked the bridle onto its peg in the tack room just as Jake walked in.

"How did it go?"

"Brilliant," she cried. "Pride took to the lunging like a duck to water, so he's obviously been properly broken. He was good for Ross to ride, too…although he was a bit green in the canter. And I had a go at lunging him myself."

"And how was that?"

"Really good. I didn't try riding him yet, of course."

Jake nodded. "There's plenty of time for that. At least you've made a start."

"Yes, and thanks so much for giving me the chance."

"After all you do for us, it's the least we can do in return," he told her. "Now I'd better go and help Ross unload the feed."

As he strode off across the yard, Maddie was consumed by another memory: she and the other stable hands unloading bags of feed from the truck that came every couple of weeks. She'd been able to carry a twenty-kilo sack as if it had been nothing back then, she remembered as she walked slowly toward the house.

Cass was in the kitchen feeding Gwen. She looked up with a smile when Maddie walked in. "You're supposed to be taking the afternoon off," she said.

"I lunged Pride," Maddie said, unable to hold back her excitement.

"And did it go well?"

Maddie reached for the kettle and filled it at the sink, suddenly feeling emotional. "Very," she eventually answered. "Anyway,

I thought you might want me to pick the kids up from school."

Cass stood, cradling the now-sleeping baby in her arms. "You don't have to. I was going to ask Jake or Bill…"

"I don't mind. I'll just make us a coffee first. It's not like I have anything else to do."

"Thanks," said Cass. "I'll just settle Gwen into her crib."

Five minutes later, the two women were sitting in companionable silence, sipping hot coffee, when Puddle, Cass's black-and-tan collie, trotted into the room. Maddie stroked her thoughtfully and the friendly young sheepdog wriggled in delight, curling her pink tongue around Maddie's fingers. "If I came across a dog I wanted, would it be okay if I brought it to work with me?" she asked.

Cass nodded. "Of course! The more the merrier, as far as I'm concerned. It would be good company for you. In fact, why don't you go to Cravendale? Bob Nelson told me they're always getting rescue dogs in and abandoned puppies. You could stop by in the morning, after you've dropped Robbie and Meg off at school."

A surge of excitement brought a flush to Maddie's pale skin. She could see Dennis then, too. "But are you sure you don't mind?" she asked.

"I wouldn't have mentioned it if I minded, would I?" Cass laughed. "Besides, I told you to take the afternoon off, and you are going on the school run, so I owe you some time."

Maddie thanked her and reached for her jacket. Life was feeling so good again...when not long ago she'd thought she had no life at all.

Part of that sense of well-being, she realized, was Ross. He'd surprised her today with his patience; up until now, she hadn't believed he *could* be patient. And his quiet skill and confidence when dealing with Pride had surprised her, too. He had an annoying arrogance, and his temper was something else, but today she had seen him in a whole new light. That kiss had been a stupid, impulsive mistake, a moment of madness, but maybe, eventually, they could become friends.

CHAPTER TWENTY-ONE

ROSS HEAVED THE last feed bag onto the truck and waited while Vince, the driver, wrote out a receipt. "Thanks," he said, handing it to Jake, who had just arrived with his loyal old sheepdog, Bess, at his heels.

Jake chuckled. "I timed that well. By the way, I heard your session with the four-year-old went well…now what does Maddie call it?"

"Pride," said Ross. "She calls it Pride."

"Well, let's hope Pride makes us all proud, then…for her sake."

"Mmm, I get the impression that she could do with a break," Ross agreed.

Jake nodded. "I get the feeling she's keeping some kind of secret, and she definitely struggles with her injuries more than she lets on."

Ross remembered the episode with the car, when she seemed completely done in just by having to walk for a while. "Yes, I see what you mean."

"Cass thinks she just wants to be treated totally normally, you know, to get some self-esteem back."

"That's probably true," Ross agreed. "She has worked with horses before, that's for sure."

Jake frowned thoughtfully. "I'm glad to hear it. She does seem to be determined to start riding. Obviously she did okay, then."

"Better than okay—she lunged the gelding herself after watching me, and she showed real feel…you know, good body language and everything."

"She probably had a pony as a kid," Jake remarked. "Did the whole pony club thing. Anyway, I'd better go and bring the two mares in from the fell field. Thanks for helping her—you're right, she does need a break."

Ross nodded, feeling strangely moved by Jake's observations. He and Maddie had gotten off to a bad start, but now he realized that despite his determination not to get close to anyone, he had come to admire Maddie. Maybe helping her with the horse had been a bad move; getting closer to her could be dangerous for them both. He wasn't up to caring for her, not properly, and he knew she wanted to get back to full strength before she committed to anyone. Sometimes he couldn't help feeling that there was something else, too... something she was holding back. "I can go and get the mares for you," he offered, changing his train of thought. "And then I'll check them over and brush them off if you like."

"Thanks," Jake said, handing over the two head collars he'd picked off the hook on the wall.

Despite his determination not to think about Maddie, Ross couldn't help but dwell on Jake's comments about her as he walked along the quiet dusty lane in the afternoon sunshine with Red running on ahead. He was probably right about her having a pony...although why would she have denied it? Perhaps she had just borrowed one. She would have been one of those middle-class girls who did the whole pony thing until they hit their teens and turned their attention to boys. Perhaps she was struggling with a broken heart as well as a broken body...not that it mattered to him, of course. There was only one woman in his life, and she was just six years old.

When he heard a car engine, he called to Red, who raced toward him and sat, waiting for the vehicle to pass. Ross looked back as it approached from the direction of the stables and was surprised to see Maddie's small car. She slowed down, opening her window. "I'm just going to pick up the kids," she told him.

He smiled...the rare, warm smile that only emerged when he thought about his daughter. "Thanks," he said, and Maddie lifted her hand, driving on.

ONCE SHE GOT back from the school run, Maddie stayed at Sky View to help give the children their tea. She hung around until Ross arrived to pick up Meg, since Cass was struggling to get Gwen to settle.

"Has she been good?" he asked when he came in the door.

"She's been an angel," Maddie replied truthfully. "She's always an angel...aren't you, Meg?"

The little girl shrugged. "I don't have any wings," she said in a serious voice.

Ross and Maddie both laughed, sharing a moment. "Thanks for the help today," Maddie said, meaning it.

"Well, I owe you, don't I, for the way you've helped with Meg," he responded.

Maddie felt a prickle of disappointment.

She thought he'd helped her with Pride because he wanted to, not just as some kind of payback.

"You don't owe me anything," she retorted, as the closeness they'd shared a minute ago faded. "I'm sure Cass would have looked after Meg for you whether I was here or not."

She thought about that conversation later, as she tried to sleep, snuggling down under her duvet and then kicking it restlessly off again. Her head ached with an unbearable thud, and her hip and leg came out in sympathy. Was she ever going to be able to do anything without having to go through all this? Suddenly, she felt really down. Why had Ross acted like helping her was just payback for Meg? Didn't he ever do anything simply to be nice? Well, she would show him, she decided; from now on, she'd train Pride when he wasn't around. She knew now that the horse was okay to ride—green, yes, but certainly rideable. She'd just have to be careful, that's all, and one day she would trot him into the yard when everyone was there and watch the amazement bloom on their faces.

WHEN MADDIE ARRIVED at Hope Farm the next morning, having dropped Meg and Robbie off at school, she felt an unfamiliar rush of excitement. Once, excitement had been her regular companion, but that was a lifetime away.

She saw Bob Nelson first, coming out of the door marked Private. He waved when he saw her and headed over. "Well, well, well. If it isn't the golden girl. Now, what can we do for you, or is it just a friendly visit?"

"Both," she told him, smiling. It was nice that someone around here knew who she really was. "I'm dying to see Dennis, but I'm also after a dog of my own and I'd rather give a badly treated one a good home than just buy one."

"Good for you," said Bob. "Ellie and Paula are both inside dealing with some new arrivals, so let's go and see them. I know we have some puppies here at the moment, and there are a couple of other dogs, too."

Maddie followed eagerly as Bob led the way to the large barn where she'd been before with Meg's rabbit. Ross had brought the little girl to watch it get released back into the wild about a week ago, and apparently it had hopped off happily to look for its siblings.

Ellie Nelson's bright blond cap of curls was

lowered over a cardboard box, into which she was making soft crooning sounds.

"Baby rabbits," announced the woman beside her, presumably Paula, the manager of Cravendale. She was attractive and curvaceous, with a wide smile and beautiful eyes. She held a jug of milk and a couple of small plastic syringes. "Sorry," she said. "I can't shake your hand. I'm Paula."

Maddie smiled. "That's okay. Are they really young, the rabbits?"

"Just a couple of days old, so we're going to have to feed them every two hours or so. A woman brought them in because her dog killed their mother. I'll help Ellie get them started, and then I'll be with you."

Maddie watched in fascination as both women began painstakingly feeding the tiny creatures.

"So," Paula finally said, standing up. "What can I help you with?"

"Are they going to be okay?" Maddie asked.

"It's early days yet, and they are very young...but we'll do our best."

"You do an amazing job here. Anyway, I'm looking for a dog. I'd like to rehome one if you have anything suitable."

"Actually, you've come at the right time,"

Paula said. "We have a bunch of pups that were handed in last week. We also have a full-grown Lab-collie mix, about a year old. He was taken from his owners by the RSPCA when neighbors reported them. He was skeletal when he came in, but he looks a lot better now, and he has a lovely nature."

"I can't believe anyone from around here would starve a dog," Maddie cried.

"That's just it," Paula told her. "He's not from around here. Since we moved to Hope Farm, we've been taking animals from as far away as Newcastle. We had three boa constrictors in from there last month—a woman had been keeping them in her furnace room, and they had grown so big, she was scared of them."

"People can be so stupid," said Maddie. "Do you still have them?"

Paula shook her head. "No, they've gone off to a zoo, where they can be looked after properly. Now come on, we'll go and see the pups."

"Can I see the other dog first, please? If you don't mind."

Paula seemed pleased by Maddie's request. "Absolutely. It's just that people usually want puppies."

"And I have nothing against them," said Maddie. "But I just want to feel that I've really helped, and puppies are easy to home, I'm sure."

Paula nodded, smiling. "That's great. Puppies are definitely snapped up quickly. And Scruff would certainly appreciate a bit of TLC."

Maddie laughed. "Scruff! Whoever called him that?"

"It was his name when he arrived...he answers to it, too. To be fair, it does suit him."

The first thing Maddie saw when she followed Paula into the room that housed the dogs was a pair of bright eyes peering at her over the side of an enclosure.

"Meet Scruff," Paula said.

The dog was the chocolate brown of a Labrador, but long-haired in certain parts with a white ruff around his neck and a thin white stripe down his nose. He was about the size of a Labrador, too, but that was where the resemblance faded. His skinny body had lost half its hair and it was growing back all rough and patchy, his ribs clearly visible beneath his skin. His eyes, however, were shining with brightness and health.

Scruff placed both paws on the side of

his cage and rested his nose on them, giving Maddie his most appealing expression.

"He's fully recovered now, really," said Paula, opening the door to let him out. "But he still needs to put on quite a bit of weight. His hair will grow back, eventually."

"He's gorgeous," Maddie said, totally taken with the dog.

Paula laughed. "Even I wouldn't go quite that far yet. He'll get there, though—he just needs a chance."

"I'll take him," Maddie said. "I mean, if that's all right."

"But you haven't even been properly introduced yet! Don't you want some time to think about it?"

Maddie shook her head as the dog bounded out of his pen, jumping up at her. "I don't need to think about it. I just know."

"But what about looking at the puppies?"

"I'd love to see them, but Scruff is the dog for me."

"Well…if you're sure," Paula said. "We usually ask for a donation, seventy pounds generally, or thereabouts."

"I'll give you a hundred," Maddie offered. "You do such a good job here."

Scruff leaped against her legs and then

flopped onto the floor, squirming with his legs in the air. Maddie dropped to her knees and scratched his belly enthusiastically.

"He does seem to have taken to you," Paula said.

Maddie smiled. "I think he'd take to anyone. Strange, isn't it—that he has been treated so badly and yet he still loves humans."

"I find that a lot," Paula said. "And it is odd, but if you think about it, they don't really know any different. Subservience is a kind of defense, I suppose, a way of being accepted into the pack."

"Hey, Scruff," Maddie crooned. "You are coming home with me."

After paying the fees, filling out a few forms and promising to come back for Scruff soon, Maddie went to find Bob. Today was already turning out to be a very special day. She had found the perfect dog—for her, anyway—and now she was going to see Dennis.

"Well," said Bob, appearing beside her as she went back out into the yard. "Which pup did you pick? I'll bet it was the little white one."

"Actually, I didn't pick a puppy at all... I chose Scruff."

Admiration shone in the old man's eyes.

"Good for you, girl…he's a lovely dog. You should have seen him when he came in. Everyone thought he wouldn't make it. I'm really glad that he has found a good home."

"He just felt right for me," said Maddie. "A bit of a misfit, I suppose, like myself."

"You are no misfit," Bob insisted. "You've just had a tough time, that's all, but you're on the other side of it now. Come on, I'll take you to see Dennis."

Grand Design was peering over his half door as Maddie and Bob approached. His eyes were shiny bright and his rich bay coat gleamed in the sunshine. "He looks well," Maddie said, a warm rush of longing flooding her veins. She was desperate to feel his power again as he surged up the gallops.

Smiling at the memory, she glanced across at Bob. "I had some crashing falls from him," she said. "Before we managed to make a truce, that is. To ride him was something else."

"He hasn't been ridden since he came here," Bob remarked. "We lunge him and he goes out into the stallion paddock most days. Perhaps, when you're totally recovered, you could give it a try."

Maddie's face fell. "I don't think I'll ever

be that recovered. Jake Munro has a scrawny youngster in that he's letting me spend time with, and maybe I can ride him eventually. He's an Irish gelding, not too big, and he's very sweet natured. But I haven't even sat on him yet, so I think I'm a long way from riding Dennis. Ross Noble rode the gelding just yesterday, though, and he seemed fine."

"Are you nervous about riding?" Bob asked bluntly. "It would be perfectly understandable if you were."

Maddie considered the question. "Not so much nervous of actually riding—just scared of being a failure…of not being able to do it anymore."

Bob nodded. "And that's understandable, too. Is it the pain that makes it difficult for you?"

Maddie ran her hand down the stallion's face; he pressed his nose to her cheek and she felt tears welling in her eyes. "The pain I can deal with," she said. "I have medication for that. It's more my balance and coordination that are likely to let me down, and I don't really know how much more they will improve…no one does."

"And maybe they won't let you down," Bob suggested. "Maybe all your old instincts will kick in and help you rise above your injuries. You have to believe in yourself, young lady."

Maddie couldn't help but smile. "You're right… I have to believe in myself to make it work."

"And after all," Bob reminded her, "you once used to ride this tyrant. So a quiet hack should be a piece of cake."

"Thanks, Bob, for helping me to get a grip. I think my determination was beginning to slip."

"You've come a long way, by all accounts, lass," he told her. "And you can make it all the way, I know you can. Just be sensible, that's all. Now why don't you spend some time with Dennis before you go collect your new dog?"

Maddie brightened. "Can I brush him off?"

"It looks like he would love you to," said Bob, smiling.

The horse hooked his head around her to hold her back as she reached for the grooming box, and Maddie laughed. Bob was certainly right about that.

After twenty minutes of grooming and bonding with Dennis, Maddie stood back to admire her handiwork.

"You look like a million dollars," she told the stallion. He snorted gently as she turned him loose, and with a final pat she said a reluctant goodbye and headed off across the yard. Scruff was waiting eagerly in his enclosure. He leaped up and down when he saw Maddie approach, almost as if he knew she was his new mistress. She opened the door, and he bounded out just as Paula approached with some documents in a plastic envelope. "He's had all the necessary shots," she said, handing the package to Maddie. "And he's been neutered, too. Oh, and I'll get you a small bag of what we've been feeding him here—you can keep him on the same brand, if you like, or just change it gradually."

Maddie thanked her, trying to stay calm when excitement fluttered inside her. She had groomed Dennis, and she had her own dog—it all felt too good to be true.

"He's all yours, then," Paula said. "You'll stay in touch?"

"Definitely. I'll bring him to see you on a regular basis."

Maddie led Scruff back to the car and settled him on the backseat. He curled up instantly.

"We will stay in touch with everyone here, just like I promised," she told him. "I'm going to keep on coming here to see Dennis…and wherever I go, boy, you come with me."

Scruff wagged his tail, gazing at her with such affection that she just had to give him a quick hug. Why hadn't she gotten herself a dog sooner? she wondered. Her lonely months of recovery would have been so much easier if she'd had a companion like Scruff. She could have told a dog all her darkest thoughts and not worried about being judged.

"Come on, boy," she said, getting laboriously into the driver's seat. "Let's go home."

CHAPTER TWENTY-TWO

ROSS CALLED TO RED, who bounded after him as he made his way up the hill to the far field. He looked back, taking in the scene with a sense of satisfaction. He belonged somewhere at last. Horses grazed in the field beside the house and he could see a small red car approaching along the narrow road that snaked up the hillside. Something stirred inside him; it was Maddie, back from her trip to Hope Farm. Cass had told him about her decision to get a dog. Had she found one? What would it be? A cute little puppy, he'd guess.

He watched her climb from the car, moving awkwardly. She may have lunged the four-year-old with good feel, but would she ever be able to ride him? What if she couldn't cope or wasn't even able to get on? That would do nothing for her confidence. Perhaps he should encourage her to just spend time with Pride for a while. She could groom him and care for him, and he would school him under saddle until she was ready…but would she ever be ready? He was worrying too much, he decided. Maybe it was time to back off and let her get on with it in her own time.

She opened the back door of her car, and a small whirlwind leaped out and bounced around her ecstatically. So she hadn't gone for a puppy. She never failed to surprise him. Turning away, he headed for the gate, where the two yearlings were tracking his approach with interest. "Come on, lads," he called, shaking the buckets he carried, and they cantered away in a circle before coming back for their feed.

MADDIE COULDN'T WAIT to introduce Scruff to Cass, Jake, Robbie and all the dogs at Sky View. She'd have to keep him in the barn during the day, at least until he was settled in and they could trust he wouldn't be too disruptive around the baby. And she'd have to introduce him to Pride, too. She imagined herself cantering across the fell with Scruff running behind, and her heart lifted. Later on, she decided, when Ross had gone home and the place was quiet, she would tack up Pride and try riding him. She didn't need Ross Noble's misplaced help, or anyone else's for that matter; she could do it by herself. She'd certainly had enough experience in the past.

The day went by quickly; Cass loved Scruff at once, as did the other dogs. Choco and Scruff were best buddies within fifteen minutes of meeting each other, and both Puddle and Bess seemed to take to him at once.

"He's settling right in already," Cass declared, watching the dogs race around the yard.

When Robbie came in to set the table for dinner, Maddie went on her way, feeling a sudden rush of nerves about her plan. Her apprehension annoyed her. How could she, who had once reveled in riding Grand Design without a moment's worry, be nervous about getting on a quiet little Irish cob?

"Pull yourself together, girl," she said out loud. Scruff whined, sensing her mood, and she crouched down to stroke him. "I can do this, can't I, Scruff? I'm afraid you'll have to stay in the house, though… I can't afford to have any distractions." It was early evening and everything at Sky View was quiet. Maddie could see Jake, Cass and Robbie through the window, sitting down for their evening meal, totally absorbed by each other; Ross must be long gone. She had kept Pride in a stable instead of turning him out in the field, and she'd slipped the spare key to the tack room into her pocket before she left the house. Hopefully, she could just tack him up, walk him to the school and lunge him before getting on from the fence. It was the mounting that worried her most; what if her leg just wouldn't stretch itself over his back?

Thrusting her doubts from her mind, she collected Pride's tack and the equipment she needed, placing it outside his stable. He nickered at her over his door, restoring her confidence.

"We can do this," she repeated over and over as she got him ready.

Leading him to the school—which was well out of sight of the house—proved easy enough. She moved slowly, but he was patient, standing still while she fumbled with the lunge line, dropping her whip on the ground more than once as her fingers turned to thumbs.

Eventually, they were ready, and she sent him out onto a circle. He was obedient, listening to her commands and trotting around her in a steady rhythm. "Right, then," she said, turning him in and adjusting her hat. "This is it, Pride."

The scrawny bay gelding looked at her with kind eyes, tossing his nose up and down as if in agreement.

ROSS APPROACHED SKY VIEW from the back. He'd been fixing a fence in the broodmare's field that afternoon and hadn't noticed how time had flown. When he'd rung to say he was going to be late collecting Meg, Jake had asked him to finish the job and told him they would give the little girl her tea. It was closer to dinnertime now, but Jake had insisted he take as long as he needed. "We can't risk the horses getting out," Jake had said.

Noticing movement in the school, Ross stopped behind the cover of a dry stone wall. Who could be there at this time of day?

Not wanting to intrude, he followed the wall to get closer to the school and see who it was before they saw him. To his amazement, it was Maddie...lunging Pride. She gave the command to halt and then went over to the horse, removed the lunging cavesson from over his bridle and unfastened the reins from his throat latch before running down the stirrups on his saddle.

Surely, Ross thought, *she's not going to try riding him all on her own?*

He almost stepped forward to attract her attention, but something held him back. Obviously, she didn't want his help, though he would have given it if she'd asked. After a moment's indecision, he decided to just stay and watch the proceedings. If she really was pigheaded enough to try to do this on her own, he would be wise to stick around...just in case.

MADDIE CHECKED THE stirrups and tightened Pride's girth, taking a deep breath before leading him to the post-and-rail fence.

"There, boy," she crooned, stroking his neck to make sure he was settled before attempting to clamber awkwardly onto the second rail. Mounting the horse had been her worry; she hadn't even thought about having to climb up the dratted fence.

Holding the reins in one hand, she used the other to heave herself upward, cursing her legs when they wobbled beneath her. She clung to the top rail and steadied herself. She could do this...she *had* to do this. Pride sidled, unnerved by her unfamiliar movements, and she took a minute to calm him again before putting her foot in the stirrup.

At last, she was in position to mount. Gathering up the reins, she reached determinedly for the stirrup with her left toe, a simple thing she had once taken for granted, and with a cry of annoyance at her objecting body, she made her move.

Somewhere between her foot connecting with the stirrup and her attempt to follow through, Pride swung away from her. With a massive effort, she launched herself...too late. She felt a heavy thud as her body met the sand. From the corner of her eye, she saw Pride buck and gallop off, reins trailing and stirrups banging against his sides.

Maddie lay motionless, unable to breathe, waiting for the pain that coursed through her back to subside and fighting off tears of disappointment and frustration. Finally, she took a gasp of air and slowly tried to lift her head. She had to catch Pride; what if he hurt himself?

"Stay still. I'll get him."

Ross's firm voice was the last thing she wanted to hear, and a hot rush of embarrassment flooded her face. He had seen her pathetic attempt to mount. Still, she did as she was told, knowing she needed a few more minutes to recover. By the time he came back into her line of vision, leading a subdued Pride, she had managed to haul herself into a sitting position.

"Are you okay?" he asked.

When she nodded without meeting his gaze, he sighed. "Then can you please explain why you did something so stupid?"

She stared at him, her defenses down. "I wanted to surprise everyone and prove I could do it by myself."

"But you couldn't do it by yourself, could you? So you proved nothing. Why take such a risk when I'd already said I'd help you?"

"Only because you had to," she said as he reached out to help her up.

"No." His answer was instantaneous. "I wanted to."

In one smooth movement, he pulled her to her feet. She fell against him and his arms closed around her, holding her hard against his chest. For an endless moment, she was frozen, listening to the beat of his heart so close to her ear. The warmth of his skin burned her cheek through the thin fabric of his blue checked shirt.

"I *wanted* to help you," he repeated. "Still can, if you'll let me."

She looked up, meeting his dark eyes; they flickered with the softness she had only seen him reveal to Meg. Her lips tingled with the memory of their kiss. "Yes…please," she said.

His arm fell suddenly away from her, as if he regretted his impulsive actions, and Maddie felt a pang of disappointment. For the first time in over eighteen months, she realized, she had felt safe.

"Come on, then," he said. "I'll ride him around to make sure he hasn't been too spooked, and you can have another try tomorrow."

"No," she objected. "I need to do it now."

He frowned. "But you had a fall. You might…"

"I'm not made of glass," she shouted, cutting him off. "I can do this—I know I can. Once I'm on, I'll be fine."

"But it's not that easy, especially when… How much riding have you actually done, anyway?"

"Enough to get by," she said fiercely.

"So basically what you're saying is that you haven't ridden since you were a kid."

"I'll be fine," she repeated. "I just need you to help get me on, and then you can go."

"No," he told her. "I'm not comfortable with that. It was obvious you were going to struggle with riding, even before you had the fall. If I don't keep an eye out, you might do yourself serious damage. So I'll just have to stay."

"I guess you will," she agreed, and suddenly he was smiling.

Meeting his eyes, she smiled back, feeling warm inside.

Twenty minutes later, Maddie had to admit that things were going better with Ross's help. He rode Pride around first, to make sure he had fully calmed down, then he gave her a leg up. She settled into the saddle with an unexpected confidence, feeling as if she was home at last.

When Ross led Pride forward, however, she swayed and struggled for balance. Discouragement hit hard as she took hold of the saddle to steady herself.

"It's only what you expected," Ross reminded her, taking hold of Pride's rein with one hand while holding her calf firmly with the other. The warmth of his hand against her leg seemed to seep into her very core, lending confidence as she gazed down at his upturned face. When their eyes connected, she smiled, nodding. It *was* what she'd expected, but to her, riding was as natural as breathing. She had imagined herself slipping straight back into it. Her hips and back ached, but she didn't care about that; it was having no balance that upset her. What if it never came back?

"You'll be fine," Ross insisted. "Just give it time."

His words bolstered her, and she took up the reins again, ready to prove herself.

"How're you doing?" he asked after they had completed a full circuit of the school.

"A bit dizzy," she admitted.

"Well, you knew that it was going to be hard. In fact, I'm not sure why you wanted to put yourself through it in the first place."

She wanted to tell him why, to say, "Because it's what I do," but instead she forced a smile onto her face. "It's a start," she allowed.

"You need to set yourself goals," Ross suggested. "You know, have a plan. When you can easily walk unaided around the school without getting dizzy, then you can try a trot and so on. Don't rush it—that's the key."

She nodded. "Take small steps, you mean?"

"Exactly," he agreed. "A bit at a time. Do you want to get off now?"

She shook her head. "No, not yet. You said I needed to have goals, and my goal for today is to ride him once around the school on my own."

Concern crossed Ross's face, but he didn't try to stop her. Taking up the reins, she took a deep breath, trying to focus and remember everything the physiotherapist had told her when she was learning to walk again.

"Okay," she said. "You can let go of the bridle now."

For the first few steps she felt fine, and then the familiar feeling of losing her balance kicked in again. She wanted to scream an objection, but instead she reined in. Pride immediately stopped, and her confidence came rushing back. It felt as if he was on her side, helping her. Glancing over at Ross, she had a surreal desire to giggle. Here she was, being helped by a man who had felt like her enemy a short while ago, trying to do what she was born for.

"Anything is possible if you truly believe," she murmured, repeating the motto that had carried her to success in her racing career.

She gave Pride the command to walk on, and he moved willingly forward. She tried to go with his movement, allowing her body to relax, and for a few minutes everything fell into place. When she felt the dizziness come back, she stopped, remembering Ross's advice. "Step one completed," she called out, smiling back at him.

He walked toward her with long, easy strides and took hold of Pride's rein before reaching up for her.

"Promise me you won't try to do this on your own again," he said as she slid into his arms.

"I promise," she agreed. She just wanted to stay there, safe in his arms, but common sense kicked in. She had enough problems in her life without falling in love…and she was getting dangerously near to that no matter how hard she tried to contain her feelings. "Thanks for that," she said, stepping away from him.

"You'll get there," he told her.

"Do you know," she said, "I really do think I will."

CHAPTER TWENTY-THREE

MADDIE SETTLED SCRUFF in the new dog bed she had bought him and went to bed early, hoping a good night's rest might relieve the dull thud in her head. Within minutes of crawling under the covers, however, the patchy brown dog appeared in her bedroom doorway and jumped up onto the end of her bed, lying down immediately as if that was where he was supposed to be.

"So much for spending money on an expensive dog bed," she muttered, and when he wagged his tail, smiling at her, she lay down again, glad of his companionship. "Okay," she told him. "You can stay."

She expected a sleepless night. There was so much going on in her head, and her body was sure to voice its objection to all the activity she'd put it through. She closed her eyes, trying to relive those precious moments on horseback, feeling as if she had taken a huge stride rather than just one small step.

Her thoughts kept flickering back to Ross; she owed him, big-time. Perhaps she should come clean and tell him the truth about herself... Somehow, though, she knew she couldn't. He'd change how he felt about and acted toward her if he knew her real background, knew she had once been a successful jockey who'd gone down on her luck. It was fortunate that he didn't follow racing, because if he recognized her, he'd realize she'd been less than honest about herself. She was enjoying their growing friendship, and she didn't want to spoil it.

"Well done," he'd told her when he helped her down from Pride. His eyes had held nothing but admiration...she liked that.

"Small steps," she murmured against her pillow. Revealing her true identity would be a huge step—one she wasn't prepared to take just yet.

AT ROSE COTTAGE, sitting in his favorite armchair and sipping a whiskey before bed, Ross relived the moment when Maddie had taken up the reins and urged Pride forward. The expression on her face as she'd looked back at him had said it all. It was clear she'd had a tough time, but she was so plucky and determined. And the way she sat on the horse, despite some obvious discomfort from both today's fall and her past injuries, had seemed so natural. It was strange, considering she hadn't done that much riding, or at least not for a long time. He had enjoyed helping her, he realized, and he intended to carry on helping her if she wanted him to.

He couldn't let himself get emotionally entangled with her, though. Even if he wanted to, he didn't deserve another chance at love. Deep down, in his heart of hearts, he didn't believe he was fit to be with any woman ever again.

Still, he couldn't help but remember the moment he'd taken Maddie in his arms. She was so small and slight, yet she'd shown such emotional strength.

He felt an unexpected admiration for her courage. Had he been less than courageous, he found himself wondering, to have run away like that with Meg? He'd come back, he reminded himself. Maybe that was his saving grace.

MADDIE WAS WOKEN at dawn by Scruff licking her cheek. She gave him a hug and reached for her robe. It was nice having someone to greet her in the morning, she decided. She noted the time on her bedside clock. Yes, it was nice…even if she did have to get up and take him out at the crack of dawn. "I hope you appreciate it," she told him with a smile in her eyes.

Scruff wriggled his whole body, madly wagging his tail, and with a sigh she eased her protesting body upright. Every morning was an effort for the first half hour or so, but the fall she'd suffered had amplified her discomfort. "Come on, then," she said, and the happy brown dog leaped around her in circles, racing down the stairs to the back door.

An hour later, Maddie pulled into her usual parking space at Sky View and headed for the house with Scruff at her heels. Cass was already making breakfast in the bright and sunny kitchen. Maddie loved the kitchen at Sky View.

"Oh, good," Cass said. "You're early. Do you mind taking over while I go and see to Gwen?"

"Of course not," Maddie said, taking off her jacket.

Scruff rushed over to Cass to say hello, sneaking past Maddie, who had intended to leave him in the yard. She smiled, stroking his head. "You picked a good one, Maddie. Puppies are cute, but they're hard work, and it's so much more rewarding to think you've helped give a neglected dog a better life."

Maddie nodded in agreement. "That's what I thought, and he does have a lovely, friendly nature. All the other dogs seemed to like him when we introduced them yesterday, too."

As she spoke, Robbie burst in from the hallway with Choco at his heels, and the two young dogs immediately began bounding around each other ecstatically. "I'll let them out, shall I?" he suggested.

"Good idea," Cass said. "They can't get into too much trouble in the garden, and it looks like they need to burn off a bit of energy."

Once the dogs were outside, Maddie busied herself making breakfast for Robbie, Jake and Bill. She wondered if she should tell them she'd ridden Pride last night but thought better of it. What if Jake felt she should have asked first? After all, Pride did belong to him.

However, when Ross came through the door with Meg, the truth came out. "Well, did Maddie tell you?" he asked.

Jake looked up with a frown. "Tell us what?"

Ross grinned. "That she actually rode the four-year-old."

"Pride," Maddie clarified, and he smiled just for her.

"That's right," he said. "She rode Pride."

"And?" Jake asked, putting down his knife and fork and pushing his plate away.

"And she did great."

Maddie glanced at him, grateful that he'd refrained from telling them about her initial attempt to mount. For a fleeting moment their eyes held, sharing a secret.

"And are you going to ride him again today?" asked Bill.

Yet again, Maddie found herself looking across at Ross, unsure of how to answer. He nodded firmly. "Can't stop now that she's started, can she? I'll give her a hand again tonight, after work. Meg can come and watch."

"Hey," Robbie piped up. "Maybe Meg can get a pony, too, and then I'll have someone to ride with."

Meg glowed with happiness, and her honey-brown eyes sparkled in anticipation. "Can I please, Daddy? Can I really get a pony?"

"Why don't you have a try on Robbie's and see how you get on?" Jake suggested before

Ross could get a word in. "And then we'll see what we can do."

"Thanks," Ross spluttered. "And of course I'll pay whatever it costs."

Jake shrugged. "Robbie will enjoy the company, and I'll keep my eyes open for the right pony at the right price. As long as everything goes well with her lessons. Now, if we're going to get that fence finished today, we need to get going. There are some horses still left to muck out, too, and the muck pile needs forking back."

Ross headed for the door. "I'll get started," he said, looking back at Meg. "See you after school, Nutmeg."

The little girl waved. "Bye…and, Daddy?"
"Yes?"

"Am I really going to get a pony?"

"We'll have to see how you do with Robbie's pony…and you'd better be good."

"I will," she promised, her little face alight with excitement.

"Right, then," Cass announced as the men disappeared out the door. "Time for school, I think."

Maddie picked up her car keys. She hoped to be able to manage the Munros' 4x4 soon, but she still needed to use her specially adapted car, which meant driving the short distance to the stables each day, when she would much rather walk. "Come on, kids," she called. "You're going to be late if you don't hurry."

As Ross strolled into the yard, he felt better than he had in a long while. It had rained overnight, and everything gleamed in the morning sunshine, making the world look fresh and new. He felt fresh and new, too, he realized, as if this place was slowly cleansing him of all the bitterness he'd been storing in his heart. He was settled at last among friends who didn't judge him, people he could trust...

It was time to let go. When an image of Maddie slipped into his mind's eye, he didn't push it away. Luminous hazel eyes that seemed to change color with her every mood, delicate features in a face that showed fewer signs of strain every day...and the way she so courageously tried to overcome her injuries.

"You look thoughtful," said Jake, falling into step beside him.

Ross shrugged. "Not really...just thinking about where to start."

"At the beginning?" suggested Jake with a broad grin.

As PROMISED, WHEN his work was done for the day, Ross appeared in the kitchen to collect Meg. "Has she been good?" he asked Maddie.

"She's always good," she answered. "Aren't you, Meg?"

The little girl nodded enthusiastically. "I have to be good if I'm going to get a pony."

"Very good, I should think," Maddie said.

Ross ruffled his daughter's curls and caught Maddie's eye. "So are we going to ride this horse, then?"

Maddie felt a sudden prickle of apprehension. "Right now?"

"No point in going home and coming back, is there? Have you brought your riding gear?"

She nodded slowly. "Yes...but what about Scruff?"

"We'll tie him to the fence, and he can watch. He has to get used to being around horses, too."

Cass had been listening in on the conversation. "Go on, then," she insisted. "I can finish up here."

Still, Maddie hung back, overwhelmed by nerves. What if yesterday had been a fluke? "Are you sure?"

"Of course I am...now go."

Maddie still hadn't shaken her uncertainty

half an hour later, when she stood next to Pride inside the school. "You've done it once, and you can do it again," Ross told her, his lips close to her ear.

She glanced back at him and smiled, noticing the little lines around his intense, dark eyes. "You're right," she agreed. "I can."

Meg gave her a thumbs-up from where she sat with Red and Scruff on the far side of the fence.

Murmuring to Pride, Maddie took up the reins and bent her left knee. Ross took a firm hold of her calf, and in seconds she was settled in the saddle. It felt so right, her nerves instantly evaporated. Then a wave of dizziness came over her, reminding her of her limitations, and Ross placed his hand on her thigh for support.

"You can do it," he repeated as she waited for the dizzy spell to pass. His hand felt warm and strong and so alive.

"I can, can't I," she said, urging the gelding forward. Suddenly, to her delight, they were moving as one. Old instincts, it seemed, were taking over. Instead of thinking too hard and worrying about failure, she needed to give in to them.

When she reined in twenty minutes later,

having managed to trot and circle without falling off, she was ecstatic.

Ross walked over to her. "Now how was that?"

"Amazing," she cried, slipping into his arms. For just a second, he held her, his lips close to hers.

"That was brilliant!" Meg called, running toward them, and the moment was gone. *Just as well*, thought Maddie. It was just the elation that had drawn them together, and she shouldn't let herself get carried away.

"It's hard to believe you're not a more experienced rider," Ross remarked. "I guess you must be a natural." He smiled playfully. "Unless you're keeping secrets from us, of course."

Maddie felt as if a cold hand had clasped her heart. How had she gotten so deep into this lie? She had to tell him. Now. "Actually, I—"

"Can I ride him now?" Meg cut in, and Ross laughed.

"Better start with something a bit smaller," he suggested, looking back at Maddie. "Sorry... what were you saying?"

"Nothing," she told him, losing her nerve. "I mean...that was great. I did feel a bit dizzy, but to be honest, I just tried to relax and go with the movement."

"We've come a long way from where we were when we first met, haven't we?" Ross said thoughtfully.

She nodded, her eyes shining. "I feel like a new person. And I think maybe you've chased off a few of your demons, too."

"Friends?" he said, holding out his hand. She took it, holding it firm.

"Friends," she repeated, liking the idea.

Ross, Meg, Red and Scruff followed her as she proudly led Pride back to his stable. She noticed Ross was quick to step forward and take her tack when she put it on the stable door.

"You don't need to wait for me," she said when he came back from the tack room. "I can manage now."

"I thought we might go and get fish and chips again," he suggested. "If you're hungry, that is."

"I am," cried Meg in delight. "Please come with us, Maddie."

Maddie smiled at the little girl. "How could I refuse when you ask so nicely? My treat, though, since you got them last time?"

"I'll drive, then," Ross offered. "My truck's just over there."

"We could go to Rose Cottage," Meg said. "I can show Maddie my room."

As they drove down the hill toward Little Dale, Maddie could see the lake way below, sparkling in the late-evening sun. It was so beautiful. She settled back into her seat, glancing across at Ross; he was leaning forward over the wheel, obviously deep in thought.

"Would you ever have believed that you and I would be doing this?" she asked.

"And me," Meg added. "I'm doing it, too."

"Ah," Maddie said. "But you and I have always liked each other."

Meg frowned. "So you mean you don't like my daddy?"

Ross raised his eyebrows, sneaking a sideways glance at Maddie. "Well, aren't you going to answer her?"

Maddie hesitated before deciding that honesty was the best policy. "I didn't used to," she began, "but…"

"But you do now?" urged Meg.

Maddie laughed. "Well, I guess I must, or I wouldn't be sitting in this truck with you and the dogs going to get fish and chips. Anyway, I owe your dad for helping me with Pride."

"Here's the thing," Ross said. "If I help you get your riding sorted, then you'll be able to help Meg when she learns to ride."

Maddie nudged his shoulder teasingly. "So you have an ulterior motive, then?"

They ate their fish and chips while they were still hot, sitting on a low wall by the side of the lane and watching the sun set behind the dark mass of the fell.

"I never tire of this view," Ross remarked.

Maddie nodded in agreement. "It's so peaceful here. It feels as if we're the only living things left in the world."

"Except for the sheep." Meg giggled as three black-faced fell sheep came trotting by. "Now can we go and see my room?"

Maddie was surprised when she walked into Rose Cottage to find that Ross had already put his stamp on it. The white walls had been painted in warmer shades of cream, and the whole place looked softer and more mellow. "You've worked hard," she said. "It looks nice."

"You should see my room," cried Meg, grabbing hold of her hand. "Come on!"

"Get ready for bed while you're up there," Ross told his daughter. "I'll follow you."

"It's beautiful," Maddie said as she took in the pink and cream walls decorated with princesses and ponies.

Meg glowed with pride. "Daddy did it," she said. "He's clever."

"Then you must be clever, too," Ross told her. "Because you chose both the colors and the pictures. Now get into your pajamas and maybe Maddie will read you a story."

"I'd love to," said Maddie. "I might even make one up...like your daddy does."

She caught Ross's eye, and he smiled. "I'll wait downstairs," he said.

Almost as soon as Maddie started on her story, Meg stuffed her thumb into her mouth, eyelids drooping, and within minutes she was fast asleep. Maddie leaned down to brush her lips against the little girl's forehead, pulling the duvet up around her before going quietly down the stairs.

"Thanks for that," Ross said when she walked into the kitchen.

Maddie smiled. "I should be thanking *you*... I feel as if you've given me my life back."

"You're the one who's rebuilding your life," he told her. "Now, why don't we go and sit outside for a bit. It's such a lovely night. I'll bring us a drink."

Maddie sat tentatively on a wooden bench in the small back garden, suddenly apprehensive about being alone with Ross in what felt like a very intimate setting. When he appeared with a smile on his face, carrying a bottle of wine and two glasses, she realized she was actually looking forward to spending some quality time with him. As he popped the cork and poured her a glass, for once she felt totally comfortable in his company.

"To celebrate your success," he said, raising his glass. She clinked hers against it with a glow of happiness.

They sipped in silence, taking in the sounds of the evening: birds settling for the night, the gentle hoot of an owl and, in the distance, the sharp yelp of a fox.

"It's so quiet here," she murmured. "And yet, when you listen, the night is full of activity. I feel more alive than I have in a long time."

"I feel as if I'm getting my life back, too," he told her, meeting her steady gaze. "Perhaps it's finally time to move on."

"It must have been tough," she said softly. "With your wife and everything."

For a moment, he said nothing, and she thought she had overstepped the boundaries of their budding friendship. Then he let out a sigh. "I blamed myself—still do—for being too selfish to see what she was going through."

She placed her hand on his forearm. "Regret is a waste of time. How could you have known what she was going through if she didn't confide in you? If she had, I'm sure you would have been there for her. Look how great you are with Meg—Jenny can see that, I'm sure."

"I hope so," he said, refilling their glasses. "Now I've just had a thought…how are you going to get home?"

Maddie laughed. "I hadn't thought about that."

"I'd offer my truck, but—"

"But I'm not up to it," she finished for him. His truck was huge and she wasn't sure she could handle a vehicle without the special adaptations her car had, but still, his lack of confidence stung.

Without warning, he reached across and cupped her chin with his thumb and forefingers, just as she'd seen him do to Meg. "That's not what I was going to say. You can do it, Maddie. You can do anything if you really believe it. But maybe not tonight. It's dark and we've had this wine… You could stay in the trailer, though. I'll drive you to work in the morning."

She hesitated for a moment then relented. "I guess I don't have any other option," she said, smiling.

CHAPTER TWENTY-FOUR

ON SATURDAY, MADDIE decided to walk to Sky View. She didn't need to bring her car since there was no school, and it was only a few minutes to the stables if she took the shortcut through the copse. As she headed into the trees with Scruff madly sniffing for rabbits behind her, she felt a surge of happiness. Never, she thought, had she been anywhere so heartrendingly beautiful.

The Lakeland hills, magnificent in their isolation, soared into an eggshell-blue sky, where one lonely white cloud was rimmed with gold from the morning sun. She looked way up the slopes, where the green of the tufty grass gave way to gorse and bracken and the gray of Lakeland stone. The half-wild, hardy fell sheep grazed up there, white spots in the distance, surviving in the habitat they loved, close to the skyline.

There was a time, she remembered, not so very long ago, when she'd felt as if she didn't fit in anywhere anymore; now, she had found Sky View and the Munros…and Ross Noble. Over the past few weeks, since he'd started to help her with her riding and they had spent more time together, she and Ross had become almost friends. Almost. Because behind their friendship lurked something more, something both of them recognized…something they were both afraid to face up to.

As she approached the house, Meg skipped across the grass toward her with her curly chestnut hair bouncing on her shoulders. Ross might be an *almost* friend, thought Maddie, but Meg had become so much more. She welcomed the feelings she had for the little girl, whereas her feelings for Ross were confusing.

True to his promise, Jake had found Meg a quiet little Welsh pony mare to call her own after she'd tried out Robbie's pony. She had named it Rainbow, much to her dad's disgust. "You can't call her that," he'd insisted. Maddie smiled to herself as she remembered Ross's reaction.

Jake had just laughed. "Technically, she still belongs to me," he'd told Meg. "Until your dad has paid all the money off, of course.

But as far as I'm concerned, she's yours, and you can call her whatever you like."

So Rainbow she had become, and in spending time with her new charge, Meg had blossomed. She was often seen around the yard riding the little gray pony with Red—who was almost as big as Rainbow—following them.

"You must stay in the yard and in sight of us," Ross had told her again and again. He confided in Maddie that he was worried he'd given his daughter too much freedom. Having Red as her protector, however, gave him confidence.

"Morning, Meg," called Maddie, and the big dog lumbered ahead of the little girl to say hello, circling around Scruff with his plumed tail waving.

"Robbie and I are riding after breakfast," Meg said, grabbing hold of Maddie's hand. "Cass is going to bring Gwen over to watch us in the school. Come on, we need to hurry."

Maddie laughed, increasing her pace. "Hang on—I'm not as fast as you, remember."

"You're faster than you used to be."

"I am, aren't I?" Maddie agreed, taking stock of how much stronger she was feeling lately. Just a few short weeks ago, she would probably have fallen if she'd tried to hurry like this. Before, she had to consider her every stride and movement; now, her coordination was much better and her limbs were stronger. She was beginning to become her real self again, and she had to admit she owed a lot of that to Ross's insistence that she keep up with her riding. She'd had her setbacks—falls and dizzy spells that had threatened her confidence—but Ross had refused to let her give up and it had proved to be better therapy than any physio. By allowing her instincts to take over when she was in the saddle, she had learned to trust her own body again.

Cass was already putting little Gwen into her stroller when Maddie and Meg appeared in the kitchen. "I'm just going over to watch the kids ride," she said. "Are you okay to see to Jake and Bill's breakfast?"

"Of course," Maddie replied. "Is Ross eating, too, or did he have his at home?"

"He's long gone…something to do with a sheep stuck in a fence somewhere."

Maddie felt a flicker of disappointment, but she pushed it aside. "Am I still okay to have this afternoon off?" she asked.

Cass nodded, carefully negotiating the step.

"Of course. Go straight after lunch if you like. Are you doing anything nice?"

"I promised to take Meg to Hope Farm, to the animal rescue center… Robbie can come, too, if he wants."

"Thanks, but he's helping his dad with something this afternoon—they were planning it all evening. I'll be back before long."

It was nice to feel so much a part of this place, Maddie thought as she listened to Jake and his dad chat about the day ahead over breakfast. They included her in their conversation, too, as if her opinion really mattered. When they headed out into the yard, still talking, it occurred to her how very far away her life in racing seemed when it had once felt like the be-all and end-all of everything.

Cass came back around eleven, pushing Gwen in her stroller with Robbie and Meg bouncing along behind her. They were full of energy from their ride, chattering like two magpies.

"I went over a jump today," cried Meg. "Rainbow was brilliant."

"Not as good as Splodge," Robbie insisted.

Cass laughed. "No arguments now, you two. You were both brilliant. Why don't you go out and play in the garden—run off a bit more steam—while I feed Gwen?" The kids ran off, and Cass turned to Maddie. "I'll make us a coffee."

"Let me," urged Maddie.

She was filling the kettle at the sink when Ross appeared in the doorway.

"Is Jake around?" he asked.

"He'll be back in a minute," Cass said. "You may as well have a coffee while you're waiting. Maddie's making some."

Pulling off his boots, he stepped inside. "Thanks. That would be very welcome."

Cass motioned him to a chair. "Well, sit down, then. You've been here for hours already, so you must want to take the weight off your feet for a bit. In fact…"

Ross looked across at Maddie with a smile in his eyes, and her hand wobbled as she poured milk into three mugs.

He turned back to Cass. "In fact what?"

"Why don't you take a couple of hours off this afternoon and go with Maddie and Meg to Hope Farm?"

Maddie's first instinct was to object. Being around Ross was one thing, but a proper outing with him and Meg felt too formal…like a date. She wasn't ready for that yet.

Her heart began to race as she waited for his response.

Ross frowned. "I don't think Jake would be too happy about that…"

"I wouldn't be too happy about what?" Jake had apparently walked in unnoticed and had overheard at least part of the conversation.

"About Ross having a couple hours off this afternoon to go to Hope Farm with Meg and Maddie," Cass explained.

Jake nodded and looked at Ross. "Of course you can have some time off. You've certainly earned it these past few weeks."

"There you are, then." Cass smiled. "You can go after lunch. Meg will be so pleased."

"WE MIGHT AS well go in my truck," Ross suggested as the three of them headed off across the yard after lunch with Red and Scruff running behind them, sniffing at enticing scents.

"I can just stay here," Maddie said. "If you want to take Meg on your own, I mean."

Glancing sideways at her, he grinned; she couldn't help but think how much softer he looked when he smiled.

"Now, why would I want to do that?" he asked.

"Well…" She was suddenly tongue-tied. "I mean…she doesn't need both of us."

"Yes, I do," Meg interrupted, hanging on to both their hands.

"Seems like she does," he said. "So I guess you have no choice."

A warm and unexpected rush of pleasure brought a smile to Maddie's face. "Okay," she agreed.

"You look quite pretty when you smile," he told her, holding her eyes with his. "Doesn't she, Nutmeg?"

"Maddie looks pretty whether she's smiling or not," she said.

"Hmm." Ross's eyes sparkled. "I don't know if I'd go as far as that."

Maddie cuffed him on the arm and they all burst into laughter.

Meg beamed as they drove into the yard at Hope Farm. "Do you think they'll have some puppies?" she asked eagerly.

"It's definitely possible," said Maddie.

Ross parked and cut the engine. "Let's go and find out."

This felt good, Maddie thought, as the three of them trooped across to the animal center. As though they were a family.

Bob Nelson was the first person they saw when they walked through the entrance.

"Well, hello," he said, addressing Meg. "Have you brought us another rabbit?"

She shook her head, leaning against her dad's leg.

"Well…have you perhaps come for a dog, then?"

When the little girl looked hopefully up at Ross, he ruffled her hair, answering for her. "Not today, I'm afraid. Maybe when she's a bit bigger."

Noting the disappointment on her face, Maddie spoke up. "You can share Scruff if you want," she said.

Meg's face shone. "Really? Can he really be half-mine?"

For a moment, Maddie regretted her impulsive gesture, but the little girl was so excited that she couldn't go back on her word. She hadn't considered the commitment it would require from Ross as well as Meg. She glanced across at him, and when their eyes connected, her heart thudded so loudly she thought he would hear it. Four became two as he held her eyes with his for an endless moment, and the memory of their kiss brought a tingling sensation to her lips.

"Why don't I take Meg in to see the animals?" Bob suggested, obviously aware of the tension between them.

Maddie dragged her gaze away from Ross. "Why don't we all go? We promised to look at them with her...if that's all right?"

"Of course. Ellie is in the main barn—she'll show you around, and then why don't you come over to the house for a coffee?"

"That would be great," Ross said. "I'd like to hear more about your stallions."

Bob glowed with pride. "I'll show them to you."

To Meg's delight, there was a new intake of puppies. She and Ellie Nelson sat playing with them, while Maddie and Ross stood side by side, watching their antics.

"It's nice to see her so happy and settled," Maddie murmured for his ears only. "I've never really said this, but I'm glad you finally got Rose Cottage back...and I'm sorry we had such a rocky start."

Ross stepped closer, curling his little finger around hers. "Truce?"

"Truce," she agreed, feeling warm inside.

Ellie led them over to some baby hedgehogs that had to be fed twice a day on a mix of special hedgehog and cat food, then they visited a neglected pig that took a shine to Meg.

"I know you two are going to see Dad, so why doesn't Meg stay here with me for a bit?" Ellie suggested. "I'm going to feed the animals soon—she can help me."

"Please?" Meg clasped her hands together. "Please let me stay."

"How can I say no to that?" Ross laughed. "Be good, though."

"I will," she promised. Ross and Maddie wandered slowly toward the house, their conversation suddenly drying up. Maddie felt very aware of his tall frame beside her, so close she could feel the heat of him. When his hand brushed against hers and their fingers automatically linked again, the intensity of her emotions told her this was the moment to make her decision: pull away from him now or allow him into her heart forever. Her every fiber screamed to stay, so she entwined her fingers more tightly with his. There was no need for words; she knew he was feeling the same way she was...as if they were one being, in total harmony. And as they walked across the quiet farmyard beneath the sun's golden canopy, listening to the sweet song of a blackbird and the low, distant whinny of a horse, she never wanted this moment to end.

At the end of the yard, he stopped, turning her to face him, his expression dark and fierce. "We're friends, Maddie," he said. "But you need to understand that after...after Jenny, I realized I wasn't fit to be anyone's husband...never would be. I do my best to be as good a dad to Meg as I can, but that's it."

"Well, that suits me," responded Maddie, forcing brightness into her tone. "Because there's no way I want to get romantically involved with anyone for a long time."

"Friends, then," he said, keeping hold of her hand.

"Friends," she repeated as they carried on walking.

To get to the farmhouse, they had to cross a small orchard. The apples on the trees were fully formed, ripe for picking, and suddenly Ross reached up and plucked one, holding it to Maddie's lips. She took a bite, crunching down on the sweet, juicy fruit, and when he swung her around to face him, the atmosphere between them sizzled. "What's happening to us?" he asked, his voice low and urgent.

"I…" Maddie began, but the words froze in her throat as his lips came close to hers.

"We shouldn't be doing this," he murmured, his breath warm against her skin.

Her response was automatic; it felt so right to just lift her face to his. And when his lips descended onto hers, it was like the last time…as if she was drowning in a sea of emotion and desire.

When she pulled away, breathless, he refused to let her go. "Friends," she reminded him. "No complications."

He dropped his arms. "I'm sorry. I don't know what came over me."

"No…" She reached up to run her hand down his cheek, feeling the roughness of his stubble beneath her fingers. "Don't be sorry—I'm not."

He pulled her close again, and she went limp in his arms, knowing this was where she wanted to be. "I can't just be friends with you, Ross," she confessed as his lips found hers again.

When he finally pulled back, he held her at arm's length, looking deep into her eyes. "Me, neither," he said. "I thought I could, but obviously there's something more between us. I never thought I'd meet someone like you…someone I can totally trust."

A loud bang from somewhere nearby broke the moment, and they stepped apart, their hands still firmly locked together.

"Let's take it one step at a time," said Maddie. "And see where it goes. Perhaps it's time to finally let go of the past."

"I'd like that," he told her just as Bob Nelson appeared, swinging a hammer in his hand.

"Darned rats," Bob cried. "I've just had to seal yet another hole in the barn—they seem to be able to get in anywhere."

Ross and Maddie blinked at him, and Ross was the first to recover. "I've heard that wherever you are in the world, you're never less than ten feet from a rat," he said, smiling. "Taking away their food source is the answer."

"It may be," Bob mused. "Come on, then—let's go and get a coffee, and you can have a look at the stallions afterward."

CHAPTER TWENTY-FIVE

THE KITCHEN AT Hope Farm reminded Maddie of so many of the other horsey kitchens she'd visited when she was in the racing world, riding out at the crack of dawn and returning, elated and hungry, for breakfast.

Like the Munros' kitchen, the Nelsons' sported piles of *Horse & Hound* magazine, but at Sky View everything was neat and tidy and in its place. Here, she noted, with a lurch of nostalgia, all types of equestrian items were strewn around: racing magazines, stud cards and even bloodstock sale catalogs... not to mention the tack on the back of the sofa and the dirty boots just inside the door. It felt familiar and homey, a guilty reminder that Ross knew nothing of her life before Little Dale. She needed to rectify that as soon as possible, she realized. He believed he had finally found someone he could trust, yet all this time she'd been keeping secrets. As soon as she got him alone, she'd come clean about her whole life, she decided, suddenly eager for him to share in her past—both the achievements and the disappointments. And then she would tell everyone else—Cass, Jake and Bill, too.

They sat down on the well-used sofa after Bob had cleared away some clutter.

"Right," he said. "I'll get that coffee and then we'll go see Blue and Dennis. There are stud cards somewhere around here if you want to look at them."

Ross rooted around and unearthed them from beneath a cushion. He whistled, studying a picture of Dennis. "What a beauty. A real quality Thoroughbred."

Maddie wanted to say, "I used to look after him…and ride him," wanted to share her memories. But the moment wasn't right; she would wait until they were alone.

"Carlotta is going to have an amazing foal," Ross continued.

Bob caught her eye as he poured coffee from a large jug. He raised his eyebrows and she knew what he was going to say to her when he got the chance: come clean and be honest before it's too late.

Ross handed her the stud card and picked up a magazine, flipping through the pages.

Maddie glanced over at the pictures of triumphant trainers, owners and jockeys glorying in their victories. "Here," he said, handing the magazine to Maddie. "Read this article called, 'Back from the Brink.' It's about a race horse that nearly died and then went on to win a top-class race."

Maddie stared at the picture she knew so well. Noble Lord looked out at her, so familiar, so brave; he had been one of her charges for a little while. Guilt hit again, clawing at her guts.

Bob remarked on the article, too, leaning over to look at the picture with Maddie. She tried to stay calm. There was no way Ross would discover her secret in one of these magazines. It would be too much of a coincidence, wouldn't it?

ROSS IDLY THUMBED through another issue. Then he stopped. Right in the center of the photo, dressed in blue-and-gold silks, was Maddie. She smiled at him from the back of a gleaming chestnut race horse, her fingers entwined with those of a tweed-clad, handsome young man on horseback next to her. There were other pictures, too. One showed Maddie punching the air, the other man's arm draped across her shoulders; in another she held the stem of a huge silver goblet with a jubilant expression on her oh-so-familiar face. The title of the article glared out at him: Racing's Golden Couple Does It Again.

Throwing down the magazine, he stood, feeling sick. There was no doubt in his mind; the girl in the photograph was Maddie—his Maddie. But no…she wasn't his Maddie, was she? She was a liar and a cheat who was keeping huge secrets. And he had believed in her, trusted her…everyone had. He felt like a fool, teaching her to ride when she was obviously way more of an expert than he.

"Sorry," he mumbled, heading for the door. "I need a bit of air."

She followed him; huge, sympathetic eyes that he no longer recognized trying to see into his soul. Her hand burned his arm as she caught up with him in the yard, and he snatched it away, torn apart by anger at what felt like her betrayal.

"Ross? Ross, what is it?"

Just like before, when he'd hidden his feelings after the whole world had seemed to turn on him, he hardened his heart, closing the door on his emotions.

Shrugging her off, he turned toward Bob,

who was watching with concern from the kitchen doorway. "I'm so sorry," he said. "But I'm afraid I'm going to have to take a rain check on seeing the stallions. I…I don't feel so good."

"Don't worry—that's fine," Bob said. "Come back when you're feeling better. I hope it's nothing major."

"No, I'm sure it's not. And thanks." Ross was already heading off across the yard. "I'll go and get Meg."

"I'll come with you," Maddie offered, and for a second he looked back.

"Don't bother," he said before sighing in frustration. He still had to drive her back to Sky View. "We'll be at the truck in five minutes. Be there, or you can find your own way home."

WITH A HEAVY HEART, Maddie watched Ross go, then she returned to the kitchen.

When she stepped inside, Bob beckoned her over, shaking his head slowly. She knew what he was about to say, but she still dreaded it.

"I told you to come clean," he said. "He saw the pictures."

Bob reached down to pick up Ross's discarded magazine. It had fallen onto the floor with the center pages open. Maddie swallowed a lump in her throat. Bob had told her to be truthful, told her that everyone would understand... She should have listened. Now what? Trust was something Ross Noble had been loath to give, and by the expression on his face and the way he had shaken her off, it was unlikely he was going to give it again anytime soon. Maddie went across to take the magazine from Bob, and she gasped when she saw the pictures, remembering the day they were taken. Her nostalgia was quickly replaced by misery. No wonder Ross had stormed out; she'd destroyed what they had with her lack of honesty. "The glory days," she murmured. "When I used to believe I was a success... You were right, Bob. I should have been honest from the start, and now I've ruined everything. The worst part is, I'd already decided to come clean the next time we had a moment alone."

"So you don't think you're a success anymore?" asked Bob.

"Well, what do you think?"

He looked at her, considering. "I think you're brave and courageous to have overcome everything and found a whole new life," he said quietly. "If you were my daughter, Maddie, then I'd be very proud of you. You have a successful future ahead of you here in Little Dale. Maybe not with the glamor and fame you were once used to, but there are different kinds of success. You are needed here by so many—surely that means something."

Maddie hesitated, thinking about it. "It means everything," she said. "But it might not matter to Ross now...or to the Munros, when they find out I've lied."

"Then don't you think you'd better go and explain yourself...to everybody? Before it really is too late."

She gave him a grateful peck on the cheek. "Thanks, Bob. I'll let you know how it goes."

ROSS DROVE IN SILENCE, a million miles away from Meg's excited chatter and Maddie's sad eyes. For the first time in six years, he had allowed himself to weaken, allowed love to flicker in his cold, cynical heart... What a fool he'd been. How she must have smiled to herself when he tried to teach her how to ride. He wondered what other lies she'd told. What was it the magazine had called them, Maddie and the man who had held her hand

and shared her glory? "Racing's golden couple," that was it.

She reached across to touch his arm, her hazel eyes dark with emotion. She'd tried to talk to him when he came back with Meg, but he'd cut her short. She tried again. "I need to talk to you, Ross...to explain."

Ignoring her touch, he kept his eyes firmly fixed on the road. "There's nothing to explain. Except that you're obviously not the person I thought you were. You've duped us all—me, Meg, the Munros..."

"Please," she begged, her voice a whisper only he could hear. "It's not like that..."

Glancing sideways for a second, he saw the pain in her face and the tears that filled her eyes...the tears of a liar. Had she even cared at all, or was she just using him to help her get her old life back? Pain seared through the protective layer around his heart. He'd believed in her, trusted her...loved her.

"Forget it," he told her, his voice flat and emotionless. He had gotten over one woman, and he would get over this one. At least he'd found out what she was really like before it was too late to go back.

Pulling up outside Sky View Cottage, Ross

stared into space as he waited for Maddie to get out.

"Can't we go and get fish and chips again?" Meg pleaded.

He shook his head. "Not tonight. I have some work to do still, so you'll have to go back and stay with Cass and Robbie for a while."

"She can stay here with me if she wants," Maddie offered.

"No, thanks," he said curtly. He wasn't about to leave her alone with his little girl.

"Just go home, Maddie," he murmured for her ears only. "And leave us alone... permanently."

CHAPTER TWENTY-SIX

Ross FINISHED OFF the yard jobs, trying to ignore the dead weight of his heart, taking comfort in the quiet company of the horses who asked for nothing and gave so much in return. If only he'd stuck with his instincts and stayed away. How had Maddie managed to get so entangled in his life, anyway?

With Jenny it had been very different. She had been so pretty and naive, he'd wanted to protect her. His attraction to Maddie had crept up on him through a friendship borne of shared interests and admiration. She'd seemed so tough and brave, learning to ride when it was obviously so hard for her, stoically and single-mindedly carrying on, even when she lost her balance and fell, again and again… And then there was Meg. She had drawn Maddie into their lives, too. And he had let her.

Tying up Carlotta's bulging hay net, he ran his hand down her gentle face, feeling her warmth. "I'm a fool, lass. I let her pull me in with her lies… It was my help she needed, not me. She's made me look like an idiot."

When he stepped out into the early evening sunshine, Red was waiting patiently, wagging his plumed tail almost as if he understood his master's anguish. "I should have stuck with the company of animals and my little Meg," he told the dog. "Like I promised to do after—"

Unable to bear the pain, Ross crumpled, falling to his knees. He dropped his head into his hands. He'd actually been contemplating a future with Maddie…maybe even kids one day. What a joke he must seem to her, the golden girl of racing.

When he felt something brush his arm, he looked up to see Meg staring at him. "Daddy, what's wrong?"

He tried to pull down the shutters on his emotions. "Nothing, Nutmeg. I'm fine."

"Why were you so horrid to Maddie, then?" she asked crossly.

For a moment he just stared at her…what to say? "*I* was horrid to *her*?"

Meg's little face contorted…a reflection of his own. "Yes, you were horrid to her all the way back, and she was upset—I know she was."

He fought with his emotions, losing out to anger. "We don't need her in our lives, Meg. She isn't what you think. She tells lies to get what she wants, and she'll just let us down."

The little girl stood her ground. "You are wrong—you don't know her. Maddie is good and kind, and she loves us."

"You're too young to understand, Meg," he insisted. "Leave it to the grown-ups. Now get back to the house before Cass comes looking for you."

Tears spilled from her eyes as she turned to run; he called her name, ashamed at having let his hurt and frustration spill out. Ignoring him, she continued on, and he went back to haying the horses with a heavy heart, trying to lose himself in cold, hard anger.

WHEN MADDIE ARRIVED at Sky View half an hour later, everything was quiet. Parking her car out of sight of the house, she cautiously skirted the yard, heading for the kitchen door. She didn't want to bump into Ross just yet. What she had to say was for everyone.

She could see Cass in the kitchen window; she was talking, her head thrown back in laughter, and when Jake's arms came around her from behind, she turned for his kiss. Maddie's heart lurched; there was just so much love in the Munro household, reminding her sharply of what she'd lost with her own deceit.

Had Ross left already? She hadn't seen his truck... Suddenly, there he was, on his way to the house, as well. He was walking slowly, eyes downcast and shoulders slumped. She almost called his name, wanting another chance to explain why she hadn't been honest with him. But no, she was determined to keep to her decision. She was going to tell Ross and the Munros everything all at once, as she should have done long ago. After that, it was up to them.

When Maddie appeared in the kitchen immediately after Ross, three pairs of eyes swiveled in her direction.

"I need to talk to you all," she said. "Please... just for a few minutes."

"You have nothing of interest to say to any of us, except goodbye," Ross said in a harsh tone.

Cass stepped forward, holding up her hand. "No," she told him. "I don't know what happened between you two, Ross, but you can at least listen to what she has to say… We all can. Now go on, Maddie. The children are watching TV, so they won't interrupt you."

For several seconds Maddie stayed silent. Now that she had her moment, she was at a loss for words.

"I've been less than honest with you all," she finally began. "And I know you probably won't believe me, but I had already decided to tell you all the truth about myself tomorrow."

"Go on," prompted Cass.

Maddie locked her fingers together. "I…I'm not the person you think I am. Well, I mean, I *am* still me, but…I *did* get knocked off my bike on my way to work about a year and a half ago, that's true, and everything I've told you about my accident and my injuries is true, too…except that perhaps it was worse than I led you to believe. My full name is *Lucy* Madeline Maguire, and before my accident I was an up-and-coming jockey with good prospects. I used the name Lucy back then, but everyone called me Lucky…until I lost my career, my fiancé and my whole future in the lane that day." The thought brought a half smile to her lips. "I guess the nickname didn't fit after that. Anyway, after the accident and everything else, it was hard to get back to any kind of normality. Don't get me wrong, I had care and support from my parents, but it wasn't enough. I was lost in self-pity. It came to a head when the doctors told me that not only would I never race again, but that any kind of riding was off-limits. I would be lucky to even walk properly. And then when my fiancé left me for someone else, I felt as if I had nothing left. Everything I knew had been whisked away from me—horses, racing, the life I thought I was going to live. It was the sympathy on people's faces, though, that I really couldn't stand. Visits dropped off as the months went by, probably because my bitterness made me less than easy company, but I was glad of it."

Maddie hesitated, daring to glance up at the surprised expressions on Jake's and Cass's faces. Ross was just staring at the ground.

"And then one day," she went on, determined now to finish what she'd started, "I looked at my surroundings and at all the beauty in the world, and I decided to prove the doctors wrong, to prove to myself that I *could* have a life again, a life that was worth something. And then I saw this job advertised…a job where I could be around horses again and be accepted for myself, not judged by what

I once was or pitied and coddled. My main goal was to ride again, and here, thanks to all of you, that has been possible. I never wanted to lie. I always intended to tell you the truth eventually...when the time was right and you could accept me for what I've become."

Maddie looked straight at Ross with her head held high. "The thing is, Ross, I didn't expect to fall in love with you. I realize you will probably never be able to forgive me for keeping all this from you, especially once we'd gotten so close. I've messed up and I am so, so sorry...for what it's worth."

For a moment, Ross met her eyes, and then suddenly he turned and went out the door, letting it bang shut behind him.

"Go after him," Cass urged.

Maddie shook her head. "No point. He's way too proud to ever let himself trust me again. And anyway...I don't deserve it."

Cass squeezed Maddie's shoulders. "Well, we trust you and we forgive you," she said. "Whatever you didn't tell us about yourself was for a reason, and we believe you would have explained everything eventually, when you were ready. Don't we, Jake?"

Jake nodded. "Of course. And I remember the name now—Lucky Maguire. I don't particularly follow racing, but I did read about your accident. Has no one from around here recognized you?"

"Bob Nelson did," Maddie replied. "He told me to tell you all the truth, but I wouldn't listen."

WHEN ROSS STORMED out into the yard, his one thought was to escape. He'd brought up Google on his phone and searched Lucky Maguire. Her success in the racing world awed him. Ambitious to the last, though, it seemed to him that she'd used them all to get what she wanted... He'd believed in her, trusted her, and she had let him down.

Sitting alone outside the house as dusk fell around him, thick and heavy, he went over her brave speech in his head. Had that been an act, too? An hour ago, he had believed that he hated her, but he couldn't deny that her honesty had shone through, no matter how hard he'd tried not to see it. No matter, he decided, realizing that he needed to go and get Meg. Maddie may believe right now that she loved him, but he never would have been enough for her. As soon as she was totally recovered, she'd be off with someone from the glamorous world of racing. Jenny hadn't trusted him with her fears, and now Maddie had let him down. Maybe the problem lay with him. Maybe he was unapproachable.

He heard the door open, and when Maddie appeared, he slid back into the shadows, not wanting to face her.

"I know you're there, Ross Noble," she called. "And I'm going to repeat what I said before. I love you, warts and all, and I think you love me, too. Give us a chance—that's all I ask…please."

"I have to get Meg," he muttered, rising and hurrying past her back into the kitchen. She didn't follow.

Cass was nursing Gwen at the table. She reached out to grab his sleeve as he went by. "Please reconsider, Ross."

He hesitated beside her, his expression darkening. "It would be a waste of time. Is Meg with Robbie?"

She nodded. "Through there…they're watching TV."

Ross found Robbie alone, his eyes glued to the screen. "Where's Meg?" he asked. An uneasy shiver ran down his back as he remembered how hard on her he'd been when she came to find him earlier. He'd taken his anger and disappointment with Maddie out on Meg, and that was unfair. What had he been thinking?

Robbie shrugged. "She went off to see you ages ago. I thought you'd both gone home."

The shiver turned into a cold hand that clasped his heart and took away his breath, and panic rushed in. He raced back to the kitchen. "Meg's gone. She's missing, and it's my fault. I was angry with Maddie and—"

Jake took immediate control. "Calm down," he insisted. "Try not to worry. She can't have gotten far."

Blood pounded in Ross's ears; all he could see was her sad little face. "She was mad at me because I said we weren't going to see Maddie anymore, and I dealt with it badly. That was almost an hour ago, and Robbie says he hasn't seen her since. We have to find her!"

"Come on, then." Jake jumped into action. "We'll all search—me, you, Dad and even Robbie. Cass, call one of us if you hear anything and see if you can contact Maddie to tell her what's happened."

"I'll start at the stables and the barn," Ross said. "She might be with Rainbow."

"And I'll cover the calf pens and chicken

sheds. Robbie and Dad can search the garden. Call if you find her."

The twilight deepened as Ross left the empty barn and headed for the paddock where Splodge and Meg's pony, Rainbow, were kept. When he heard Chief's frantic whinny, he started to run, knowing with a sinking heart that Rainbow was gone. Meg must have tacked the little gray pony up all by herself and ridden off somewhere in her distress... A sob rose in his throat. She was alone, probably on the dangerous fell side, and she'd only been riding for a matter of weeks. He'd done it again—let down the person he loved, the person who depended on him most.

His phone vibrated in his pocket and he answered without checking the caller ID.

"Ross, where are you? Have you found her?"

"Oh, Maddie..." His voice sounded hollow and empty to his own ears. "Meg's gone. She's out on her pony all alone, and she can barely even ride."

Hearing her familiar voice, calm and determined, brought some relief. "We'll find her," she promised. "Rainbow is a sweet, steady old thing, and they can't have made it very far. Try to think which direction she might have gone in. Where are you? I'm on my way."

MADDIE'S HEART RACED as she hurried across the yard on foot. Not much point in driving when she was looking for a little girl on a pony. It crossed her mind that Meg might go to the cottage to find her…and Maddie wouldn't be there to meet her. But she decided she'd be more use searching out on the fell—if Meg showed up at Sky View Cottage, they'd just have to hope she stayed put. What had she been thinking, going off on her own? Was she hoping to teach her dad a lesson by running away? Who knew what might be going on in the mind of a six-year-old. Jogging along the grassy path that led to the fell, Maddie called Meg's name over and over, trying to keep a level head. She needed to be strong for Ross; he'd sounded so desperate on the phone.

She saw him at the gate to the fell, outlined by the evening sky, Red a dark shape beside him. His phone rang out into the silence and he put it to his ear; his voice was tight and urgent. "No luck? Well, just keep on looking…

please. We have to find her before it gets too dark."

Maddie caught her breath; the thought of the little girl, lost and alone somewhere in the darkness, brought a rush of raw panic. She touched Ross's arm. "Don't worry—we'll find her," she told him with a confidence she was far from feeling. When he gave her a grateful glance, hot tears pressed against the backs of her eyelids; resolutely, she held them back.

"I was angry with her," he admitted. "I took my... I took it out on her."

"We'll find her," Maddie repeated firmly. "That's all that matters. Now let's think where she could have gone."

"I always tell her she's not allowed to ride out by herself or go onto the fell alone because it's too dangerous."

"So you think that that's where she might have gone...to get back at you?"

"I have no idea, but it's a start at least."

Maddie took control. "Okay, you go up one side of the slope and I'll take the other. Red will find her if she's up here, I'm sure."

Ross jumped into action. "Red—find Meg," he urged.

The big dog wagged his tail, pricking his

ears and cocking his head to one side. "Find Meg," Ross said again in a sharper tone. Suddenly, the dog was off, racing up the steep hill.

"Maybe he's got her scent already," Maddie cried. "You follow him, and I'll look farther over—shout if you find anything."

When Ross and Red had disappeared into the rapidly descending gloom of night, Maddie set off to the left. The moon was rising now, improving visibility, but not enough for her to clearly see the ground ahead. Her wavering flashlight wasn't helping much, either. Rocks and tussocks of grass made it difficult to keep her balance, and she stumbled again and again, cursing her stupid, useless legs. "Meg!" she shouted over and over. "Meg… it's Maddie. Where are you?"

In the distance she could hear Ross calling, too, and her heart ached as she felt his anguish.

Half an hour went by and the darkness thickened as clouds rolled across the moon. Maddie could no longer hear Ross's voice; she felt alone and lost and helpless. And then she saw something against a crooked tree up ahead, a white, blurry shape. The shape moved, and she trembled so violently that her legs gave up. "Rainbow," she called gently, standing motionless. "Is that you?"

The pony approached her, warm and real, whickering softly. She took hold of the broken rein. "Meg!" she screamed. "Meg!"

The rising wind took her voice away. She stumbled on and the pony followed obediently, a ghostly shape behind her. A few minutes later, Rainbow stopped abruptly, snorting loudly. Maddie followed her gaze and saw a small figure lying awkwardly on the rough ground.

"Meg!" she cried, rushing over as fast as her legs would let her. "Ross…Ross! I've found her."

Again, the wind ripped away her cry. For a moment, she couldn't decide whether to call Ross first or tend to Meg. Helping the little girl had to be her priority, she realized; every second could be vital. She knelt down beside her. "Meg…oh, Meg. Are you okay? It's Maddie—I'm here to help you."

Meg didn't respond. Maddie's instincts screamed at her to scoop up the little girl and cradle her close, but common sense kicked in. She had to find out if she was injured. Her eyes were closed and her skin pale, but her body felt warm and vibrant. When Maddie stroked her small face, she felt the sticky wetness of blood…but Meg was breathing steadily, her little chest rising and falling relentlessly.

Maddie grabbed her phone, dialing Ross with shaking fingers. "Ross, I've got her. We need an ambulance. Come quick. I'll keep on shouting until you get here."

Red arrived like a whirlwind, a few paces ahead of Ross, and when he saw Meg, he sniffed her cheek and whined.

Ross spoke between ragged gasps. "Is she okay?"

Maddie grabbed hold of his hand. "She's unconscious and she has blood on her face. I think she must have fallen and hit her head, but I don't want to move her in case she's broken something."

The moon burst out from behind the clouds, lighting the scene dramatically. Ross ran his hands over his daughter's slight body, feeling gently for broken bones. Maddie held her breath, watching his face. *She's going to be okay*, she repeated again and again inside her head, willing it to be true.

With a doubtful glance back at her, Ross leaned down and gathered Meg into his arms, cradling her against his chest. "We have to take a chance," he said, getting to his feet. "She needs to get to the hospital. Tell Cass to get the car ready and to call the hospital to let them know we're on our way. We can get her there faster than waiting for the ambulance. Red, stay here with Maddie."

He set off down the steep slope before she'd even picked up her phone.

By the time Maddie had spoken to Cass and caught Rainbow, Ross and Meg were gone, gulped up by the night. Maddie felt so alone and afraid, realizing more than ever how much they both meant to her. No matter what Ross believed about her, there was no way she was going to let him and Meg out of her life so easily.

CHAPTER TWENTY-SEVEN

MADDIE HEARD AN engine roar to life as she arrived back at Sky View, and then everything seemed to happen at once. Robbie was there, taking Rainbow's rein from her numb fingers, while Cass bundled her into the backseat of Jake's 4x4.

"You need to go with them," the other woman said, slamming the door shut. "Call us," she mouthed as the big vehicle pulled away.

Ross sat next to her with Meg in his arms, stroking her pale, still face with gentle fingers. Maddie fought to contain her emotions; she had to stay strong...for him.

On impulse, she reached across and squeezed his forearm, wanting to show her support. "She'll get through this," she told him fiercely. "She has to."

He glanced at her and glanced away again, his eyes cold and glassy. "What is it to you?"

"You know what it means to me," she said quietly.

"And maybe if you'd been honest from the start, this never would have happened to her."

Maddie couldn't believe what he had just said. He was trying to make this *her* fault? Then again, perhaps he was right.

Ross took a deep breath. "Look, I'm sorry. I shouldn't have said that."

His apology did little to relieve her guilt. If she had told the truth from the start, then Meg wouldn't have felt the need to run away. She turned to the window. "Yes, you should have, because you're right. I'm the one who should be sorry."

"Laying blame isn't the answer," Ross responded sadly as the hospital lights came into view. "Meg is the only person who counts now."

A doctor and two nurses were waiting for them at the ER, brisk and professional. The next minutes were a blur: lights and voices and cool, hurried action. And then Meg was on a gurney being whisked along corridors with Ross beside her and Maddie right behind.

The words circled in Maddie's head, matching the repetitive rhythm of the gurney wheels: *she's going to be okay...she's going to be okay...she's going to be okay.* As if saying them over and over would make them true.

At the open door to a treatment room, a dark-haired nurse with a firm smile blocked Ross and Maddie's way. "Sorry," she said. "We need to assess her condition. If you wait here, we'll let you know how she is just as soon as we've examined her."

"No!" Ross began, but Maddie took hold of his arm.

"Let them do their job," she urged, ushering him to a blue plastic chair and sitting down beside him. "She's in good hands now."

"But I can't leave her...what if she wakes up and I'm not there?"

He looked so vulnerable, so very afraid, and on impulse she put her arms around him. "If they think she's waking up, they'll get you at once, I'm sure."

For a moment Ross just sat there, lost in his own shock and distress, and then suddenly he pulled away, dropping his head into his hands. Maddie longed to stroke his smooth sweep of dark hair, to comfort him, but she knew her sympathy wouldn't be welcome. When he stood up and began pacing, a heavy pain pressed against her heart. If anything happened to Meg, it would finish him.

The next half hour felt like an eternity, and then at last the doctor appeared. Maddie took hold of Ross's hand, and he didn't pull away.

"Well," he said, smiling gently. "Your daughter has a concussion, but that seems to be her only injury. We'll need to monitor her carefully for the next twenty-four hours or so, but she is showing signs of regaining consciousness. You can go in now, but—" he placed a restraining hand on Ross's arm "—you must understand that we won't know the full extent of the damage until she wakes up. All her vital signs are good, and we're hoping for the best but she had a nasty knock on the head—it's imperative that she is kept very quiet and still."

Ross made a beeline for the door, but Maddie held back—she was desperate to follow but unsure if she was welcome. Suddenly, Ross stopped and looked back. "Come on," he said.

Meg lay on the bed, so tiny beneath the white sheet that covered her. Her face was white as alabaster and there was a large bandage around her head, but her eyelids were flickering. Ross let out a strangled sob as he reached for her hand. "Meg…Meg," he murmured. "I'm here now. You're going to be fine."

Maddie stood beside him, willing the little girl to open her eyes, longing to hear her voice. And then she was looking at them and trying to smile through the tears that fell from her eyes. "My head hurts. And where is Rainbow?" she cried. "I'm glad Maddie's here, and I'm sorry for running away, Daddy."

"It's not your fault, Nutmeg," he told her, reaching down to touch his lips to her forehead.

"Rainbow is fine and so are you." Maddie smiled, taking hold of her other hand.

The doctor bustled back into the room. "Ah...good," he announced. "She's conscious. Hello, young lady, I'm Dr. Brewster. Did you know that you are a very lucky girl?"

After five minutes of tests and questions, he stood back from the bed, a broad smile on his tired face. "Well," he said, "it seems your daughter may just be okay. She's going to need a lot of rest, and there will be more tests to do but for now we'll let her sleep. It would be a good idea for the two of you to try to get some rest, too."

"I'm not leaving her," Ross insisted.

The doctor nodded. "Of course. That's

fine, but maybe you should go and get some refreshments, then. You need to keep your strength up, too."

Once the doctor left, Meg drifted off almost immediately into a peaceful, relaxed sleep, and Ross seemed to slump, as if all the worry and fear had finally weighed him down.

"We should get some fresh air," suggested Maddie. "And I need to call Cass and Jake. They'll be worried."

He hung back for a moment more, reluctant to leave, but Maddie pulled his sleeve. "Come on," she insisted. "We'll just be five minutes…unless you want me to just go home. Jake said when he dropped us off that he'd come back right away if we need him to."

Ross's response was instant and sincere. "No… I need you here."

His words were like music to Maddie's ears.

"And anyway," she said quietly as they headed down the corridor, "I'm going to be sticking around whether you like it or not."

Ross TURNED TO look at her. He had thought Maddie Maguire was frail, vulnerable, a woman whose needs he couldn't possibly meet…like Jenny. He had been so wrong. The woman who stood beside him had overcome all odds, both to get her life back and, today, to help save his daughter. And here she was, at the hospital, lending strength when *he* needed it. How could he ever live up to a woman like that?

"Can't you see?" he said. "We'll never be enough for you. I understand, now, why you kept the truth from me, but this is just a lull in your life—a healing time. When you're totally well again, you'll be off, back to the glamor of racing."

She took a firm hold of his arm and led him out into the cool night air. The sound of the hospital filled his ears: busy people caring for others and saving lives, the distant whine of an ambulance. Taking both his hands in hers, she drew him around to face her, holding his eyes with a ferocity born of love.

"You are so wrong," she said. "I will never pine for that life again. It was great when I had it…for a while, but at Sky View I've discovered what I really want, what really matters in life—love and companionship, genuine partnership…a family."

Ross let go of her hands and cupped her

face in his palms. "With me?" he asked, his voice deep and husky.

"With you," she said as he pulled her toward him. "I already told you, Ross Noble, I love you, warts and all…and Meg, I love her, too."

"Warts and all it is, then," he agreed, lowering his lips to hers. "Forever?"

"Forever," she breathed as he closed his arms around her. "Promise?"

There was no need for an answer, as her lips opened for his kiss.

* * * * *

LARGER-PRINT BOOKS!

GET 2 FREE LARGER-PRINT NOVELS PLUS 2 FREE MYSTERY GIFTS

Love Inspired®

SUSPENSE

RIVETING INSPIRATIONAL ROMANCE

Larger-print novels are now available...

YES! Please send me **The Montana Mavericks Collection** in Larger Print. This collection begins with 3 FREE books and 2 FREE gifts (gifts valued at approx. $20.00 retail) in the first shipment, along with the other first 4 books from the collection! If I do not cancel, I will receive 8 monthly shipments until I have the entire 51-book Montana Mavericks collection. I will receive 2 or 3 FREE books in each shipment and I will pay just $4.99 US/ $5.89 CDN for each of the other four books in each shipment, plus $2.99 for shipping and handling per shipment.*If I decide to keep the entire collection, I'll have paid for only 32 books, because 19 books are FREE! I understand that accepting the 3 free books and gifts places me under no obligation to buy anything. I can always return a shipment and cancel at any time. My free books and gifts are mine to keep no matter what I decide.

263 HCN 2404   463 HCN 2404

Name	(PLEASE PRINT)
Address	Apt. #
City	State/Prov. Zip/Postal Code

Signature (if under 18, a parent or guardian must sign)

Mail to the **Reader Service**:

IN U.S.A.: P.O. Box 1867, Buffalo, NY 14240-1867
IN CANADA: P.O. Box 609, Fort Erie, Ontario L2A 5X3

* Terms and prices subject to change without notice. Prices do not include applicable taxes. Sales tax applicable in N.Y. Canadian residents will be charged applicable taxes. This offer is limited to one order per household. All orders subject to approval. Credit or debit balances in a customer's account(s) may be offset by any other outstanding balance owed by or to the customer. Please allow 4 to 6 weeks for delivery. Offer available while quantities last. Offer not available to Quebec residents.

Your Privacy—The Reader Service is committed to protecting your privacy. Our Privacy Policy is available online at www.ReaderService.com or upon request from the Reader Service.

We make a portion of our mailing list available to reputable third parties that offer products we believe may interest you. If you prefer that we not exchange your name with third parties, or if you wish to clarify or modify your communication preferences, please visit us at www.ReaderService.com/consumerschoice or write to us at Reader Service Preference Service, P.O. Box 9062, Buffalo, NY 14269. Include your complete name and address.

MMLPBPA15

LARGER-PRINT BOOKS!
GET 2 FREE LARGER-PRINT NOVELS PLUS
2 FREE GIFTS!

◇ HARLEQUIN®

super romance®

More Story...More Romance